PRAISE FOR *The Broken Detective*

"Joel Nedecky's debut, The Broken Detective, is dark, twisty, and uncompromising. It's a bruising noir filled with broken glass, broken promises, and one desperately broken but unforgettable protagonist in PI Jake Joelsen, who learns the hard way that not everyone deserves saving, least of all himself. I couldn't put it down and neither will you ..."

–J. Todd Scott, best-selling author of *This Side of Night*

"Cults, corrupt cops, and crystal meth–if you swap out Albuquerque for Winnipeg and change the title from *Breaking Bad* to *The Broken Detective*, you'll find yourself hard-pressed to notice a difference between the quality of storytelling of one of television's best crime shows and this stunning debut by Joel Nedecky."

–AJ Devlin, screenwriter and award-winning author of Bronco Buster and "Hammerhead" Jed pro-wrestler PI mystery-comedy series

"Both hard-boiled and achingly vulnerable, *The Broken Detective* is an old-school private investigator thriller with emotional resonance for contemporary readers. Nedecky's talented hand combines tenderness and tension to pull readers into an edgy, beautifully crafted mystery."

–Amber Cowie, award-winning author of *The Off Season*

"A stellar debut from Joel Nedecky, *The Broken Detective* is one of the best crime novels I've read this year–a propulsive and engaging page-turner with addictive tendencies. The desperation and ticking-clock intensity sucked me in from the first page. With a flawed and relatable hero, a believable assemblage of dirtbags, drug dealers, shady cops, and a megachurch cult leader, it calls to mind George Pelecanos and Lawrence Block. This is modern noir at its finest."

–J.T. Siemens, award-winning author of the Sloane Donovan novels

Praise for *The Broken Detective*

"In *The Broken Detective*, Joel Nedecky conjures a mystery deeper than any plot or familiar narrative can deliver. How is it that one can care more for another than for oneself? The answer, of course, is love. Or personal obligation. Or faith. Or some distant promise one makes. Or perhaps the best of us are addicted to being needed. Despite his failures and inadequacies, Jake is more assembled than most of us ever will be–here, Nedecky has crafted a necessary and modern yarn for the rich tradition of detective fiction."

-Matt Phillips, award-winning author of *A Good Rush of Blood*

"*The Broken Detective*, Joel Nedecky's debut novel, is one of the grittiest and most compelling examples of crime noir I've read in recent years, featuring private investigator Jake Joelsen, the kind of flawed, cynical but big-hearted anti-hero that readers can root for in a big way. Authentic dialogue, lean, detailed prose with moments of breathtaking lyricism and an underlying current of wry humour make this an intense page-turner. Add to that a cast of genuine, complex characters and an original and fast-paced plot revolving around corruption and indoctrination in a powerful religious cult, and you have a stunning debut by an exciting new crime author."

-M.M. DeLuca, author of Amazon and Apple bestselling novels, *The Secret Sister* and *The Perfect Family Man*

"*The Broken Detective* is a wonderfully crafted, highly original story and Jake Joelsen a refreshing protagonist who I hope to see more of."

-David Swinson, author of *The Second Girl*

Editor: Krysta Winsheimer of Muse Retrospect

Book Design: Gary Anderson

Cover Photograph: Garth Jackson

Cover Design: Garth Jackson

ISBN: 979-8-9904851-3-6
Run Amok Crime, 2025
First Edition

RunAmok

Printed in the USA

THE BROKEN DETECTIVE

A NOVEL

by

JOEL NEDECKY

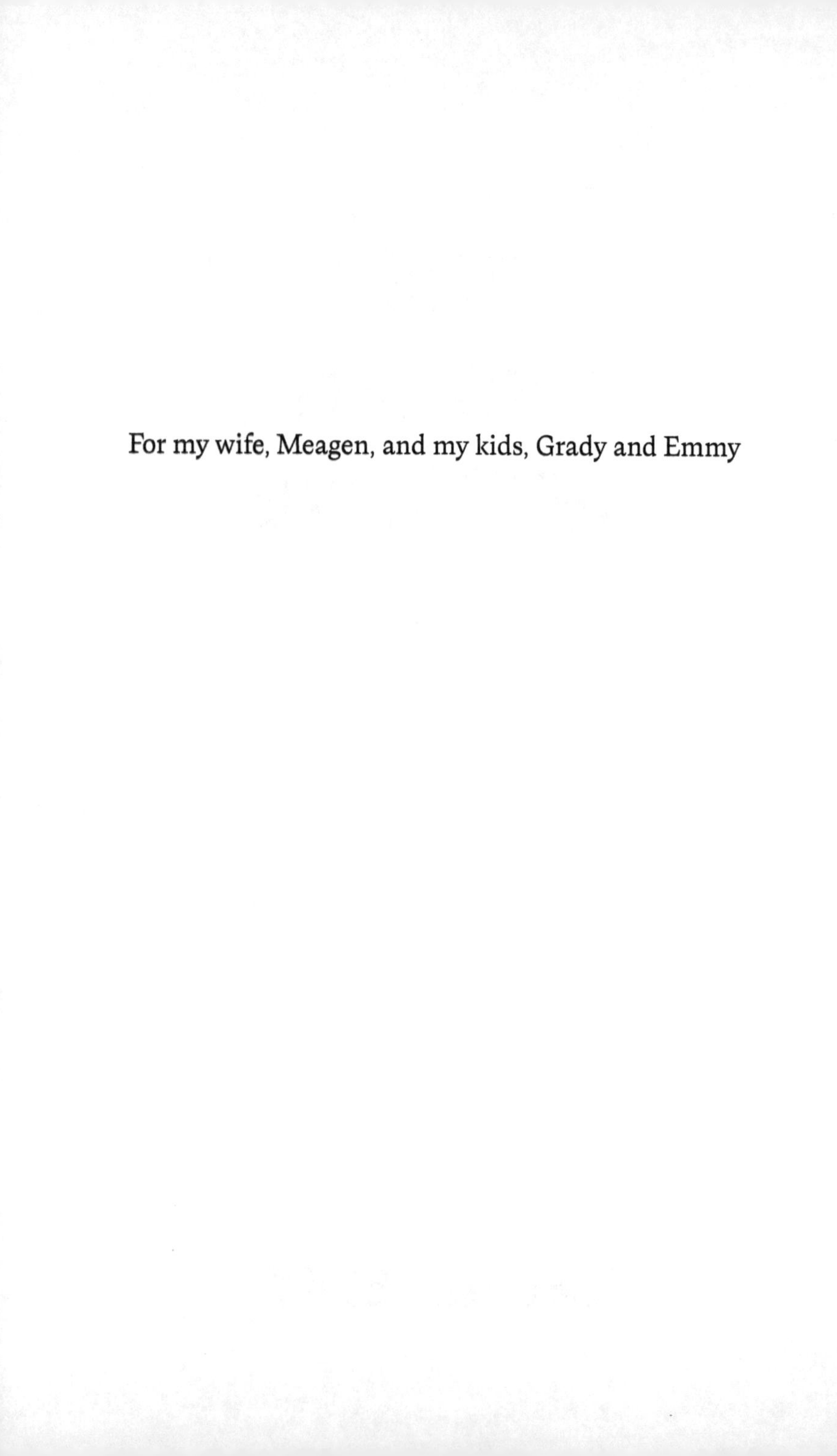

For my wife, Meagen, and my kids, Grady and Emmy

"There is something at work in my soul which I do not understand."
–*Frankenstein* by Mary Shelley

PART 1

OLD HABITS

1

Wednesday, October 16, 2019

I walked into Prairie Credit Union at 10 a.m., hungover and completely broke. Six months ago, I'd fractured the jaw of a man who'd hit my mom. I'd pleaded guilty, and yesterday, my lawyer, Roger Bancroft, had asked for a suspended sentence.

Bancroft said, "Your Honour, my client is the sole caregiver of his mother, Mary Joelsen, who suffers from depression and alcoholism. She's unable to work, and my client subsidizes the meagre income she gets from the government in the way of social assistance. We ask that Jake be provided with a suspended sentence of at least six months to organize Mary Joelsen's finances, living conditions, and situation in preparation for his time away. Thank you."

Judge Evelyn Leaf stared at me like I was a forlorn child, and I wondered if pleading guilty had been the right decision. She put on glasses and read from a paper on the judge's bench.

"Pursuant to section 731, article one of the criminal code, a suspended sentence is called for when 'the nature of the offence and the circumstances surrounding its commission make it appropriate,'" Leaf said, looking up from the paper. "Jake, I am providing two weeks from today for you to establish a plan for the care of your mom. I'm not comfortable with any longer than that. As part of this decision, you are required to present yourself here, in Her Majesty's court, on October twenty-ninth. I suggest you speak with your counsel and act wisely. I will take into consideration how you spend this time."

Her decision meant I had fourteen days to get my affairs in order and raise enough money to support my mom while I was inside.

Earlier, I'd spoken to a lender at Prairie Credit Union named Jason Bremnar, who was now twenty minutes late. On the phone, when I'd asked him how he was doing, he'd commented that his Sunday ticket had been a winner, and that he'd made nine hundred bucks. I played along like I cared, and he went off. Aaron Rodgers this and Aaron Rodgers that. Interceptions and incompletes. Yards after the catch and team defence. I didn't watch football, but I knew enough to pretend, so I said how my ticket hadn't panned out because of the "fucking Vikings." He seemed to really like that, so along with black Dockers and a brown fitted sweater underneath a navy bomber jacket, I picked up a second-hand Green Bay Packers hat from Value Village. It sat on my head now, faded from heavy use. I also wore a decent pair of Timberland boots.

As I waited for my appointment, I thought about the woes of my city. The summer had been one of the bloodiest in Winnipeg's history, and the trend had only continued into the fall. The city had just recorded its thirty-second homicide of the year, ten more than all of 2018. In addition to that grisly statistic, I couldn't go a day without hearing about property crimes, the meth crisis, kids apprehended by child and family services, or a police headquarters that had run eighty million dollars over budget. How does that even happen? I could see eight million, but eighty? Mayor Bowman wanted a full investigation, Premier Pallister did not, and the good citizens just kept on keeping on, trying to survive and pay the bills. Finally, my name was called, and I followed a young woman to Bremnar's office.

Bremnar stood behind an IKEA desk, trying hard to look younger than someone in their late fifties, and it rubbed me the wrong way. His dark blue suit was stylishly too tight, and when he came around the desk to shake my hand, I noticed he was wearing dress shoes without socks. His crisp white shirt sparkled next to a baby-blue tie, and his close fade had white and grey sprinkled above the ears. The office smelled of Brut aftershave. Behind the desk, a row of built-in cabinets held manuals and binders. Two pictures on his desk showed extended family, his children and grandkids, I presumed.

He asked for my driver's license, and I hesitated, worried it'd be tarnished with coke residue from last night. I pointed to the pictures on his desk as a distraction.

"Grandkids?" I asked.

The pictures had been taken at a cabin, the sun causing everyone to squint. With his attention elsewhere, I wiped the card on my pants and laid it on the desk.

"Yeah, three and five years old," he said. "Little hellions, but they're awesome."

He chuckled and so did I. It pained me to do so, but I needed this loan.

"You got kids?" he said.

"No, no kids. Maybe one day, though."

"Well, you have lots of time." He noticed my hat. "You a fan?"

I perked up. "Lifelong. I came out of the womb wearing the green and gold. You?"

"Die-hard all the way, baby. Third-generation cheesehead."

"My lucky hat," I bullshitted, tugging on the beak.

Bremnar and I chatted for another few minutes about the Pack, then he got down to business, reading from two monitors on the desk and frowning like he'd read something of concern. He reminded me of a doctor about to impart a death sentence on a patient, but it seemed like he was acting, playing the role.

"Mr. Joelsen," he said, "you have a combined thirty thousand dollars of debt on three credit cards, and each is at their limit. We just can't approve a line of credit or loan at this time."

My piss up last night had drained my account and maxed out the last card that had any space. I'd tried to get other cards and secure loans from other banks, but I'd been declined.

"Is there nothing you can do?" I said.

Bremnar shuffled. "I'm afraid not."

"Your website says 'Helping people live their best lives.'"

"Let me take another look." Bremnar read from the monitors again. He hemmed and hawed and acted like he was reconsidering, but I could tell he wasn't.

"I'm sorry, Mr. Joelsen," he said mildly, "but you need to qualify for the services advertised on our website."

"Listen," I said. "I have responsibilities. My mom's less than fully functional. I don't need a lot. I could manage with twenty thousand, and I'll tackle the credit card debt soon."

Bremnar gathered loose papers and placed them on the corner of his desk as a whiff of Brut smacked me in the face. He mumbled something.

"What's that?" I said, leaning in.

"Nothing ... It's just–I noticed how many transactions on your account are from the liquor store and two a.m. withdrawals from ATMs."

My first instinct was to reach across and bang his head off the desk until he approved the loan. Instead, I counted to ten and slowed my breathing. Bremnar stared at me, waiting.

"The Packers suck," I said, and got up to leave, stopping at the doorway of his office. "And go fuck yourself."

He looked like I'd slapped him.

***

When I got to my mom's, she was asleep. I put the groceries away, tossed anything expired or mouldy from the fridge, and then went to the bedroom and sat on a wooden chair in the corner. There was an ashtray full of butts on the night table that looked like a Jenga puzzle, like it could topple over at any second. A litre of cheap wine sat next to the ashtray. I didn't see a glass. A putrid smell wafted from my mom like a living thing, and as her body rose and fell with each breath, I wondered how the hell she'd manage when I went away.

I closed my eyes.

Then I emptied the ashtray and poured the wine down the drain. I checked on my mom again before leaving.

2

The McCinnis Law offices, located in a building east of downtown on Henderson Highway, left a lot to be desired. Small and largely in disrepair, the building should have been externally renovated years ago. The first time I'd been there, the cracked stucco, motley windows with hazy glass, and garish signage had made me think I might have chosen wrong. Inside, worn furniture and outdated decor gave the same impression, but that's where the shoddiness ended.

A young woman had greeted me at the desk, friendly and professional, and Roger Bancroft followed that intro with more of the same. Bancroft's off-the-rack suit, loose, messy hair, and average height and weight presented a mundane air, but he was anything but. He spoke strongly and with a deep knowledge of the law in the province of Manitoba, working efficiently and with complete confidence. My opinion of Bancroft had only improved during the months he'd been my lawyer, and I visited him directly from Prairie Credit Union.

"You look like an unmade bed," he said.

"I feel like shit."

I sat down as he made coffee, taking his time about it. Once he'd finished the task, he placed a mug in front of me and sat down behind his desk.

"Have you processed Judge Leaf's decision?" he said.

"That's what I want to talk to you about."

I removed my phone from my pocket, opened it, and found my notes. I started to talk, and he held up a hand, hushing me.

"Leaf is a hard-ass," he said. "But she isn't wrong. You haven't been to A.A. and counseling, nor have you apologized." He leveled a finger at me. "I told you months ago the apology needs to happen, and I also told you to get your ass to an A.A. meeting."

Bancroft's face had gotten red, but his voice remained calm.

"So, now, you have two weeks to get your shit together. And I can't believe I need to say this, but I will, one last time: The maximum sentence for aggravated assault is ten years. Ten fucking years," he whispered. "You won't get that, but you could get two, maybe even three. That's thirty-six months inside. Why won't you go to A.A.? Why won't you apologize to the victim? What's his name–Cory Francis?"

I adjusted myself in the chair. "If I apologize to Francis, then that means I did something wrong. It also means I regret breaking his jaw. I didn't do anything wrong, and I don't regret it. As far as A.A. goes, it just doesn't feel right."

"And you'd go to prison for three years because it doesn't feel right? What's wrong with you? You say you love your mom, but you are willing to leave her on her own for two, maybe three, times longer than necessary. And if you do get more than two years, you'll go to a federal prison with inmates serving long stretches. Lifers. People who have done all kinds of heinous shit. Give your head a shake. Even apologizing gets you under two years. If you join A.A., I bet you'll get eighteen months. Probably serve twelve."

"So you're asking me to lie?"

"No. I'm asking you to find some measure of truth in the situation. I'm asking you to take responsibility for your actions. To look after your mom. Come on, Jake. Do the right thing."

"Mom's rent is $1,000 a month," I said, launching into a speech of my own, ignoring what he'd said. I understood where he was coming from, but his reality wasn't mine.

Bancroft shook his head and smiled, part frustration, part sheer bewilderment at my stubbornness.

"Utilities ... $200," I continued, reading from my phone as I spoke. "Food ... around $800. Clothes ... let's say $50. Miscellaneous $100."

I knew my mom's finances because I paid her bills when she'd forgotten or pissed away the money. My mom didn't do much other than drink, but she watched a lot of television and spent half the day on YouTube.

"Phone ... $100. TV and internet ... $150."

It hurt me to do it, but I had to be honest.

"Cigarettes ... two packs a day times thirty days ... round up to $700. Booze ... $1,000. Total ..." I said, and did a little mental math. "... $4,100. She gets $880 a month in social assistance, let's call it $900. That means she needs $3,200 a month to live. I also have thirty grand in credit card debt, and before you ask, the answer is no, I can't get a loan. I was just at Prairie Credit Union, and they told me to eat shit."

"What are the minimum payments on the cards?"

"About $650 a month."

"So then you're looking at almost $4,000 a month. If you get lucky–and that's a big fucking if–and you get two years inside ... that's $96,000 to take care of your mom–ninety-six grand!" Bancroft let the number hang in the air like a foul odour. "No way you earn that money in two weeks without robbing a bank."

Banks were usually robbed by idiots or addicts in need of quick cash for a fix. An article online told me that the average payout per robbery in 2018 was only four grand. To get more than that you needed to get into a vault, and that was close to impossible. It was situations like the one I was in that prompted bad decisions, but robbing a bank was just plain stupid.

I could blackmail someone, but that took time. You had to find a suitable mark, research what they did and how much money they had access to. Then, you had to stake them out and learn their routine. You had to know their families, friends, and coworkers. Their hobbies and favourite restaurants. You needed it all. It was possible, but blackmail never sat right with me, not because it's illegal or immoral, but because I'd be taking money for nothing. I would not cross that line, become dependent on others again. Ever.

"Do you know anyone who can lend you the money?" Bancroft said.

"Ninety-six thousand dollars? Fuck no. I can sell my truck and probably get twenty. Maybe sell a few other things, but not ninety-six grand worth."

I hated making excuses, and I hated apologizing when I didn't mean it, but what choice did I have?

"Okay. I'll write an apology," I said. "And I'll go to A.A."

It almost killed me to say it.

"All right," Bancroft said, slapping the desk for emphasis. "Finally, some common sense." He worked it out. "Eighteen months, serving twelve, means you need $48,000. In two weeks. That's a lot of money, but not impossible. You'll need to sell everything you own, and you need a client. And fast."

I nodded.

"Perfect," Bancroft continued. "I can't guarantee Judge Leaf will sentence you to eighteen months, but I've been doing this a long time, and she always factors the Crown's recommendation into her decision. You do your part, and I'll get to work on it."

I stood, shook his hand, and walked out.

3

I lived in a small one-bedroom apartment on Colony Street and kept an office on Osborne Avenue above an aesthetician and next to a Chinese food restaurant. I'd set up a couch, mini fridge, and two wicker chairs in front of a heavy wooden teacher's desk with a rickety adjustable chair behind it that was here when I rented the place. I'd covered the bare walls with movie posters in cheap frames. Seven Samurai. Reservoir Dogs. Taxi Driver.

I opened the fridge and yanked out a bottle of vodka, but returned it when Bancroft's words echoed in my mind.

"What's wrong with you? You say you love your mom, but you are willing to leave her on her own for two, maybe three, times longer than necessary."

I put on a pot of coffee instead, fired up the laptop, and hit play on the album *Victory Lap* by Propagandhi. With atomic drums, wicked guitar, and Chris Hannah's intense vocals in the background, I listed my truck, a 2011 Sierra, on Kijiji for twenty-three grand, and returned calls to two insurance companies who'd left messages for me last week regarding contract work. Initially, I hadn't responded to their inquiries because I thought I'd be in prison. Both hung up the phone like they were allergic to it when I told them I no longer held a valid investigator's license.

What did it matter?

Even the most lucrative insurance work wouldn't net me twenty-five thousand dollars in two weeks, and that's how much I'd need if I sold my truck. I had been listening to the rumble of the coffee maker for several minutes when someone knocked. I got up and answered the door.

"You Jake?" a young Black woman said, sans greeting.

She looked between twenty-six and thirty years old, with warm, green eyes and short black hair. Her curves were on display in a white blouse tucked into light grey high-waisted pants. A Kate Spade purse was slung over her left shoulder, and she used her right hand to remove gold-rimmed Aviator sunglasses as she stepped into the small room. In her left hand was a cell phone.

"I'm Jake," I confirmed, and the woman looked at me with desperation strewn upon her face.

"I ... well ... I'm not sure where to begin," she said, like any words she spoke would cause her grief.

"Why don't you sit?"

She examined the couch like she was looking for stains, then slowly sat down in one of the chairs.

"Take your time," I said.

Tears slid down her cheeks, and when she dabbed her eyes with a tissue from her purse, I noticed how small and delicate her hands were. It made me self-conscious of my scarred, beat-up mitts.

"Can I get you a coffee?" I asked. "Or maybe something stronger?"

She frowned. "I don't drink."

"Ever?"

"It always seemed like a great way to mess up my life. I got drunk a few times as a teenager and didn't like it. I'll take a coffee, though."

I thought about the vodka in the fridge, pushed the fantasy from my mind, and poured two cups of coffee, one for each of us, with cream and sugar on the side. She wrapped both hands around the mug.

"Thanks."

"No problem." I sat down and opened a Notes page on my phone. "How can I help?"

"Read this ..." She turned her phone around so I could see the screen. It was a text message sent from someone named Sadie.

I read the text aloud:

"I'm sorry, N. I don't know what I was thinking. I was just so angry all the time. Don't hate me."

Tears formed behind her eyes again, and she bent her head to the side as she turned away.

"You're N?" I asked.

"Nia."

"And Sadie?"

"My sister."

I lit a cigarette, even though it had been illegal to smoke inside buildings in the city since 2004. Nia opened her mouth to say something, but let it go, as if speaking would be a great burden she didn't have the energy to take on.

"When did you get the text?" I asked.

"Today. She left for work yesterday morning at eight but didn't come home. We live together. She's not answering her phone or responding to texts, and she was a no-show at work today."

"How old is Sadie?"

"Twenty-three."

"Twenty-three-year-olds stay out all night sometimes," I said. "It's kind of what they do."

"I understand that, and I'm not going to lie, Sadie doesn't always come home. But she always answers texts from me. Always."

I blew smoke, then tapped the dart to drop the ash in a ceramic frog I used as an ashtray. "It's been, what, thirty hours?"

"Give or take."

I considered this information as Nia frowned. She looked at the frog, then over my shoulder at the posters. She peered up to the exposed rafters above us, dropped her eyes to the mini fridge, coffee maker, and finally, those beautiful greens landed on me. I felt something shift, a slight quake in my chest, or maybe it just felt that way, the dramatic longing of a sober man who sat in front of a gorgeous woman, jonesing for a drink.

"Logan Bergel recommended you," she said, voice clearer now.

"Logan?"

"Yeah, he said he knows you from a group home, that you lived together when you were teenagers? I'm not entirely sure. He described you like you were his younger brother."

I shifted in my seat.

Logan Bergel.

I thought about him often, and what I'd done for him. Nia

wasn't wrong, he had been like a brother, but I hadn't spoken to him in years. He'd become a spectre in my rearview mirror, a ghost haunting me from afar. Why would he recommend me for a job?

"How do you know Logan?" I said. "Are the two of you an item?"

"An item?" She laughed. "What is this, 1980?"

"You know what I mean."

Nia gave me an odd, slightly incredulous look. "I wouldn't say we're an item. But we are–or were–casual. Now ... it's complicated. I see him from time to time."

"Fair enough," I said. "Does your sister–"

"Sadie."

"Does Sadie have a boyfriend or a recent ex?"

"No."

Nia seemed unwilling or unable to say more. The text was ominous, but people sent texts that didn't make sense all the time. Maybe Sadie was drunk, or stressed, or it could have been a joke. The possibilities were endless.

"Why don't you wait until tomorrow," I said, "and if you haven't spoken to her by then, make a police report. The police have resources that I don't have."

She stiffened. "I don't want the police involved."

I sat forward, placed my elbows on the desk. "Why not?"

"There's no point. You said yourself, twenty-three-year-olds stay out all night. The cops won't do anything. I want you to find her."

I wasn't sure how to respond because I couldn't say for sure she wasn't right. Clients tended to shy away from the police, especially people of colour.

"Does Sadie work?" I asked.

"She's an assistant at Sport Sphere. It's a marketing firm."

"On Fort?"

"That's right." Nia retrieved the Kate Spade, opened it, and removed a typed paper, then placed it in front of me. "Here's a list of her coworkers. Well, the ones I know. I also wrote down her vehicle information and social media handles. You'll find pictures of her there."

I extinguished my butt, read the paper, and opened Instagram, entering @hardcoresadie. I scrolled, tapped a picture, and stared at a young white woman, with skin so naturally tanned it could only be described as golden, sitting on the patio of a bar. It was summer, and Sadie sat cross-legged, the folds of a simple dress breaking across each thigh like waves. Her bare shoulders were delicate, and her pronounced collarbones created the air of a model. A long nose that would usually be considered too much, fit with a large mouth, heavily lidded dark eyes, and blonde hair that held streaks of blue. One side of her head had been shaved, and her cloth handbag was plastered with buttons like Meat is Murder, Feminist, and Make Love, Not War. People drank and laughed in the background, yet Sadie's expression remained neutral.

"Sadie's white," I blurted before I had a chance to think it through.

"Yeah, no shit, Sherlock."

Nia looked at me like I'd just teleported in from another planet, her expression screaming "What the fuck?"

"Sorry," I said. "Sometimes I speak before I think."

"It's fine," she said in a way that let me know it wasn't.

I wanted to ask why Sadie was white and she was Black, but that sounded stupid, not to mention racist, so I pointed at the screen of my phone and asked, "The buttons–are these causes she's involved with?"

Nia craned her neck to see the photo, then sighed. "Sadie was a member of a church called Watershed Moments. She left the church six months ago."

I drank coffee and typed the name. "Any changes since she left Watershed Moments?"

"Sadie's always struggled with depression, and she's always partied, but now ... it's worse."

I typed brief notes, looked up. "How much does she party?"

"Three or four nights a week." Nia looked at her phone and checked the time. "That's why I'm here with you right now and not at one of the other agencies. Logan told me this is your world. Dive bars and nightclubs. Pubs and lounges. No offence, but he said you live one step above a homeless person."

"No offence taken," I said, and meant it. She wasn't wrong. I was a drunk, and drunks knew their own. There were certain places and people I'd have access to that someone in a more upscale organization might not. "Before yesterday, did she seem off? Was she agitated?"

"No more than usual."

"Do you have other siblings? Parents in the city?" I asked.

A shadow crossed her face. "No other siblings. My parents are here."

"What do they say?"

"I haven't spoken to them about this," she said. "They aren't part of our lives."

"Maybe they've talked to her," I suggested, prodding her to say more.

"They haven't, and I don't trust them. We barely communicate."

"Why don't you trust them?"

"Lots of reasons," she barked.

"Can you be more specific?"

"What is this, twenty questions? Do you want the job or not?"

"It's a question-based job, you realize."

She didn't say anything to that.

Nia's refusal to talk about her parents seemed odd, but not unheard of. Nevertheless, the fury she'd shown as I pestered her with questions told me there was something there.

"Why did Sadie leave the church?"

"What do you mean?"

"People are creatures of habit. They don't usually make changes unless they're forced to. There must be a reason."

Nia's eyes were tawny, teary, and unblinking. "I guess it was a combination of things."

"And you think they're involved in this sudden disappearance?"

"I-I don't know. I mention Watershed Moments only to give you the full picture."

I nodded. It was time to get down to business.

"My rate isa hundred dollars an hour," I said, raising it from the usual eighty. "Plus any costsI incur throughout the investigation."

"What kind of costs?"

I pulled a contract from my desk. "Here, read this. It explains the ins and outs. Sign if you agree to the terms."

She read thoroughly, and I watched her, the way she used a pen to guide her eyes, licking her finger before turning to the second page.

"What do you do?" I asked.

"I'm an actuary."

She signed, e-transferred me five hundred dollars, and left the contract where it lay. Her last name was Rowe. Nia Rowe.

"Is Sadie's last name Rowe?"

"Yes." She paused, then said, "I have a one thirty appointment with a client, and I can't be late." She stood. "That does it then."

It wasn't a question.

"I'll let you know when I know something," I said.

I watched her walk onto Osborne Avenue without looking back, then stared at the contract, thinking about Logan Bergel.

I hated that fucking guy.

4

My weather app informed me the high was 12 degrees Celsius, mild for mid-October but cool. Outside my office building, I smoked a cigarette and watched two cops, one man, one woman, interact with a homeless guy sitting on the sidewalk. The guy's hair peeked out from under a Winnipeg Blue Bombers toque. He sat cross-legged with a checkered blanket covering his legs, speaking passionately, waving his arms and pointing. The male cop kneeled, and the woman stood. The kneeling policemen listened intently before responding. The seated man threw his arms up in defeat, rummaged around under the blanket, and produced a needle, which he placed in the cop's gloved hand. The officers went on their way.

A new billboard advertised condos with two bedrooms starting at $499,000, displaying an interior of modern greys and whites and hip furniture that I knew nothing about. Construction on Osborne caused numerous delays, horn honks, and middle-finger salutes. I extinguished the butt on the brick façade, dropped it in a coffee tin.

At my desk, I opened Instagram again, this time on my laptop. It's inaccurate to boil a person down to details learned by viewing their social media, but it somehow makes them more human, too. Nia's bio said she'd graduated from Western University in London, Ontario. Her smile in most pictures said the photographer and everyone else should be grateful they had the pleasure of taking her picture, as if they were in the presence of greatness.

I took a more thorough look at Sadie's account, and as I scrolled through her pictures from past to present, I saw the transformation Nia had described. Sadie never smiled, and I wondered if it was purposeful. Recently, she had a fondness for posting self-help quotes, and several pictures showed her with the same person, a young woman with the physique of a bodybuilder. Sadie had the genetics to stay thin, but it was out-of-shape thin, whereas this woman had muscle and a V-shape to her frame.

I logged into Facebook and Twitter next. Sadie's inactive Facebook account told me little. In fact, she hadn't posted in months, which didn't surprise me. I'd heard Facebook had become passé for young people, and now only stay-at-home moms and grandparents used it. Sadie's Twitter and Instagram accounts were insane; busy would be an understatement. In the days before her disappearance, she had tweeted ten times a day on average, often more. She'd also posted multiple pictures a day on Instagram. The activity had come to an abrupt halt on October 14.

I followed a link on Sadie's Twitter account to @fitness_gyrl and found the name Arkell Lightfoot, the friend in the pictures. Two pictures showed her onstage with a trophy. She had dyed blonde hair, skin the colour of flax, and thick, sinewy muscles. A painted bronze statue with pink lips, she resembled a Potato Head toy, like you could snap her mouth off and on. Arkell worked at Rupert's Gym and competed as a sponsored fitness competitor.

I stopped when I got to a picture of Sadie and Arkell together. It was a picture of a picture, and it was dated 2010. Sadie would have been in grade 9. Fourteen years old. She was dressed conservatively in a tan sweater. Her hair had been parted in the centre, and she wasn't wearing makeup or jewelry. Again, she didn't smile. She looked angry. But behind the plain appearance, I saw the potential of physical beauty, the kind on display in the other pictures.

Arkell had a round face and thick black hair, not chubby, but young and healthy in an immature way. She wore a shirt in support of her Indigenous roots, white words ironed onto a black T-shirt. "La culture, les traditions et les langues autochtones ont subsisté." I Googled the sentence. "Indigenous cultures, traditions and languages have survived."

The picture made me nostalgic. I leaned back and scrolled through the albums on my phone to the one I'd labeled Parents.

People act like morons when they're having their pictures taken. Women pucker their lips, arch their backs, and bend slightly at the knees to give them that aura of desirability. Men, especially the ones I know, mean mug the camera or wear their best deadpan and a slight upshot of a smile, everyone posing, putting their arms around each other and slapping high fives.

I found the picture I was looking for, the original taken around 2000. I stood between my parents in front of my dad's white Chevy Silverado. We looked happy, intertwined like a braid. It was one of the only pictures I had of my dad. We'd load up and rumble down to the old Winnipeg Arena on Maroons Road. With no frills and terrible sightlines, the basic, rugged nature of the arena reflected our city. That building was now gone, but I loved those nights and thought about them often.

We drove down to Minneapolis in that truck in '02 to watch the Minnesota Wild, the last hockey game I went to with my dad before he disappeared. I was thirteen, and I'd played hockey since I was six years old. I could skate like the wind, and I had good hands, but I'd miss games and practices when my parents were drunk or fighting. When I entered foster care, I stopped playing on a team, and the only ice I got was at the outdoor rinks.

At the intermission of the Wild game, Dad bought me a beer, a hooded sweater, and a bunch of hockey cards, which I collected and obsessed over.

"Anything you want," he said. "Anything you want."

My dad glowed from the alcohol, a glossy look that started with his eyes and swept across his face. Tiny crow's-feet extended from the corner of each eye like a road map. He worked sporadically, odd jobs, and we didn't have much money. But at those games we were millionaires.

We watched the second and third periods, ate popcorn, and drank more beers, which I'd done with him at home, but this was my first time getting drunk.

"Lightweight," my dad said, joking, and he smacked me on the back.

My dad gave the manager of our hotel a fifty to let me into the bar, and that night we ate steaks and drank wine, talked about hockey. He told me the story of how the Jets had left Winnipeg after the 1995-96 season, a riveting tale he painted as a David (Winnipeg) versus Goliath (capitalism). He didn't know, how could he, that the team would return in 2011. The conversation moved to music, movies, and TV.

"Jake," he said, an arm around me. "You're my boy and I'm so proud of you. I'll always be proud of you, you know that, right? Big things for you, my boy. Big things."

My dad turned every act into a lesson, but his drinking undermined most of them. He'd be the only adult playing street hockey with the neighbourhood kids, and then go for a beer and come home two days later. My mom wasn't much better, but she had to take care of me, and I think that saved her. For a while.

I was stumble drunk by the end of that night in Minneapolis, leaning on my dad as we navigated the hallway of the hotel together, bouncing off the walls, unsteady, giggling like children.

"As long as you're in bed by midnight," my dad said, "you're golden. Nothing good happens after midnight. It's the witching hour. Remember that."

He helped me into bed and pulled the covers tight at 11:58. Then he left the room, completely ignoring his own advice. When I woke up in the middle of the night, he wasn't in the room, but he was back by 8 a.m. for coffee and a cheap buffet breakfast.

A month later, my dad went on a bender and didn't come home. My mom started drinking seriously not long after. She'd always been a drinker, but it became dire when my dad left. Bleak, even.

I quit going to school, dropped out in grade 8, and some days I'd spend nine or ten hours on the bus, until the driver would ask me to leave. I checked bars he frequented, spoke to bartenders and patrons. I walked the streets downtown and got to know people. At one point, I thought I'd found him, but it amounted to nothing.

The cops made little progress. I returned to school, but my mom had gotten worse, and by the end of 2003, I was in the care of the province.

I broke my reverie, found the number for Rupert's Gym, and dialed.

5

The guy I spoke to said Arkell Lightfoot was in, so I drove out to Pembina Highway in the South End. This part of the city had a massive shift in demographics around 2010. It used to be predominantly white until its proximity to the university made it a beacon for foreign students, refugees, and new Canadians from around the world. Now, bus stops were plastered with the names of Nigerian real estate teams, banks had signage with Mandarin as the dominant language, and Sikh gurdwaras were a staple of the neighbourhood. Middle Eastern restaurants and markets could be found on every second block.

Rupert's Gym was in the basement of a strip mall, underneath a collectibles store with images of Pokémon and Yu-Gi-Oh! next to Steph Curry and Sidney Crosby on the exterior glass.

Inside, a trainer with a nametag that said *Seung* sat behind a desk to the right. He wore a navy-blue polo shirt with the gym's logo, a white stallion standing on its hind legs. Seung looked around five nine, one eighty. He had broad shoulders layered with muscle, Popeye forearms, and massive hands that smacked the keyboard like he was mad at it. He looked like he could squeeze the head off a chicken. I told him I needed to see Arkell Lightfoot.

"You called earlier?" he asked.

"Yes"

"New talent?"

"No."

He eyeballed me as he moved out from behind the desk to get a complete look. "You got muscle on you. Some fat on there, too. I'd guess ... seventeen or eighteen percent body fat. Big arms. Solid glutes. Decent delts. Wrists and forearms need work, though. If Arkell doesn't take you on, maybe I will."

He was pissing me off more with every word.

"What'd ya say?" he asked.

"Zero fucking chance, pal," I said, and walked in.

"Hey, you need to pay!"

I stopped, turned, and stared at him. "I won't be long."

"All right, man," Seung said, putting his arms up in mock surrender. "Arkell's inside."

I'd expected Arkell to train in a modern gym with slick new weights, state-of-the-art treadmills, ellipticals, and other cardio machines. What I stepped into had little in common with anything modern, as if I'd traveled back in time. Metal plates hung on ancient racks, and dumbbells ranged from five to a hundred and fifty pounds, much higher than most gyms. Haggard weight benches and not a machine in the place, other than the traditional pulleys for seated rows and lateral pulldowns. Four treadmills. I half expected Arnold Schwarzenegger and Lou Ferrigno to walk in. The patrons were that big.

The men wore spaghetti straps and short shorts for better visual access to their muscles. The women wore spandex trunks and sports bras. A guy in the far corner held a bowl in one hand and a small paint brush in the other. He dipped the brush into the bowl and swiped it across his skin, painting himself a metallic brown. The behemoth smiled when he'd finished, happy with his handiwork. A woman sat on a weight bench eating a chicken breast, brown rice, and beans from a Tupperware container. A mid-workout meal. Another guy posed shirtless in front of a mirror, grunting loudly as he contorted himself into various positions. Practicing, I supposed. And it smelled bad, like mould, sweat, and those powdery workout drinks. Wall-to-wall mirrors gave the impression of a fun house for meatheads.

These people meant business, and it both intimidated and fascinated me, a culture unto itself.

I spotted Arkell, and she fit in with the ethos of the place, wearing pink, oversized headphones above white-blonde hair and a face free of makeup, as she hammered out a set of dumbbell flys. Her chest muscles, swollen from stress, glistened with perspiration. She finished her set, dropped the weights, and stood. Her body was so overdeveloped that she looked unreal.

"Arkell," I said.

She took off her headphones. "Hey."

"You have a minute?"

She smiled. "I got a minute. What's up?"

"I've been hired to find Sadie Rowe. I understand you two know each other."

Arkell paused. "Who are you?"

"My name's Jake Joelsen."

"Are you a cop?"

"No, private."

She nodded. "Hired by Nia?"

I shrugged a "maybe."

Arkell drank deeply from a four-litre jug filled with a lightly coloured red liquid. Her eyes never left mine as she considered me. People often told me I was direct. Some said blunt. Others called it harsh.

"Anyone ever tell you that you look like that guy–the actor–what's his name?"

She kept staring at me as she tried to recall the name, but there was curiosity there, too, like she was trying to figure me out. I gave her time, thought about my next words, and reminded myself to soften my voice as best I could. I needed her to know I cared, even if I asked tough questions.

"It'll come to me," she said.

I waited, but she couldn't recall the actor.

"I'm here because I want to find Sadie," I said, moving on. "She might be in trouble. Anything you say will stay between us."

"Okay ..."

"When was the last time you spoke with her?"

Arkell checked her phone and said, "By text ... October fourteenth. I've texted her since then, called, DM'd, sent her Snaps, but she hasn't responded."

I nodded as I made notes in my phone. "Have you talked to her parents?"

"No." Arkell took another sip. "Her parents are losers. I doubt they even know she's gone."

"I heard about Watershed Moments."

"Yeah, it's a cult of epic proportions. Mind-control-type shit."

"What can you tell me about it?

"Well, they have a congregation of, like, thousands of people. That's not exaggeration, either. I'm talking for real, thousands." Arkell stiffened, then loosened up. "The minister is a man called Uncle Walton ..."

It took me a second to realize she wasn't joking. I hesitated and she read my mind.

"I'm not shitting you," she said. "That's what members of the church call him–Uncle."

"That's fucked up."

She nodded as I added the name Walton to my notes.

"Have you been there?" I said.

"To the church? Hell, no. You couldn't pay me to step foot in that place."

I was averse to most kinds of authority, and religion was no different. "Maybe you can help me understand why anyone would want to be a part of a church like that?"

Arkell shook her head. "They get 'em young, and like anything when you're young, you buy in with"–she paused, searching for the right words–"blind commitment. And then you're part of something, and once you're part of something, it becomes who you are. What you do. It takes up all your time, shapes your identity, your worldview, and it gets to where you don't know how to live any other way."

That was the best description of human beings that I'd heard in a while. She'd summarized my drinking career in less than ten seconds. It's just what I did.

"I've been told Sadie quit the church six months ago. You know why she left?"

"No ... not why. Maybe she finally wanted out. Despite what I said, people do change." Arkell looked around the gym like she was seeing it for the first time. "Five years ago, if you would have told me I'd be here, lifting weights, training every day, I'd never have believed it. Never."

"I know," I said, and smiled. "I saw your grade nine picture."

"How?" she said, and then answered her own question. "Instagram. Sadie posted it."

I nodded and paused, trying to picture the two of them in high school. A white kid from a wicked-strict religious family, and a young Indigenous kid. It seemed like an unlikely duo.

"What drew you to her?" I asked.

Her eyes narrowed as she thought about it. "Sadie and I were outsiders. In hindsight, I think we were both very afraid. We didn't have friends, and people generally stayed away from us. I was angry. Sadie was just weird."

"How so?"

"The way she dressed, the way she talked. She knew almost nothing about movies, music, celebrities, and forget about anything in the news. I don't think the Rowes owned a TV. She was so naive, but old in other ways, she seemed ... world-weary. Like she'd seen it all yet knew nothing." Arkell shook her head. "It was just bizarre."

I let her finish, then took the time to type a summary of what she'd said. I looked up and Arkell was staring at me. I didn't not like it.

"Did she have a boyfriend in high school? Other friends?" I asked.

"Nah, only me. And Nia, of course. I didn't know anyone from the church."

"Do you know if she has a boyfriend now?"

Arkell took another sip. "Sadie's not the way she was in high school. I'm sure she has lots of boyfriends now."

"Why's that?"

She paused. "In high school she rarely made eye contact, couldn't make friends, and people just stayed away from her. Not long after high school, Sadie started partying, and the shift was immediate. She got louder, more intense about social justice and protests and shit like that. She never backed down from a fight. She got involved in women's rights, LGBTQ+ issues, Black Lives Matter. If there was a protest, march, or rally," Arkell said, "Sadie was there. It didn't hurt that she's gorgeous. People were just drawn to her. Vulnerable people. People who needed someone to admire."

I updated my notes. "Do you have any idea where she might be?"

Arkell didn't hesitate. "I think she probably went out of town."

"She'd do that? Leave on her own?"

"Sure," she said. "Or she's been partying too much and in one of her funks. Pouting. She does that, too."

"I heard she was depressed."

"I don't know about depressed, but when you party like a maniac, there's bound to be negative consequences. Shaky mental health is one of them. Is that depression or a side effect? I'm not sure."

"Does Sadie use drugs?"

Arkell nodded. "It isn't a secret."

"Do you know what she's using, and maybe where she gets it?"

"Oh, man. You're really going there." She stopped to collect her thoughts. "I haven't partied with her in a long time. She smokes dope. Together, we had a rougher phase where we were doing coke. Where she gets it now? I wouldn't know." Her hands moved to her headphones. "Listen, I need to get back to my workout. Provincials are in three weeks."

"You compete?"

"I do. Physique category."

"Well, I'll let you get to it, then. Call me if you hear anything."

I gave Arkell my number and she typed it in her phone.

"Tom Hardy ..." she said, readying for her set.

"What's that?"

She smiled. "The actor you look like. It's Tom Hardy."

Headphones on, she picked up the weights, seemingly satisfied that she'd recalled the name she could not earlier. As I headed for the exit, I wondered if Arkell Lightfoot had a boyfriend. Then I remembered that I was going to prison in two weeks, so what did it matter?

Fuck.

6

I drove down Pembina Highway behind a Ford Focus with an Every Child Matters sticker on the rear window, stopping every hundred feet at a light. It seemed other cities had mastered the art of planning, but city planners in Winnipeg liked to haphazardly string together freeways and add streetlights until the speed limit was eighty, but you were lucky if you hit fifty.

On the radio, the talking heads were lambasting the effort of the Winnipeg Jets, who'd lost 4 to 2 to the Arizona Coyotes at home the previous night, calling the team a "longshot to make the playoffs."

An urge struck, so I moved through traffic to an exit and parked in the lot of a Best Buy. I Googled Watershed Moments, found it, and recorded the address. I set the GPS and followed directions to Bishop Grandin Boulevard, drove for five minutes, turned right headed south on St. Mary's Road, and continued past St. Vital mall, all the way to the perimeter where the city proper ended, to a satellite community called St. Adolphe. On the outskirts of that town, I saw two huge buildings that were set back from a newly paved Gauthier Road, on a massive property stretching the better part of ten acres. The first enormous building had a sign that read Watershed Moments: The Church of Spiritual Enlightenment. The slightly smaller, but still huge, building was labeled Christian Academy. Dozens of vehicles were parked on a football-field-sized parking lot, in the shadows of a fifty-foot outdoor screen, stage, and an eight-foot-high wrought-iron fence that surrounded the plot.

The church was only accessible via a no-name access road, which I drove slowly until I found a driveway and turned in. To the left was a shack, and there were two men inside. Straight ahead, a heavy gate blocked my way. One of the men came to my window. He wore a uniform, boots, and a serious expression. His hands were free, and he placed them inside the frame of my rolled-down window. I didn't like it.

"Do you have business here today?" he said.

"No, I must have gotten turned around. Do you know how I can get back to the freeway? Can I keep going this way?" I said, pointing opposite to the way I'd come.

"That's a dead end. The only way out is to go back to Gauthier and hang a right," he said.

"Thanks. You've been helpful."

I smiled at the man as I reversed and drove off. I considered waving, but that would have been overkill. I pulled onto the shoulder of Gauthier where I had a view of the church but was far enough away so that the guard probably couldn't see my vehicle, and Googled Watershed Moments again. On their website, there was very little about beliefs or denomination. Contact information was only a phone number, but there were biographies of the leadership. Brad Walton–Uncle Walton–was the senior minister. Walton's biography read: *Brad Walton is an inspiring public speaker, a true leader, and the righteous one to lead us into Heaven.*

The picture showed a man approaching sixty, with a full head of grey hair swept back and parted on the right side of his head. He had tanned skin, a thick moustache, and dark eyebrows hanging like curtains, shading his eyes, making him look stern. He wore a light grey suit over a white shirt, and a red tie crawled down the front of his body like a tongue.

Could Sadie have gone back to the church?

Nia said it was unlikely, but a church had talons and, like Arkell said, once they'd pierced skin, it was difficult to get them out. I needed to speak with Brad Walton.

I dialed the number on the site and a woman answered.

"Hello," she said.

"Hi, can I please speak with Brad Walton?"

"Mr. Walton is unavailable. Can I take a message?"

"I'm looking to join Watershed Moments. What time are your services?"

"It doesn't work like that. If you'd like to attend, you need to qualify."

"Qualify ... for what?"

"Salvation."

I wasn't sure if I should laugh or cry.

"How do I qualify?" I asked.

"We send someone out and there's an interview. I can make an appointment for you if you'd like."

"Thank you for your time," I said, ending the call.

I sat back and watched the church. Growing up, my family had attended church once a year, on Christmas Day, before Christmas dinner with my mom's side of the family. At one of these dinners in the late nineties, my dad stood behind me in the buffet line, surveying a spread of dumplings, cabbage rolls, perogies, ham, turkey, stuffing, corn, salad, and meatballs.

He carried a plate in one hand and a drink in the other. His shaky legs caused drops to spill over the rim of the glass. Dad speared a piece of ham with the serving fork and bit off a chunk. My mom gently pushed his arm to guide the fork back onto the table, but Dad jerked his arm away, and his drink flew across the room. The glass hit the floor and blew up like a water balloon, covering people in whiskey and Coke.

My five-year-old cousin, Robbie, looked at the stains on his shirt as liquid ran down his face. Slowly, his expression drooped, and his eyes filled with tears. A spastic cry erupted from his tiny body and, of course, my Auntie Syd consoled him.

"Well, Jesus Christ!" Dad said. "What a waste of good drinkin' booze!"

Robbie continued to howl.

"Oh, come on, little man. Suck it up," my dad said. "Nothing to cry about."

"He's five, Uncle John," Syd said.

"I know that. When I was five, I smoked a pack a day and had two jobs."

"John!" my mom said, tugging at his arm.

"Get your hand off of me!"

People stared.

Cousins watched my dad, their faces showing concern, but

they didn't know what to do. Uncles and aunts looked at my mom, wondering how she managed. Some averted their eyes altogether.

A variation of the same situation happened every few months. My dad would get smashed and hurl insults, break a glass, or pass out at the table. It wasn't uncommon for him to be puking drunk on the car ride home and not remember a damn thing the next day. My mom handled these situations with dignity. She appeared embarrassed and helpless, but she never backed down from him.

As the entire family waited for a resolution, Mom simply offered one last comment: "John, you owe Robbie an apology."

The earlier drunk version of my dad in Minneapolis had been giddy. But the version on display in the buffet line was the angry asshole. People chose not to get involved with the asshole, eating their dumplings, turkey, and perogies with their heads down and mouths shut.

My dad didn't apologize, so Mom dragged him into the kitchen and they had it out. He called her dramatic, and she told him she'd never have more kids with him. It angered me at the time, but I understood it now. My dad would vanish for days without explanation. He'd lost jobs, friends, family–everything he valued. We declared bankruptcy and Dad's mental health deteriorated to the point where he needed to be hospitalized more than once. Psyche wards, mental hospitals, stints in rehab and sober houses. You name it and he tried it. I guess he finally said "fuck it" and didn't want to be with us anymore. Gave up. Or maybe tragedy befell him. Who knew?

But marriage required a partner, and John Joelsen couldn't carry the weight. How could you raise children with a man like that?

A white Toyota 4Runner left the parking lot of Watershed Moments, pulling me out of the waking nightmare. The vehicle headed toward me, a man in his forties behind the wheel. I let him drive past, pulled out and followed, the church shrinking in my rearview mirror.

I wished some memories would do the same.

7

I followed the 4Runner to St Mary's, crossed the perimeter highway, and drove into the city. I made sure to stay at least two cars behind him, which wasn't hard to do in the bumper-to-bumper traffic. He turned right onto Bishop, left on Lagimodière, and took Laj until we got to Concordia Avenue, where he exited into a middle-class neighbourhood called East Kildonan. The traffic was steady, enough for me to stay back and hidden while not losing him at a light. He pulled into a bungalow on Louelda, the garage door opened, and he drove in. I waited for the door to close, drove past, and parked on the next street.

A blow-up witch had been mounted on the lawn, and pumpkins lined the front walk. There were poorly drawn pictures–jack-o'-lanterns, bats, more pumpkins–taped to the windows. I knocked and two kids answered the door, jostling for position.

"Hi," I said. "Is your dad home?"

The girl turned and shouted "Dad!" and the man behind the wheel came to the door.

"Hi," he said. "How can I help you?"

I waited until the kids were back in the house, out of earshot.

"My name's Jake Joelsen, and I've been hired to find a missing woman. She was a member at Watershed Moments, and I'm hoping you know her."

He stepped out of the house, closed the door, and I backed up. I stood on the steps as he came closer, hovering over me. He seemed to be deciding how to approach the situation. He wasn't huge, but he had the build of a rugby player with a sturdy base and thick upper body.

"What brought you here?" he asked, folding his arms across his chest.

"I tried to get into the church but couldn't. I watched you pull out of the lot after me, and I followed you."

"You followed me?" he said, his voice hard. "To my house? Where I live with my family? What's the matter with you?"

He had a point.

"I don't want to cause you trouble," I said, "but I have questions, and right now you're my only in."

He took another step toward me, uncrossed his arms, and I thought he'd swing. I transferred weight to my back foot and held my ground. It surprised me when he said, "Please leave."

He didn't turn to go back in the house, though, and I took that as my cue to carry on.

"What if it was your child?" I said. "Or your sister?"

"Hey ... you don't talk about my family."

"It's hard to think about, isn't it? That's the situation for my client. They just want to know where Sadie is and that she's okay."

I had dropped the name on purpose.

"Sadie?" he said.

"Sadie Rowe."

Recognition showed on his face, and he froze, rubbed his chin and scratched a cheek. He brought the hand to his head and ran it through his hair. "Let's go in the garage."

We walked over and he typed a code into a little box. The door opened and we walked in. The 4Runner occupied half of the space, and the other stall had been converted into a man cave. A couch, recliner, and coffee table sat before a big-screen TV mounted on the wall. He closed the garage door halfway but didn't sit down.

"What do you want to know?"

"Why Sadie left the church," I said. "Did something happen that made her leave? Was she forced out? I get the sense Watershed Moments does that."

He shook his head, like he couldn't believe his rotten luck, then whispered "shit" to himself, walked to a freezer near the door to the house, and pulled out a pack of cigarettes from behind it. He opened the pack, removed a smoke and lighter, and lit up. The tough-guy exterior melted away, replaced with hesitancy and a lack of confidence. He looked rattled.

"Sadie ..." he said, sighing.

"You knew her?"

He waved the cigarette and began pacing. I lit one, too.

"Not really," he said. "I know her parents, that's about it. But her departure was an event."

"What do you mean?"

"I–well–it's unusual for a member to leave." He took a hit as he walked, then stopped abruptly. "It's not that I don't want to help, you know. It's that I can't. I just–"

"I understand," I said. "You have to think of your standing within the church."

"Yeah, there's that, but ... we were directed not to talk about Sadie."

"With outsiders?"

"With anyone."

"Even within the church?"

"With anyone in or out of the church."

"If you can't talk about the reasons Sadie left," I said, hoping there was a way around this, "maybe you can tell me what she was like."

"I didn't know her."

I blew smoke across the room. "How long have you been a member?"

"My whole life."

"My understanding is that Sadie was born into the church, too. If you saw her there for twenty-plus years, you must have an impression. You know her parents, and I suspect the Watershed Moments community is a tight one."

He returned to pacing, took a final drag, dropped the smoke and stepped on it. "Sadie always seemed unhappy, like she didn't want to be there."

"Where?"

"At church services, concerts, fundraisers, congregational meals. Anything. Just a miserable-looking human, you know. One of those people that had problems. But as she got older ..." he said, searching for the words, "she was also, what's the word? Like, magnetic."

He got embarrassed by his choice of words.

"Magnetic?" I said.

"Well, I get a bit, umm ... uncomfortable talking about it, you know. I'm not good with my words."

"That's okay. Most people aren't. Do your best."

He thought about it, then lit a new cigarette. "I watched her front teeth get knocked out, and she didn't even cry."

"Jesus ..."

"She was like ten years old."

"She's twenty-three now, so 2006?"

"Around then, yeah, that sounds right. It was at a church event. Middle of winter. We rented one of those tents, the ones they use for weddings, and set it up over by the Valley Gardens hills. Even heated it. The kids went tobogganing, you know. Those crazy carpets."

He shook his head as he recalled a detail.

"Sadie lost control of her carpet and collided with the monkey bars at the bottom of the hill. She kneeled, mitts to her mouth, blood soaking through them. Nia ran over, but she didn't know what to do."

"Shit ..." I said to prompt him.

"That's not the part that made an impact on me."

"Sadie panicked?"

"No, the opposite. Sadie was calm, showed no signs of stress. Nia froze. *She* panicked. Sadie actually made sure Nia was okay. Can you believe that? Her teeth had been knocked out, and she consoled her sister. Then she scoured the snow."

"For the teeth?" I said, impressed.

"That's right. Sadie found her own teeth, placed them in the pocket of her coat. Even pulled Nia to her feet. When they got to the tent, their parents put the teeth in a glass of milk and drove the girls to the hospital."

"Why do you remember this story? After so many years?"

He took a moment. "Sadie scared me."

She was ten, I thought. What could make a grown man fear a ten-year-old girl?

"Why?"

"She had a ..." he said, and stopped, unsure of himself. "She had a sadness. It seemed inevitable something bad would happen to her."

I wasn't sure how to process his last comments. I didn't believe in fate, and I sure didn't agree that Sadie's life was affected by an unstoppable sadness.

"There must be others," I said.

"What do you mean?"

"Others who've left. Sadie can't have been the only one."

"My nephew." He plopped onto the couch and hung his head. "He was friends with Sadie."

"What's his name?" I asked.

He hesitated, took a drag. "Tracy Remple."

I wrote the name in my phone. "When did he leave?"

The man stared at the smoke like it would give him answers. "It was a little more than a year ago. I'm not sure why he left. He was just gone, and then, umm ... the congregation was directed not to speak on it. Same as with Sadie." He drooped and seemed to blend into the sofa. He shook his head, and his eyes became watery. "I miss Tracy, you know. I really miss him. My sister's boy."

"You know where I'd find him?"

He shook his head. "Nah, he moved from his old apartment, and we haven't spoken since he left. His parents aren't in touch with him, either."

"How old is he?"

"Twenty. I heard, through the grapevine, that he's an apprentice plumber. Works for a place called Crestman or Crestway. Something like that."

The door to the house opened, and the man dropped the cigarette, extinguishing it with his shoe. Two women in their mid-thirties stepped onto the landing at the top of the stairs leading to the house. The first one said, "Henry, will your friend be staying for supper? It's almost ready."

Henry spun toward them.

"No," he said.

"Five minutes, sweetie," the second woman said.

"I'll be right in."

I thought the one who called him "sweetie" must be his wife, the other one a sister, or maybe his wife's sister.

"Thank you," I said, and turned to go, but stopped. "Your name's Henry?"

"Yeah. Henry Formenton."

I nodded. "When you're directed not to talk about these people, who is it delivering that message?"

Henry located the stepped-on butts and put them in a Ziplock bag he kept hidden on a shelf. The bag was three-quarters full. He looked at me but didn't say a word, his face a mask, part fear, part indecision.

"Was it Brad Walton?" I asked.

Henry nodded. "I-I can't ..."

"I understand," I said, and turned to go.

"Hey," he called out, "if you find him, umm ... Tracy, I mean. Let me know."

I stopped.

"Only if he wants me to," I said, and ducked under the garage door.

***

That night, I toured Sadie's haunts, two nightclubs and a dive bar next to a laundromat that didn't even have a name. In the bar, I listened to two middle-aged men argue over which of their trucks had more power, a Chevy Silverado or a Ford F-150. I went outside with the crowd when they parked rear to rear, hooked a thick chain from the hitches of each vehicle, got in, and hammered on the gas. The Ford's engine blew up, smoke billowed from the hood, and the crowd hooted and hollered as if cheering on their favourite team. Cash changed hands, people swore, and the owner of the Chevy danced in a circle, taunting his opponent, a move that cost him a right hand to the chin. He lay there for a moment, got up, and declared, with a shit-eating grin on his mug, that he was owed a beer.

No one had spoken to Sadie, and they didn't know any men

named Tracy.

At the Palomino Club, I watched young people dance like malfunctioning robots, shimmying back and forth, dropping low, and caressing each other with wild abandon. I spoke to three bartenders, five servers, and the manager. None of them had heard of Tracy Remple, but everyone knew Sadie. They hadn't seen her recently.

I wanted to drink so badly I could barely breathe, but I kept hearing Roger Bancroft's words. I thought about my mom and abstained.

The night ended with a bang in a place called the Disco, an older joint clinging to Portage Avenue like a threat. I met a woman from Alberta who took me to an after-party at a Victorian mansion in Old Tuxedo. We had awkward, uncomfortable sex before I tiptoed out at 3 a.m. to a round of applause from three middle-aged men, who were still up, playing poker and drinking. If this was what sober life was like, I'd rather be drunk.

8

Thursday, October 17 (two days missing)

I woke up disoriented with a dry mouth and a slight headache behind my right eye. My body, used to a daily dose of alcohol, felt weak. I got out of bed and checked my Kijiji account. Three people had contacted me about my truck. I read their profiles and messages. One asked if I'd accept fifteen thousand, which was a hard pass, and the other two wanted to see the truck, so I replied and said I could meet later that day. I gave my cell number.

I ate a bowl of Vector, showered, shaved, and brushed my teeth, feeling somewhat human again. Henry Formenton had speculated that Remple worked for a plumbing company that started with a C. My search revealed there were eighteen in the city. I narrowed the search to include only those that started with Cr. Two. Crestview and Crescentwood.

I could call both and ask if Tracy Remple was available. Might work, but unlikely. Remple was probably on a job site, and I couldn't see them releasing personal details like that. I searched Crestview AND 2019 and found three jobs listed on their website that were current. I did the same with Crescentwood but didn't get much. It seemed like they were a smaller outfit. I'd start with Crestview.

I found my Carhartt overalls, put on a T-shirt and a Dickies coat I'd had for years, with steel-toed boots and a hard hat I'd kept from my construction days.

Twenty minutes later, I arrived at the first site, a hotel in St. Boniface. I did a thorough walk-through, talked to a handful of people, and when it became clear Remple wasn't there, I left.

I drove to site number two, an addition to the University of Winnipeg, walked around again, spoke to more people with no luck, and was back on the road within the hour.

The third and final site on my list was the Health Sciences Centre, a sprawling hospital in the heart of downtown. It took ten minutes to park and another fifteen to navigate the network of complex walkways and confusing signage. My head ached and frustration grew. I could really go for a pint and a shot of vodka, but I had neither, just a swelling irritation.

I found the site, tarped off and secured with a makeshift door built into the wall. I opened the door and walked in. Tradespeople worked, mostly men, but a few women, too. They pulled wire, climbed ladders, drilled, trimmed lumber, laid pipe, ran tin, and hauled supplies. Two men pored over drawings, flipping pages and talking with their hands. Another group of three pointed at something in the ceiling. One man described a problem and outlined a plan to fix it. He walked along to show the others as he spoke. It was like a colony of ants, everyone with a task. You did your job, the others did theirs. Walls were framed and open, exposing wires. Pipes ran here and there, in various stages of completion. I saw the Crestview name and logo on several hard hats, but none of the people were the right age. It didn't take long before I found one who fit.

A man lay on his back, contorting himself to work on a pipe. He had a thin, narrow frame, and his hair stopped just above his shoulders–he reminded me of Eddie Vedder. I tried my luck.

"Remple, you have a sec?"

He looked up from his back like a mechanic under a vehicle might.

"What's up?" he said, skeptical.

"Are you Tracy Remple?"

"I am." He slid out from under the pipe, picked up his hard hat, and smiled cautiously.

"My name's Jake Joelsen. I'd like to ask you a few questions."

"Do you work here?" he said, looking around to see if anyone watched us.

"No."

"What do you want to talk about?"

"Sadie Rowe," I said.

His expression changed from unsure to confused as he stood up, placed the hard hat on his head, and wiped his brow.

He shook his head. "Sadie?" His eyes took on a sheen, not tears, but a glaze of emotion. "I haven't spoken to her in ... a long time."

"She left the church about six months ago."

"That's good," he said, and looked like he meant it. "I'm glad she got out." He paused. "One second ..."

Remple walked to a porta-potty, opened the door, and stepped inside. As I waited, strange memories from my past rose to the surface. One after another, they arrived, unwelcome and hostile.

I saw scarred wooden tables in nameless pubs, saw myself drinking beers and telling stories.

The boys I'd lived with in group, sitting on the couch, cracking wise and acting tough.

My dad, reading the newspaper on the recliner, football on the TV.

My mom, rustling around in the kitchen, preparing supper.

I was restless, anger flaring in my chest, glad when Remple returned a moment later. It took an incredible amount of willpower not to shake him, not to scream "Sadie's missing! Tell me what you know!" but that would cause him to shut down. I waited for him to speak, what felt like hours.

"Why are you here?" he finally said.

"Sadie's missing, and I've been hired to find her."

"And you think I know where she is?"

"I don't know. I understand you used to know her, and I'd like you to tell me about that."

"You're asking a lot," Remple said.

He turned and stared off into the distance, pondering what I'd said. Then he looked me in the eye.

"Okay," he said. "My lunch is in twenty minutes. Meet me in the cafeteria."

I nodded. "I'll buy you lunch."

"I'll take you up on that offer," he said, and got back to work on the pipe.

***

Remple opened a chicken salad sandwich, took two huge bites, and then sipped from a bottle of iced tea. I opened my ham and Swiss but left it untouched.

"Thanks for speaking to me," I said.

He nodded. "Let's begin the interrogation."

I smiled and watched as he chewed the food slowly, like if it took long enough, maybe I'd go away. He didn't seem like a bad guy, and his movements were steady, eyes alert, pupils normal. I hadn't seen any scabs or needle marks, no obvious signs of hard drug use, but whatever happened at that church had obviously left a mark on him. He swallowed and had another sip of tea.

I bit into my sandwich. "I heard you left Watershed Moments."

"Yeah, August of last year."

"Why'd you leave?"

He scoffed. "Where to begin ..."

"Let's start with Sadie."

He rolled his neck from side to side, working the kinks out.

"I was told she uses drugs," I added. "You know if that's true?"

Remple shifted and broke eye contact. Eventually, he returned to me, nodding yes.

"You know that for a fact?" I said.

"Yeah ... I was in that life, too. I'm not anymore," he said quickly, as if he wanted to get that out in the open before I could chastise him. "But I was a mess."

"On drugs?"

He laughed under his breath at a private joke, but the humour left his face so fast it gave me a start.

"Why should I tell you anything?" he said.

I took a bite and washed it down with water, contemplating my next move and how I'd play it. I had to be careful. Most people wanted to relieve themselves of secrets, especially if those secrets had caused them or others harm. From past mistakes grew heavy burdens, and the weight of them could hold you down as if drowning. But if you hammered a damaged person too hard, too fast, they'd clam up and you'd get nothing. Remple seemed like he was like that, the type for whom sharing didn't come easily. I wondered if this was his natural disposition or if it had been beaten into him. I chose honesty and gave it my best shot.

"I don't know why you'd help me," I began, "but you could have said no at the site and you're sitting here, so that means you care. Maybe it has to do with why you left the church, like helping me is redemption for you, a way to ease the guilt you've felt since you left. Or maybe you're here to see what I know, because you're worried I might dig into your past. I don't know, but Sadie's been missing for two days. I don't think I need to tell you how serious this is. Anything you say to me now, I'll use only to find her. I won't get you in trouble with Watershed Moments, your family, or the law."

The cafeteria pulsed with conversation, hospital employees and people visiting loved ones. Remple smiled.

"That's some speech ..."

"I try," I said, and smiled along with him.

"Fuck ..." he said to himself, not in anger or frustration, but in release. "It's been a minute since Watershed Moments came up. That place–" He drank, finishing the bottle.

"Take your time."

"That church is a nightmare." Remple squeezed the empty iced tea bottle, pushing in the plastic and releasing it so it popped. He did it again and again. "You know I didn't say fuck until I turned nineteen. I'd sold drugs, but I'd never sworn."

He laughed, but this time he was on his own.

"You were a dealer?" I said.

He looked surprised at my question, like he'd forgotten his admission. "Sort of."

Restlessness bubbled up inside me, and I leaned forward and placed my hands in a steeple. "I don't understand."

"I sold for a while ... maybe a year."

"Sold what?"

"Meth."

I had so many questions. Who supplied you? Where'd you sell?

How'd you begin selling? But I kept the focus on the job, what I was there to do. "Was Sadie doing meth?"

Hesitation, fidgeting, and a terse nod, *Yes*. He tilted his head to the side, recalling a memory. "I'm ashamed of that time in my life. I live every day trying to make up for it. But there isn't anything I can do. It–I-I can't change what I did."

I believed his regret was genuine, but I couldn't stop anger from rising in my chest, an animal burrowing its way up to the light. I worked hard to keep it under control. I also felt guilty for my degenerate lifestyle, and the combination made me weary.

I asked how he went from drug dealer to apprentice plumber, and he shrugged.

"My dad died about a year and a half ago," he said. "He was one of the founding members of the church. Brad Walton is senior minister. He's also co-founder. My dad was his second in command."

Remple tensed, readying himself.

"I found notebooks when I was going through my dad's stuff," he continued. "This was after he died. Boxes of notebooks. I started reading and realized each notebook was like a record of events. Marriages ... fundraisers and finances ... sex acts."

That caught me off guard. "Sex acts?"

"The pages were full of lists. Columns with rows. Names of the men and women. Dates and money exchanged. In the far column there was a brief description of what had occurred ..."

"You're telling me," I said, dumbfounded, "that your dad or someone else at Watershed Moments kept records of their sexual lives?"

"Not their lives. People who had paid to have sex with women in the church." Remple thought about it. "I shouldn't have said anything ..."

"Why would they do this?"

"Money." He paused, scratched his cheek. "Power. To keep a record in case one of the women wanted to leave? Who knows. It could be they were all just sick fucks."

It was a fair point, and one I thought about often. Did people need motivation to be cruel or was it the way of a world designed to reward survival of the fittest?

"How old were these women?" I said.

"It ranged, but they were young."

A concrete block of impending doom settled in my stomach. "Was Sadie in there? In these notebooks?"

Remple twisted the iced tea bottle, and a couple at the table next to us looked over. He apologized to them for the noise and then nodded to me, head down. "Yes."

"Where are the notebooks now?" I asked.

"I burned them."

"You what?" I said loudly.

The couple turned again, but I didn't apologize. I gritted my teeth and breathed so hard through my nose that I felt the hairs move with each breath. How could someone be so stupid?

"At any point," I said, "did you bring the notebooks to the police?"

His lip quivered and his eyes filled with tears. "No."

"Did you make copies?"

More vibrations as the first tear fell. "No."

"How old was Sadie when her name was written in the notebook?"

"Sixteen," he said. "Sixteen years old."

Remple covered his face with his hands in shame. I'm sure it looked like he was grieving a family member who was in the hospital, but I knew better. I held my anger at bay by telling myself he'd been a victim, a child forced into a church, and victims needed compassion, not judgment and punishment. That didn't stop me from wanting to kick the shit out of him.

"I'm sorry you found those notebooks," I said, "and I'm sorry you grew up in that place."

We exchanged numbers, and I said I'd be in touch. Then I left the cafeteria, walked down the maze of hallways, and out into the chill of a fall afternoon. Nothing felt the same.

9

One person canceled, so that meant I had one interested party wanting to check out my truck. We met in the lot of a Walmart, and he spent more time than I would have liked inspecting and driving it. When the guy asked questions, I answered quickly, absorbed by Tracy Remple's tale and the cryptic notebooks.

I believed his emotions were honest, but was the story true? Why would Remple lie?

Sadie had been sixteen years old.

The age I'd left foster care and entered juvie.

Just a kid, really.

I thought about Judge Leaf and what she'd said to me two days ago, before she suspended my sentence.

"Jake, from what I've witnessed of your demeanour in court during the limited time I've spent in your presence, and your unwillingness to apologize to the victim, Mr. Francis, I have no option but to believe you are not remorseful for your actions. In addition to the assault against the victim, you were admittedly drunk and extremely impaired on the night of April twentieth when you drove to the victim's residence and committed the assault. I am also aware that your dad disappeared when you were thirteen, and that you were removed by family services from the care of your mother shortly after, due to her alcoholism and neglect for your well-being."

At the time, I thought, Here we go again, another person searching for excuses on my behalf, looking for reasons to explain what I'd done.

To me, it was simple: If you hurt me or my people, then I hurt you. Cory Francis hit my mom, so I hit him.

The buyer asked if I'd do eighteen, snapping me back to the moment, and I said no, countered at twenty-two, and we agreed on twenty. I gave him a bill of sale to complete, and he left to get a bank draft. We made plans to complete the transaction the next morning.

***

Sport Sphere Industries on Fort Street inhabited a building with a white stone façade, tall windows, and the name PERCIVAL carved into the block above the door like a name bar on the back of an athlete's jersey. I knew nothing about architecture, so I typed *Percival Building* into a search engine on my phone and read.

This historical landmark is in the style favoured near the turn of the century, when fired clay was used on the exterior of buildings, creating a ceramic look invented thousands of years prior. Built in 1909 by Samuel T. Thompson, the original structure was only one storey until a one-storey addition in 1912 brought it to its current size and scope. A saloon occupied the space for twenty-two years, and in 1931, Thompson sold the building to the Manitoba Federation of Businesses, who renovated it and opened a legion to support local entrepreneurs from 1932 to 1945. The building has served many purposes since 1945, including a furniture company and a manufacturer of garments. After a long period of emptiness and neglect, Barry and Estelle Robson bought the building in 2010, renovated it, and Sport Sphere Industries has occupied the space since then.

I visited the Sport Sphere site next and clicked on the About page, confused by a logo of a gold cartoon person running, its legs ending in a swirly ribbon. It dawned on me that it was a tribute to the Golden Boy, a twenty-foot-tall statue of the Greek god Hermes that sat on top of the legislative building downtown, hovering over the city like an overbearing parent. Sport Sphere provided custom website design, copy writing, and custom optimization for "elite sports-centric programs," whatever that meant.

I walked in, floored by the white walls, white couches, and a white chair.

"Woah," I said. "I need sunglasses."

The young woman who sat behind a desk, also white, smiled. Her nametag said Krista. I said I had an appointment with Dustin

Bannerman, and she said he'd be right out. As I waited, I checked out the space. The desks were attached at right angles, with partitions dividing the workspaces. Employees stared at laptops or large monitors with additional arms. Circular lights hung low from the ceiling on thin (white) cords. On the walls were charts and a whiteboard. At the far end of the room, I could see two offices and a large boardroom, glass walls, and a sliding glass door.

Nothing I heard on the phone prepared me for how Bannerman came slow walking out of his office in the back. I half expected him to stop and pose as if on the end of a runway. He stood over six feet tall, with longish, combed-back hair that blew softly in the breeze of an imaginary fan. Guy was handsome, real handsome, and he had an air of authority. He looked to be around fifty. We shook hands.

"Nice to meet you," I said.

"Of course. Follow me."

He had a slight accent from the southern United States. Texas, maybe?

"Sure," I said, and followed him to his office, where his name and title–Director of Accounts–had been stenciled on the glass door. The open blinds showed the dull clouds of an overcast day above a beige brick building, and a teenager sat on a fire escape three floors up, smoking. A painting on the wall of the office, of a cowboy riding a horse over the expanse of a desert, was familiar. The horse's auburn coat amplified its muscular body, and the cowboy gazed yonder at the setting sun. Two floating shelves held trophies and plaques. Manitoba Best Business Awards 2015, 2017, and 2018. I wondered what happened in 2016.

We both sat, and up close I could tell I was way off on my original guess of fifty. I'd say Bannerman was forty-one or two, although he seemed older.

He said, "I've created a schedule in twenty-minute increments for the people whose names you gave me on the phone, Janice Loughlin and Stu Westermann. How's that sound?"

"That works." I waited a beat, then asked, "Where are you from?"

Bannerman laughed. It was a good laugh, too, deep and genuine. "You're direct."

"Sometimes. Is it Texas?" I asked.

"Oklahoma."

"How'd you arrive on the Canadian prairies? Must have been for love."

The laugh became a smile. "No, not for love. It's a story for another time, or never, but I assure you, it wasn't love."

"Now who's direct?"

He smiled. "Touché."

I got out my phone. "Is there anything you can tell me about Sadie, before I meet with the others?"

"She's been working here for close to a year, give or take. She's an assistant to account executives."

"And how's she fitting in?"

"Well ... she's young, and she misses days too often, but she's a decent worker with room for improvement."

"Do you know why she misses?"

"It's probably better if you ask Janice about that. Janice is the account exec that works closest with Sadie," Bannerman said, smiling again, his jaw square and precise, as if built by a carpenter. "Are you ready to begin?"

"Let's do it," I said.

Bannerman stood. "Right this way."

He brushed past me, and our eyes met awkwardly. Strange guy, I thought as I shadowed him down a hallway into a small, neatly appointed lunchroom.

"There's water and glasses. Paper and pen," he said. "You need anything else?"

"No, that's it. Thanks."

Bannerman departed and a woman walked in.

She looked like an overly intense soccer mom, like if you messed with her kid on the field, she'd fight you in the parking lot in front of her minivan. Her long, mousy hair was straight, parted in the middle, and she wore a white, frilly blouse tucked into black dress pants. She was in her mid-thirties.

We shook hands and I introduced myself.

"Janice," she said.

"Thanks for seeing me."

"No problem," she said, and we sat down.

"Have you been briefed?"

"Briefed ..." she said sarcastically. "You sound like you're on a TV show. Yeah, I know what this is about."

I wondered why she was so pissed off, but that wasn't any of my business, so I kept my mouth shut and got down to business. "How long have you worked with Sadie Rowe?"

"Ten months. Since she started."

I jotted that down. "Do you work closely with her?"

"Yes and no. I coordinate account execs, as necessary, and I supervise the assistants, as well. You probably met Krista when you came in. She's in the same role as Sadie. In addition to supporting execs, assistants watch the front, complete clerical work, organizational tasks, etc."

I thought she might provide an anecdote, letting me know the nature of their relationship. Did they get along? Was Sadie a hard worker? Why did she miss so many days, as Bannerman had indicated? When she didn't elaborate, I said, "How's that going?"

"Excuse me?" she said, noticeably bothered.

"Is Sadie a good employee?"

"No."

Her answers were getting shorter, and I wondered if this would be a waste of time.

"How long have you worked here?" I asked.

"Nine years, minus two mat leaves."

"Dustin mentioned Sadie misses work more than is acceptable. Do you know why?"

"The excuses vary. Dentist appointment. The flu. That type of thing. She's on probation because of the absences."

"Probation?"

"It means she's been written up twice. If a third reprimand occurs, she'll be dismissed."

I took a little extra time, added to my notes, and considered my next question. Janice glanced at the clock again, and this time she knew I'd caught her.

She was the opposite of Tracy Remple, uptight and self-important. The only way Janice would share was if I challenged her.

"Did Sadie say if she was going out of town?" I said.

"No."

"Was Sadie at work on the fifteenth?"

Janice took a second, then said, "Yes."

"How well do you know her?"

Janice glared at me. "What do you mean?"

I looked up from my phone. "Did you spend time together outside of work?"

"We did, at the beginning." Janice checked her phone, typed quickly, then placed the phone on the table, sighing. "I like to go out once a month with my team. Most of the staff are young–twenties and thirties. It builds comradery. Sadie, well ... Sadie likes to drink."

"More than others?"

"More than everyone."

Janice looked away, and her hard disposition became something else, like she was considering sharing sensitive information.

"Is there more?" I asked.

She hesitated, then said, "She might've been using drugs."

Nia had said Sadie liked to party, and Arkell Lightfoot and Tracy Remple had said that Sadie did drugs, but if her boss knew, then it was worse than I'd thought.

I poured a glass of water, took a sip. "How do you know?"

"The absences, obviously," she said, "and there were other signs. She looked different. Skinnier."

"She lost weight from when she started?"

"Yeah, and on occasion, she smelled."

"Smelled? Like marijuana?"

Janice shook her head. "No, like BO. She had a hippie vibe that went too far. Greasy hair, bags under her eyes ..."

"Do you know what she was using?"

"I'm not sure." She shook her head. "Sadie and I were friends for a time." Janice had softened, and I thought this must be her real personality, once the veil had been removed. "She was never a great employee, but her first few months here, she was competent. She was even fun. Sadie's got attitude, and I liked that about her. But there's a fine line between someone who's tough and sticks up for themselves, and someone who causes problems. Unfortunately, she drifted into the latter category. I feel for her, and I hope she's okay, but I have kids, and I'm married. I don't want to be around drugs. This sounds bad, but it's only a matter of time before she gets that third reprimand and she's gone."

Whether it was the talk of drugs, I wasn't sure, but a wave of guilt–like the one I'd felt with Remple–threatened me with shitty thoughts. How many times had someone said that they couldn't be around me? How many times had I hurt someone without even knowing it? Dozens, maybe hundreds.

"I understand," I said. "Last question: Have you heard of a church called Watershed Moments?"

She shook her head. "No."

"Thanks for your time."

Janice left and I updated my notes.

***

Stu Westermann arrived next. He was the type of thin that looked frail, accentuated by a red polo and tight black pants.

"Hi, I'm Stu. Nice to meet you. Can't say how happy I am to help," he said, talking like it was a race, each word strung into the next with little room in between. "Sadie is like a big sister."

"Really?"

Stu's hands moved like he was performing a martial art. He spoke quickly, frantic is the word that came to mind, and I wondered if I'd found one of Sadie's drug companions.

"Yeah," Stu said. "She was always giving me advice, telling me to put myself out there and meet people, go on dates, you know."

"So, you get along well?"

"Oh yeah," he said. "We're friends."

"What kind of advice does she give you?"

"She told me not to settle for a girl that treats me like sh–"

"You can say it."

"Like shit."

He'd whispered shit like he'd assaulted my virgin ears. I smiled. "Do you work here full- or part-time?"

Stu brought one leg over the other. "Full."

"What do you do?"

"I go to the gym, I cook, I like to watch Netflix. I–"

This fucking guy thought he was hilarious.

"What do you do here?" I said.

"Oh," he said, feigning like he didn't understand my original question. "I'm a digital marketing specialist."

"These next questions might be uncomfortable. Are you ready?"

"Born ready."

"Good," I said, and leaned forward. "What drugs do you and Sadie use?"

I thought the question would bring panic–Oh shit, I'm about to be found out–Stu took it in stride, though.

"Well ..." he said, brimming ear to ear, "that's for me to know and you to find out, isn't it?" I took a moment, and when I didn't follow up, he added, "You look surprised."

"No offence, but you look like you own a hamster."

He laughed. "I have a turtle named Bender. I named him after–"

"The character in The Breakfast Club."

"You know the movie?"

"Everyone knows that movie. Look," I continued, "I don't care about your drug use, but I do care what Sadie uses and who she gets it from. It could help me find her."

Stu uncrossed his legs. "I own a turtle, but I'm not an idiot. How long has she been gone, a day?"

"Two days."

"Two days, dude. That's nothing."

"She's not answering her phone, texts and calls, and she missed work yesterday and today," I added.

Stu frowned and stiffened as he sat up straight. A poker face he did not have.

"I didn't know that. I wasn't in yesterday, so I didn't know." He pulled his phone from a pocket of his pants, typed. "Sadie always answers texts." He sank back into himself, thinking. "I can't give you a name, but ..." He got up and closed the lunchroom door. "We do a little coke."

I made a note in my phone to ask Nia about coke, then tried to imagine this dork doing rails.

Stu continued. "But she'd gotten worse. I think she was doing something else."

"Could it have been meth?"

"I don't know. I don't go harder than blow," he said, rearing back and raising his hands defensively.

"Anything else you can think of that might help me find Sadie?"

Stu scratched his arm. "No, I don't think so. Sadie is probably fine. She most likely met a guy or something and her phone died."

"For two days? Phone cords are not hard to come by."

He fidgeted, uncomfortable now. "You really think she's in trouble?"

"I don't know. That's why I'm here." I drank from my glass. "You said she most likely 'met a guy.' Does that mean Sadie's single?"

"Last I heard, yeah. She wasn't really one for long relationships, at least not in the time I've known her. There have been guys ... nothing I'd call serious."

I recorded as he rattled off a list that grew to five names. "Did she ever mention a church called Watershed Moments?"

Stu took a deep breath and let it out. He rubbed a cheek, then sat back. "Yeah, she mentioned it–said it's an awful place–but she didn't elaborate, only that leaving was the best decision she ever made."

"Thank you," I said.

Stu stood, leaving more upset than when he arrived.

I had that effect on people.

***

I left Sport Sphere and headed north on Fort.

"Hey," someone said. "Hey ... over here."

I turned to the alley next to the Percival building and saw a man in a slick suit leaning up against the wall, smoking a cigarette. His torso must have been a foot thick, but his neck was two inches long, and his suit jacket hugged his biceps as if in love. I'd put him at thirty-five years old.

"New client?" he asked.

"No," I said.

"Okay, okay. I was just wondering."

"You work at Sport Sphere?"

"Fucking rights." He tossed the butt into a puddle, causing it to sizzle before going out. "Five years."

"Maybe you can help me," I said.

"Sure, what's up?"

"Do you know Sadie Rowe?"

"Yeah," he said, curious now. "Why?"

"She's been away from her place for a couple days and her sister is worried. I've been hired to find her."

He considered it, and I waited, giving him time.

"I'm Jason Parilla. Account exec extraordinaire," he said, and we shook hands. "What do you want to know?"

"What's Sadie like?"

"I'm not in charge here ..." he said. "But if I was, and if this was her quarterly review, I'd categorize Sadie as listless, undependable, and downright lazy. She misses at least one day a week, sometimes more, and has been on probation pretty much since she got here." He thought about it. "She knows she's lazy and doesn't try to hide it. I think she's embraced it."

"How does she still have a job?"

Parilla lit a new smoke. "How close are you with Dustin?"

"Bannerman?" I said. "I'm not close with him at all. He helped me set interviews up with Janice and Stu, but that's it."

"Will he receive the information I share with you?"

"Not unless you tell him."

"I have your word on that?"

Parilla had a juicy piece of information he wanted to get off his chest.

"You have my word."

"Like I said, I've been here almost five years, working my bag off. I've recently been promised 'Senior' next to my title. Finally, the hard work's paying off." He paused and stared at me for emphasis. "Well, Dustin said I'll get it within the next year. That's twenty grand more on my salary. As you can imagine, I don't want anything to mess that up."

Parilla increased the serious look. It was like he had several versions of the same expression, each more severe than the previous one.

"I was at a wedding," he said, blowing smoke toward the sky, "like three weeks ago. My cousin lives in Toronto, but he married a girl from Winnipeg, so the wedding was here. At the Fairmont downtown. Fancy as hell. I met a girl, and around midnight, we left the wedding and walked to this little bar in Hy's restaurant. You know it?"

I nodded.

"So, I'm in there talking to this girl, Holly–who I'm still seeing by the way–and it's kind of cool. The place is dark and old. Expensive. I'm a sports-bar guy, not a fancy, highfalutin type, so I'm a bit uncomfortable. But I'm drinking with a beautiful woman, so I tell myself to enjoy the moment, you know? I get up to take a leak, and who do I see crammed in the far corner? Bannerman ... sucking face with Sadie."

"Kissing?"

"Kissing times a hundred, like they were trying to eat each other."

"Did they see you?"

"No," he said. "I mean, you never know, but they haven't mentioned it and neither have I."

"And you're sure this was three weeks ago?"

He thought about it. "It will be four weeks on Saturday."

"Are they affectionate here?"

"Not at all. I've never seen them speak to one another, never mind show affection. I don't work closely with Sadie, though. Janice does, and from what I hear, Sadie's on thin ice."

Janice had said as much, so that wasn't new, but Sadie and Bannerman hooking up? And hiding it at work? That interested me.

Could be it was a one-time thing, or, more likely, it was ongoing, and they wanted to keep it a secret. Sadie was at least fifteen years younger than Bannerman, and workplace policies usually discouraged older men in positions of power from dating younger women in entry-level positions. There might even be an explicit rule forbidding it in the Sport Sphere code of conduct. Something to look into.

"What's Bannerman like?" I said.

Parilla laughed to himself.

"Bannerman?" he said. "He reminds me of a man from another generation, you know. Like he was born in the wrong era."

"Do you have an example?"

"Not really. He's very professional, but occasionally I'll notice a look, an eerie expression at a staff meeting or when an employee gives him attitude, like there's more going on behind his eyes than he lets known. He never does anything overtly off-putting, but you just know he's seen some shit. And I get the feeling that in another context, he'd be throwing hands in those situations. Does that make sense?"

"It does," I said. "It absolutely does."

I shook Parilla's hand and he left.

I could ask Bannerman if he was romantically involved with Sadie and he might answer honestly, but my guess was he would deny it, and then he'd think Janice or Stu had told me something linking him to Sadie in that way. For the time being, I'd keep Parilla's story to myself.

***

When I got to my truck, I contemplated how I could get inside the church and talk with Brad Walton. I couldn't see it happening without the help of the Rowes, so I texted Nia, asking for their number.

A response arrived a minute later.

Why do you want my parents' number?

I need to speak with them.

They don't know anything

Let me do my job, I replied.

She texted back a number, and I called from my truck.

"Hello," Muriel Rowe answered.

"Hi, my name is Jake Hardy," I said, lying, Arkell's Tom Hardy moniker still in my head, "and I work in a law firm called Ross, Petrov, and Jove."

"How can I help you?"

"My area of expertise is corporate law, catering to a clientele with like-minded pursuits. Basically, a Christian focus."

"Keep going."

"In our annual budget we have monies allotted for community endeavours. Watershed Moments has come to our attention, and we think it might be the perfect place for our brand. We hope to invest in organizations dedicated to sharing and growing a Christian message."

"We don't handle the money at the church. Why call us?" Muriel said.

"Well, when my partners and I discussed a suitable enterprise to work with, I remembered Nia and Sadie belonged to Watershed Moments. I thought I'd touch base with you, and you could point me in the direction of the right person to speak with."

There was a long pause. "Are you still in touch with them?"

I assumed she meant her daughters.

"Well, just via Instagram and Twitter," I said. "You know, social networking and all."

"How'd you get our home number? It's unlisted."

I lightened my voice. "We have our ways."

After a quiet beat, she said, "I'll call you back in five," then she hung up.

I sat there as the heat filled the vehicle, warming my insides. She called back three minutes later.

"Seven tonight. At the church. Tell the person at the gate why you're there. You'll be on the list."

"Well, I guess I'll see you tonight. Thank you."

Best case scenario, they'd introduce me to Brad Walton.

10

Hope.

I started losing it when my mom broke down after my dad disappeared in 2002, and like an ancient engine that hadn't been maintained with regular service, you could say the breakdown was inevitable. Looking back, I'm surprised she held on as long as she did.

I'd sit in front of the TV on Saturdays, watching reruns of The Simpsons. I'd wake up early, my mom passed out in her bedroom, and I'd feel as though I were alone. The rock 'n' roll music that played well into the wee hours of the morning had ended, and friends or lovers had left or been tossed out. The silence gave me time to think, and I could finally relax. This type of alone was not the lonely kind, it was peaceful.

My world consisted of very little, and it was around this time that terror latched on to me with its vice grip. Sometimes, I'd get up in the middle of class and just leave, walk to the mall and sit on a bench across from the food court. I'd been held back a year, participated in zero extra-curricular activities, and didn't have one true friend. I lived in constant fear.

I was afraid my mom would bring home a random guy from the bar, or that I would find her drunk when I got home from school. I was afraid we would have to move again, that there would be no clean clothes to wear, of there being nothing to eat.

Fear.

But on Saturday mornings, plunked in front of the boob tube, the fear left temporarily.

If Mom's purse had been dropped haggardly at the entranceway beside the pumps she wore dancing Friday night, I'd inspect it with care. Loose change, cigarettes, a tampon, lipstick, a pen, checkbook, gum, and a condom or two. The spoils of a sad life equaled spending money for me. I'd pocket the money and lighten the cigarette pack by three or four. A full pack meant I could get bold and take seven or eight. I'd smoke the cigarettes or sell them at school for a buck a piece.

The money mostly went toward food, to supplement the little I got from home, but I allowed myself the odd indulgence. Most teenagers would have tried for Playboy, or the Sports Illustrated Swimsuit Edition, but the calendar I bought was not so hedonistic. It was, nevertheless, filled with fantasies, ones I knew I'd never achieve, but I craved them all the same. It showed a family with the perfect life. Each month presented them in a tropical destination like Hawaii, Puerto Vallarta, Cabo, or Florida. January held images of an ocean, sparkling blue water, and a bright yellow sun shining down on the family, the kids frolicking on the beach. March featured two small children building a sandcastle with their parents. In May, they splashed in the water. August was a great shot of a dad throwing a Frisbee. I'd never been to a beach, but I thought it must be heaven. A place to relax. To play. To have fun. No one felt afraid at the beach.

I'd pour a bowl of Lucky Charms, which I'd stash in my closet underneath a blanket, and check the fridge for milk. I'd be shit out of luck if Mom drank paralyzers on Friday, but I really didn't care about the milk. Those little balls of sugar that passed for charms tasted great either way.

One Saturday, hungover after a big bottle of Sangria, Mom began her usual spat. "Come here, Jake," she whined from the bedroom.

I put down the bowl and crept nervously toward her room as Bart schemed at Springfield Elementary. My mom lay on her stomach, face smooshed into the pillow. I stood at the door.

"Come here and sit down," she said.

I paused, deciding if I would oblige, and in the end, I always did. I sat on the edge of the bed, staring at the wall.

My mom rose stiffly, like a cartoon monster. "What are you doing?"

"Nothing, Mom."

"Nothing? I'll tell you who was nothing–your father. What a useless piece of shit." She reached for her cigarettes, which weren't there, then stumbled to the kitchen, arriving a moment later with a smoking dart. "He just left. Poof! Gone, like a fart in the wind."

I stared at the wall, half listening.

"Men–you can't live with 'em, and you can't shoot 'em. Well, you can shoot 'em, but then you'd end up in the slam," she said, and laughed to herself. "Don't be another asshole, okay Jake? When you're a man, don't be an asshole."

"Okay."

Mom blew smoke at the ceiling. "We got enough assholes already."

I sat on the bed, thinking about the calendar pinned to the wall in my room and my favourite month–July. A bald eagle soared across a bright blue sky, a fiery sun in the upper corner of the page. The family huddled together on the shore of a lake, pointing from below in admiration, and my heart filled with pain, not only because I wanted what the family had, but because I knew in my bones that I'd never be as free as that bird.

11

I sped home from Sport Sphere, threw on my suit, and made it to the church by seven, expecting the place to be deserted. Instead, the lot was packed. I came to a stop in front of the guard booth, and a man walked to the driver's window, a different man than yesterday, but he stuck to the same script.

"Do you have business here today?" he said.

"I'm meeting with Carl and Muriel Rowe."

"Name?"

"Jake Hardy," I lied.

The man stepped back and retrieved a smartphone from his pocket, scrolled for a moment, then said, "Yes, here you are." He produced a badge from the other pocket. "This must be worn at all times. Park in visitor parking. You have one hour from now to be out of the building."

"And if I'm not out in an hour?"

"We'll come in and gently escort you to your vehicle."

"All right, then."

***

Stained glass windows in the lobby showed Jesus with children, helping the sick, and on the cross. Wall-to-wall laminate flooring brushed up against white walls and expansive windows. A classy establishment as far as churches went, but I hadn't been in many, so maybe I wasn't fit to assess. The Rowes were waiting for me.

I shook Carl's hand. "I'm Jake."

"Carl. This is my wife, Muriel."

She didn't offer her hand.

Discomfort showed on their faces, but they invited me in, and I followed them to a boardroom. We sat and Carl sized me up. He had thick forearms covered in coarse hair and a closely cropped, greying army cut. His callused hands and rough demeanour led me to believe he'd farmed or worked with his hands, construction maybe. Muriel had brown hair with grey mixed in, and a clean complexion that made her expression seem more real than it was, like we were in an amateur video without money for actors to get their makeup and hair done.

Carl opened with, "The only reason we agreed to meet you is because my wife is gullible." Muriel shifted in her seat. "If I had answered the phone, I would have told you to hit the bricks. It's odd of you to contact us, rather than one of the authorities here at the church. Can you see my concern?"

A teenager, like fifteen years old, arrived with bottled waters and a plate of dainties. She placed water in front of each of us and put the tray in the middle of the table. Muriel sipped her water. Carl didn't move. I sampled a Nanaimo bar.

"I understand," I said. "I just thought the opportunity might interest the church."

Carl pondered that, then stood. "I won't be long."

He walked out of the room, leaving me alone with Muriel. Neither of us spoke until Carl returned a minute later with Brad Walton. I sat back, shocked at his height. He must have been six foot eight. Walton wore a white shirt rolled up at the elbows, tucked into black pants. The shirt had a crisp collar, and the top button had been left open.

Carl sat beside his wife, but Walton remained standing.

He said, "What brings you here today, Mr.–?"

"Hardy," I said, standing and offering my hand. "Jake Hardy."

He shook my hand but didn't introduce himself. "What brings you here today, Mr. Hardy?"

"I'm here to offer you a business opportunity."

Walton didn't react, but he took his time and considered me. When he was ready, he said, "What kind of man are you?"

"There are different kinds?" I said, confused.

"Are you a good man?"

"I think so. What's your name?" I asked, even though I knew the answer.

"I'm Brad Walton, Senior Minister here at Watershed Moments. Let's sit, and you can tell me about yourself."

Walton listened closely as I launched into a phony biography. Where I grew up, went to school, and the church I belonged to. When I had finished, Walton smiled, but it was forced.

"Before you arrived, I searched for a law firm employing a man named Jake Hardy," he said. "There is no one by that name working as a lawyer in Winnipeg. Or Canada for that matter. I found one in England. But when you speak, I don't hear an accent. Why don't you tell me why you're really here."

The ruse got me in, but that was as far as it would take me.

"I want to ask you about Tracy Remple," I said.

Walton's face was a blank wall. "I don't know that name."

I looked at the Rowes. They didn't move or speak, so I tried an alternate route.

"I'm friends with Nia Rowe–"

"We tolerated Nia for a short while," Walton cut in, "but it was a mistake. One we've since corrected. She's no longer allowed on these premises."

"Because she's Black?"

Muriel squirmed, and I knew that's why Nia had been tossed out of the church. Walton did not answer.

"You said Nia's not allowed on the property. What about Sadie?" I said, putting a little extra emphasis on her name.

"I won't discuss current or former members of the church, and I resent you coming here under false pretenses, wasting my time. I'm a busy person, and I value privacy. For the record, I don't know the man you asked about," Walton said, and stood.

"How do you know it's a man?"

"What's that?"

"The name is Tracy Remple. How do you know they aren't a woman?"

Walton realized his mistake and scowled. "I try to run a clean organization here. Professional. A place people can worship the Lord, away from the ills of society." He paused, and the skin on his face pulled taut as his eyes darkened. "If we run into one another again, you'll find I'm not so nice. There are no second chances where I'm from."

He walked out of the room, followed closely by the Rowes.

I kept my mouth shut, exited the church the way I'd come in, and it dawned on me that Muriel hadn't spoken the entire time. I couldn't decide if this silence made her an accomplice or a victim. Did she warrant anger or pity? Or perhaps she deserved something else. Help? Support? Comfort? Love? Did people need kindness more than reprimand? Kindness can be difficult to provide when the recipient is culpable. I waved to the guard, who opened the gate, and continued along the service road.

On Gauthier Road, I noticed headlights in my rearview mirror. With my attention on the lights, I hadn't noticed a car pulled perpendicular to the road, blocking my way. I slammed on the brakes, stopping ten feet from a big SUV with heavy tint. The vehicle coming from behind was a black Cadillac CT4, and it got closer until it stopped behind me. In my rearview mirror, I watched three men exit the Cadillac. I opened my door and stepped into the night.

The men approached me, and I didn't like what I saw. Each of them wore a white, short-sleeved dress shirt and maroon tie. There was nothing that distinguished one from the next. They were white and in their late twenties, with light brown hair, and stood five foot ten to six feet tall. Their bodies were average, and none wore jewelry or tattoos that I could see in the dim light. Their hairstyles were nondescript.

They moved in tandem, three abreast, and came at me slowly. I couldn't see into the SUV.

"Can I help you?" I said to the men.

The one in the middle said, "Do not show your face here again. Ever. Watershed Moments is not part of your investigation."

"I don't know what investigation you're talking about."

"Yes, you do," the middle man said.

The one on the left pulled out a short baton that had been tucked in the back of his pants, flicked a wrist, and extended it to its full length. The one on the right hadn't blinked.

"Am I clear?" the middle man said.

I didn't like being bullied, and I had never responded well to threats. I could fight these men now, lose, and sustain injuries that, at best, left me sore. At worst, I'd end up in the hospital. I couldn't risk it.

"I understand," I said.

The men got in the CT4 and drove away, followed closely by the SUV.

12

The encounter with the three look-alikes lit a fire under my ass, and I decided to make one more stop. Nia said Logan Bergel had recommended me to her, and I wanted to know why. She said it was because I'd go to the places the more professional outfits couldn't, or wouldn't, but there had to be more to it.

I slowed, turned into the lot of Soul Patch, and parked, preparing for a confrontation. Bergel and I were not on good terms.

The fundamentals of fighting played in my head like a teleprompter running on autopilot, little reminders in case the shit turned physical. Maybe I was just on guard after seeing that baton.

Weight balanced. Arms loose. Relax. Throw first, ask questions later. I thought about getting hit and feeling pain. I accepted it. Bergel was a lefty, so I'd pivot to the left, away from his power. Watch for the headbutt. Always breathe.

The neon sign of the strip club glowed, luring me in with the fake promise that with violence came redemption. I opened the door and walked in.

"Fifteen dollars," the girl said.

I paid and she stamped the back of my hand, then I deposited my cell phone and keys into a plastic container. A muscly bouncer waved me through a metal detector. No beep, so I picked up my possessions and the bouncer patted me down. He nodded, and I walked through a second set of doors to the main area of the club.

I approached a long wooden bar running the length of the right wall, waited in line, then ordered a bottled water, paid, and walked around, taking in the private dance area and a stage where a young brunette danced sans clothing.

I weaved through tables in the centre of the room, past a group of college kids, three middle-aged men, and a bachelor party hollering at the dancer from sniffers row. One of the hollerers wore a skin-tight onesie. When he stood up you could see a massive penis drawn on the front in black marker. The thing damn near touched his knee. A piece of paper taped to his back announced: *Last day as a free man.*

I located Bergel near the back, sitting with a guy who was probably only six feet tall but weighed in the range of two hundred and fifty pounds. He had a short mohawk, and a portrait of a Viking had been tattooed on the side of his neck. He'd have to rip his T-shirt to get it off, that's how tight it was. A bottle of SKYY Vodka sat on their table.

Bergel wore a tailored suit, hair slicked back, and an oversized watch on his left wrist. He had moved up the ladder from low-level dealer–where the average customers were teenagers, weekend warriors, and college kids–to mid-level where he supplied smaller dealers. Then, five years ago, he'd cashed out and bought Soul Patch Gentlemen's Club downtown. Quit selling drugs outright. As far as peeler bars go, the place was decent, which meant the clientele wasn't down-and-out, but it wasn't a high-roller joint either, falling somewhere in between.

Bergel and Tight Shirt held drinks, sipping occasionally as they talked. I walked over.

"Bergel!" I shouted over house music.

They stopped and turned toward me.

"Jake? Shit, brother, it's been a minute."

He'd reacted more positively than I expected, but with Bergel, that could be a feint, a ploy to get me to let my guard down.

"Give me a sec," he said to Tight Shirt, stood, and motioned to the wall, where it was quieter. We shook hands and he had a weak grip. Something about that scared me because most men liked to crush the bones in your hand, overcompensating, like a firm shake meant they were tough. Bergel never tried to impose himself physically, at least not at the beginning. That wasn't his style. Nonetheless, I was ready.

"What's with the water?" he asked.

"On the clock."

"Bro, that's never stopped you before," he said, and a big piece of me wanted to smash him in the face. "So how you been?"

"I'm all right. Same old. You?"

"I'm doing well, brother. Real well. You hear about Sadie?"

I nodded, as Tight Shirt kept a close watch on us from his table. "Yeah, Nia said she'd hired you."

"At your recommendation," I said, wondering if Nia lied about the nature of her relationship with Bergel. "I have a couple questions for you."

"Sure."

"Are Nia and Sadie close?" I asked as Tight Shirt walked toward us. Bergel sent him a glance, and he stopped dead in his tracks, turned around, and walked back to the table.

"Yes and no," Bergel said, his eyes back on me. "Nia says they used to be two peas in a pod. Together all the time. Now, not so much. They live together, but the closeness has faded. Nia says Sadie is a 'troubled soul.'" He chuckled, sipped from his drink. "Troubled soul," he repeated. "Aren't we all?"

"I'm trying to get a sense of what Sadie is like," I said. "Why she might leave, or where she could be. Do you know if she owes money? Anything like that?"

He thought about it. "I don't think she owes, but she's got bad habits."

"For example?"

"She ain't fussy, bro," he said, and a smirk spread across his face. "If you know what I mean."

The song ended and a dancer took the stage to Mötley Crüe's "Girls, Girls, Girls." The drink in Bergel's hand glowed neon blue like a lava lamp in the dark room.

"Sadie's always had a chip," Bergel said, and tapped the shoulder of his suit, "right here. She takes life just a little too seriously, brother. You gotta let some shit slide. You can't fix most problems in the world, so why bother trying? Roll with it, you know."

"How does she take life too seriously?"

"Last summer she had two weeks off in July. Most people? They go away on a holiday, go camping or some shit. Sadie? She spent the time sleeping in a tent on the grounds of a government building in protest of emergency rooms closing. It's camping, I guess." He laughed.

"Healthcare not high on the list of causes you support?"

"Bro, I wouldn't know. Politics aren't my area of expertise."

Fair enough, I thought.

"Have you heard of a church called Watershed Moments?" I asked, wondering if Nia had told him about her childhood, the time she'd spent in the church.

"Of course," he said.

"What's your take on the place?"

His head bopped side to side, weighing things a little. "I think they brainwash people. I've heard they charge big bucks for membership. It's a scam to line the pockets of the top dogs."

I nodded, uncapped the water, and brought it to my lips, pretending it was gin traveling into my body from a distant land where booze was fuel, an elixir that sustained life, brought sustenance, happiness, and a deep sense of purpose.

"Why did you recommend me to Nia?" I asked him.

"I don't care much for Sadie. She's not my cup of tea." He squinted, then slowly opened his eyes. "But I care about Nia, and I don't like seeing her upset. I'm doing it for her."

"Are you dating Nia?" I asked.

"Yeah, you could say that," he said, "but Nia's a tough nut to crack. She's got walls, brother. Big fuckin' walls. I've made headway, and I can't have her sister derailing that progress."

He was arrogant, and I didn't like how he spoke about Nia like she was a prize to be won, but I had noticed those walls, too.

"Is Nia adopted?" I said.

"She is. The Rowes adopted her as a baby, so they're the only family she's ever known. That's part of it, bro, the bond she feels with Sadie. They have a strange connection."

I wanted to know more, but Nia's personal history wasn't my reason for being there.

"Anything else?" I said.

"Yeah." He finished his drink, left the glass on the shelf along the wall. "One more thing. If you can find Sadie, I'll give you an extra ten grand on top of what Nia's paying you."

I paused, baffled. "Why?"

"I know about your legal problems, and that you're going away. If I know you like I think I do, then I'd also say that your mom is right fucked when you go in. She'll be on the street in a month. I'm not unsympathetic to your plight. I'll give you the money when you find Sadie on two conditions," he said, holding up two fingers. "One, this stays between us. Don't tell Nia about the money. And two, you don't tell Nia what you did for me way back when, that you helped me beat the charges. I've got a new venture on the horizon. I'm getting into the restaurant business. I'd like Nia on my arm at the grand opening."

The last time I'd accepted a deal from him it had led to the biggest regret of my life, but the money was just too much for me to pass up.

I held out my hand. "Okay."

We shook hands again, and I turned to walk away.

"Hey, Jake," he called out. "Stop."

I stopped.

"Come here," he said.

Bergel understood power, and it had to look like he'd won this exchange in front of his people in his club. I obeyed and walked back to where he stood.

"I haven't forgotten what you did for me," he began, "but just because you did that doesn't mean I'll let you fuck with my plan now. Keep me in the loop."

It wasn't too late to throw a punch. I might knock him out or at least knock him down. I could probably get to the door before Tight Shirt. I could ...

"I understand," I said, "and I will."

"Bro ..." He smiled again. "It was good seeing you."

"See you around, Bergel."

I left, proud of myself for not sucker punching him and glad to be finished with the conversation. I smiled at Tight Shirt on the way out, and he frowned.

Some people are no fun at all.

13

I was behind the wheel on Main, coming down from the conversation with Bergel, when my phone vibrated. I answered on Bluetooth.

"Hello," I said.

"Hey ..." It was Nia and she sounded odd, hesitant and far away. "Have you found her?"

"Not yet."

It crossed my mind that she might fire me, that she had no trust in my abilities, and that I'd never earn enough to keep my mom alive before I went to prison.

Be strong, I thought, and tossed the worries to the side.

"Why haven't you updated me?" she added.

"I've been busy, but you're right ... you deserve to know what's going on. Let's meet for breakfast in the morning."

"I'd like to meet now. I'll be at The Daily Grind in twenty. Meet me there."

I was tired, but I owed her an update. I'd give Nia what I had and hope it was enough for her not to terminate my employ.

"Okay," I said.

***

I walked in and found her at a table at the far end of the coffee shop. She wore wide-legged black-and-white-striped trousers and a top the colour of the sun, with complete makeup, but her eyes were puffy like she needed sleep. Two mugs steamed in front of her. I shook slightly, and she noticed as I sat down. Neither of us said anything until Nia broke the standoff.

"I got you a tea. Earl Grey," she said.

I added milk. "Thank you."

"Are you okay? You look off. Rattled, maybe. Did something happen?"

I placed the mug on the table and started to speak, but the words sounded stupid in my head. How to answer that. *Did something happen?*

My dad disappeared.

My mom pissed her life away.

I lived in a group home.

Three foster homes in five years.

Neglect. Abuse. Anger.

So much anger.

I shook from alcohol withdrawal.

Where to begin?

"I spoke to Sadie's coworkers," I said, sticking to the facts of the case. "More than one said she's using drugs."

Nia breathed loudly and closed her eyes, opening them quickly. "What's she using?"

"She does coke, but my gut tells me that's not it. Coke is expensive, and I'm not sure she'd be able to afford it, unless someone is supplying her with it for free, which is possible. But I also heard she was doing meth, and my feeling is that's it."

"Meth?" Nia shook her head, troubled. "I knew it was something, but meth? She wouldn't talk about it. When I asked her, she told me to mind my own business. Her hours are insane, especially on weekends. She gets home at five in the morning."

"Have you heard the name Dustin Bannerman?" I said, then sipped some tea. "He works at Sport Sphere."

Nia shook her head. "Is he involved with her disappearance?"

"Maybe ... I spoke to him, and he's a lot older than her. Another employee saw them kissing outside of work, but I think Watershed Moments is the smarter avenue to pursue right now." I paused, then said, "I met your parents and Brad Walton."

"You've been busy," she said, shuffling in her seat and crossing her arms. "And?"

"Your dad seems like a hard man. Your mom seems stuck."

"What do you mean?"

I knew about being stuck, and I knew about being trapped.

"Like she's in quicksand and can't escape," I said.

"I feel that way sometimes, like once the sand reaches my neck, I'll drown."

"When I left, three men followed me and told me to stop."

"Stop?"

"Stop investigating Watershed Moments. Why didn't you tell me what the church was like? It's got a gate and guards in front of a property the size of a shopping mall. It's completely closed to outsiders. They control who goes in and out. The only way I got in was with the help of your parents." My tone had more anger in it than I'd expected, but Nia didn't back down and came at me full force.

"I didn't tell you," she said, uncrossing her arms, "because I hate talking about that place. I fucking hate it. I get anxiety just thinking about the shit that happened to me there. It stole years of my life, and now I refuse to give it power."

"You understand that if I'm going to find Sadie, I need all the information, right? Me talking to people with half the picture won't work. I'll make mistakes, I'll–"

"I'm sorry, and it won't happen again, but we need to talk about something else." She paused, then surprised me. "How much do you drink?"

I looked out the window for a second. I could have lied, but for some reason, I told her the truth. "I used to drink every day, but I'm trying to be better. Today is my second day sober."

Nia drank from her mug, kept her eyes on me. When she spoke, her voice was lighter than it had been.

"I'm sorry you're struggling," she said, "but this is my sister. Despite Logan's recommendation, I can't have someone looking for her who isn't at the top of their game. I just can't ..." Nia sipped again to calm her nerves, or so it seemed. "Jake, you're not in the right condition to do the job. I'm not judging you. I swear I'm not, but someone else could provide a more stable commitment. This is my sister ..."

A slight surge of panic increased the speed of my words.

"Listen, everything you said is true, but those are the reasons I can find Sadie. She's suffering, and I know what that's like more than anyone. My dad disappeared in '02 and he was never found. That's why I'm the right person to do this. Because I go where the other person won't. I have no special powers, other than a fucked-up ability to accept pain. I'll never stop looking for Sadie. Never. I swear on my mom's life."

Nia held my eyes, and a beacon of something passed between us.

"Your mom ... what's going on with her?"

I inhaled deeply.

"About a year ago, I was arrested and charged with aggravated assault causing bodily harm. It's a long story, but there was this guy, and he hit my mom. I did the same to him, only I went overboard."

Nia's expression was a mixture of concern and uncertainty.

"I'm going to be sentenced on October twenty-ninth," I continued, "and I'm going away for at least a year. My mom has problems, and she can't work, so I need to earn as much money as possible to support her while I'm inside."

Something tender moved across her face. Understanding? I wasn't sure, but I knew her next words were important.

"My parents are members of the church," Nia said, "and I've been out of the church for years. And when I mean out, I mean out. I can't attend any aspect of church life. Walton tossed me in 2009. I had quit attending regularly, and I guess he saw an opportunity to get rid of me on his terms. People of colour are allowed, sort of, but it's rare, and they're excluded from marriage within the sanctity of the church."

I took a second to process what she'd said and became certain of one thing.

"Walton is a part of Sadie's disappearance," I said. "Could be directly or indirectly, I'm not sure yet." I paused, remembering Bergel's dapper suit and slicked-back hair. "You have shitty taste in men."

Nia laughed loudly and it sounded good, like relief.

"Always have," she said.

We soaked up the positivity of her laughter, and I wanted to tell her Bergel offered me ten grand if I found Sadie quickly. But I didn't.

"I came here from Soul Patch. He seems to think you're his girlfriend."

"He's not. He's not my boyfriend," she repeated, "but he wants to be. When we started seeing each other, I didn't know he owned that club. He said he was a businessman, and that he owned a restaurant."

"Technically, the place serves food," I said, smiling.

"That's not all it serves ..." she said, and we let that hang in the air a moment. "Did he tell you anything useful?"

I shrugged. "He added to the general picture of what Sadie's like, her social justice stuff, that kind of thing."

Nia nodded. "I want you to keep looking for Sadie, but I have one condition. And it's kind of a two-parter."

"Name it."

"You can't drink and you have to attend an A.A. meeting."

I sat back, surprised, then shook my head and leaned forward, placing my elbows on the table. This again.

"Come on, Nia. You can't be serious. Today is my second day sober–"

"I am serious. Two days is something, but I saw your hands shaking when you sat down. What about tomorrow? And the next day? And the day after that? I'd never forgive myself if you were drunk and the outcome was ... negative."

People sitting around talking about their drinking. It sounded awful, and even though I had told Bancroft I'd think about it, I wasn't planning to attend. I thought maybe I'd recruit someone in A.A. to back me in court. Pay them fifty bucks to say I had attended. This threw a wrench in that plan.

"One meeting's not going to do anything," I said.

"Probably not, but you never know," she said, reaching across to put her hands in mine.

I shook my head, considering my options. If staying sober and an A.A. meeting were required to keep working, I'd do it.

"I won't drink, and I'll go to one meeting, but I'm not promising anything beyond that."

"Agreed," she said, and held out her hand. "To a fresh start."

We shook hands.

Something occurred to me. "How will you know if I drink, or if I even go to the meeting? I can just lie to you."

"I'll know," she said but didn't elaborate.

I asked if there had been any more messages from Sadie, and she said no, just that initial text on the morning of the 16th. I talked a little more about next steps, then we went our separate ways.

I looked out the window as I drove, watching the people and places of my city pass by in a blur, like interchangeable statuettes. That was untrue, though, and I knew better. Each of them had a story. I couldn't save my dad, but maybe I could find Sadie. Maybe get her some help. We all needed someone to look for us when we got lost, of that much I was certain.

PART 2

TAINTED

14

Friday, October 18 (three days missing)

I woke up with excruciating pain in my side, shaking. I stumbled into the kitchen and opened the fridge with a trembling hand. A beer would relieve the shakes, but it would lead to twenty more. Dark, confusing thoughts swirled around in my head as I realized, thankfully, that there was no alcohol in my apartment.

I hadn't drunk a drop since being turned down for the loan at Prairie Credit Union, and if I didn't drink today, this would be my third day sober. I washed down two Tylenol, and soon, the pain in my side lessened. The shakes passed, too, and I got dressed.

Colder now and dark outside, shadows moved slowly across the sky. The trees held few leaves as the colours of fall transitioned to the whites of winter.

I sold my truck, and it felt more emotional than I'd expected, like the vehicle somehow legitimatized me and without it I'd be a loser. The guy handed me a bank draft for twenty thousand dollars, and we exchanged the required papers. From there, I bussed to my bank, deposited the draft, and fought every urge to withdraw five hundred bucks and get back on the sauce. Without booze, it was like a limb had been cut off, a part of me missing. I felt scatterbrained and sad.

The only thing to do was keep busy, so I spent the morning in bus depots, showing Sadie's picture to employees and street kids, punk rockers and goths who looked like they had been there a while. Winnipeg is an incredibly difficult place to be homeless. It's not easy anywhere, but at least in warmer climates you aren't battling minus-thirty-degree Celsius temperatures in the winter. October wasn't cold like that, so they were still outside.

I thought I had a lead at Thompson Bus and Freight, but

it turned out the kid was just fucking with me. He was white, probably sixteen years old, and wore a Minor Threat T-shirt under an open hoodie and winter coat.

At Maple Bus Lines, two teenaged girls, their ethnicities unclear–I'd guess South American, maybe Colombian–accused me of being a cop. They both had short hair and were dressed like teenage boys in jeans, hooded sweaters, and snapback hats. Loose, unfitted winter coats hung on their thin frames like painter sheets draped over scarecrows. I felt out of touch and stupid when I wondered at their gender and sexuality.

I wrapped it up at 11:30 and hopped on a city bus, on my way to an A.A. meeting. I found the meeting online, wanting to get it over with as quick as possible and get back to the case.

***

It was almost noon when I arrived at a congregation of people smoking in the alley behind a strip mall. I walked past them to a faded red door, opened it, and walked up a narrow flight of stairs, shifting sideways as a stranger passed going down. He said "hi" and I nodded. The room opened at the top of the stairs, outfitted with thirty or forty wonky chairs with cloth seats, the type you can buy in bulk from Costco. The chairs were arranged in rows, with a big wooden desk at the front of the room like the one in my office, and a bathroom along the wall. People talked loudly and drank coffee. I took a seat close to the door and kept my head down, a trick I'd learned as a kid in school.

Everyone stood, someone read a prayer, and a basket was passed around as people threw in change, a couple five-spots. A man three rows up read a list of rules, and another person read a story. After that, people shared, commenting on the reading, relating it to their own experiences. Sometimes the speaker talked about their own troubles, unrelated to the topic. It continued this way for a while, and my mind drifted to Sadie. I mentally compiled a list of everything I knew.

She'd left home on October 15 and had made it in to work that day. She wasn't answering texts and phone calls, and her social media accounts had been quiet. Several coworkers suspected she was doing drugs, Stu had confirmed it, and according to Tracy Remple, the ministers at Watershed Moments had sexually assaulted teenagers in the congregation, including Sadie.

Post meeting, I'd return to Sport Sphere and ask Dustin Bannerman straight up if he knew where Sadie was to see how he responded.

I checked my phone and got surly looks from people. It seemed phones during meetings were frowned upon. I put it away and let my eyes wander, stopping on a man I hadn't noticed earlier. Despite his age, he dressed like a colour-blind ten-year-old. Turquoise jacket. Navy-blue Red Sox sweater. Faded green jeans. A pair of red sneakers. It was Katz–Bogdan Katzmarek–the man who'd hired me and got me started in the business. I hadn't seen him in years.

As gregarious as they came, Katz was built like an overweight wrestler, stocky and wide, but he carried the bulk well. His ability to get the most out of his people made him a great leader. You might think he used intimidation to motivate, but Katz wasn't like that. He spoke loudly, but never threateningly.

I'd met Katz in 2013 when a foreman of mine, Paul Sigurdson, took a shine to me. Siggy had sobered up years earlier, and I guess I reminded him of himself at my age. He convinced me to get a GED, and I even sobered up for a year. This was when he introduced me to Katz, who Siggy knew through the program. Katz operated his own agency, after twenty years on the WPS, and although he never said it, Siggy must have greased the wheels to get me an interview. Sober, I handled myself well and got the job. I quit working construction two weeks later and joined Katz's team, Red River Investigative.

Life was good.

Katz became my mentor and dragged me through the ropes, provided training on the job and a stiff kick in the ass when I needed it. He taught me to slow down, observe, and that the mind is the most powerful weapon a person has.

"Notice the details and write them down," he liked to say. "Always be watching, always be alert. Think, then act. Create good habits, routine, and do that shit every day."

I started lifting weights, running, and practicing jiu jitsu. We worked out together, ate together, and even lived together for a while.

I've thought about it hundreds of times, but I'm not sure why I started drinking again in 2014. Using, too. One day on the way home from work, I put my blinker on and turned into the lot of a bar. That was all. No big event prompted it. I wanted a drink, so I got one.

Katz let me off the hook more times than I care to remember, but he'd finally had enough, and I got fired in 2017. Broke his heart. I loved the guy, even if he had let me go. He loved me, too, and told me as much, but he had a business to run, and the behaviour of his employees reflected on him. He'd tried to convince me to sober up, said he'd take me back on if I did, but I said "no thank you" and kept on drinking. Neither of us held a grudge.

I opened Joelsen Private Services in 2018 and catered to the client who needed a job done and didn't want the fanfare of a larger corporate team. It was a better fit for me until this situation with Cory Francis cost me my license and, pretty soon, my freedom.

The meeting continued, and when it was Katz's turn to share, he told one hell of a story.

"Amends, shit, let me tell you about amends. Sometimes it's not possible, and you need to accept that. But usually, it is. There are different ways to do it, too." He paused, like every good storyteller, and made his audience wait. "There's a golf course here in the city that I used to play every Saturday in the summer. These rounds were a piss up more than anything. The course has one of those flagpoles you see outside of schools, and what I did is, I brought bolt cutters, and after a round, I cut the chain on the lock, lowered the flag, and cut the cords. I stole the flag. My buddies thought this was a riot, and this was the late eighties, way before security cameras and cell phones, so I got away with it scot-free. That flag hung on the wall of my basement for a decade, right above the couch, and when I sobered up, going back twenty years now, it started to bother me.

"Every time I sat down, there it was, that damn flag. Staring at me like it had something to say, you know? Watching TV. Grabbing a nap. Folding laundry. There it was. It finally dawned on me that it wasn't the flag that bothered me, but what the flag symbolized. It represented the way I used to carry myself. The way I used to live. But I had the power to do something about it. I was maybe a year sober when I decided to mail the flag back to the golf course, along with a new one and a note of apology. I included my name, address, and phone number."

A splattering of laughter moved through the crowd.

"I've never heard back from anyone at the course. No one called. Nothing. I couldn't believe the manager didn't thank me or at least acknowledge that I'd returned the damn thing. How's that for an alcoholic mind? I stole from them, and I thought deserved acknowledgment."

More laughter.

"I eventually calmed down and realized all we can do is take care of our side of the street. We can't control people, and we can't expect them to thank us or care about our amends. They have a right to be angry. Thanks for letting me share."

The crowd said, "Thanks, Katz."

The meeting continued, and ten minutes later, the woman two seats down from me spoke, meaning I was next. As the woman finished, I panicked, my hands tightening on the arms of the chair.

What should I say?

"My name's Jake," I began, and sweat grew under my arms and on my forehead like moss at the base of a tree. "And I'm ..."

A chorus of voices saved me. "Hi, Jake."

"I uh, I-what I mean is ... pass."

"Thanks, Jake," the crowd said.

The meeting ended at one. Some people left directly, most stayed and chatted. Katz caught me before I could escape, put out his hand, and we shook.

"How's it hangin'?" I said.

"Short and stocky. You?"

"Average but adequate."

He howled at that.

We had slid right into our usual banter, but there was a thin veil of awkwardness, sort of like when you've dated someone, broken up, and then gotten back together. It's familiar but uncomfortable. It also rarely works.

"First meeting?" he asked.

"Yeah."

"Keep coming back."

I didn't know what to say. I'd known this man for years, but not here. This was different. People talked about their feelings, shared stories. I'd done so little of that, and it made me nervous.

"You okay?" he said. "You got a ride home? A place to stay?"

I shuffled. "Yeah, I'm good."

"Listen, we should go for coffee," Katz said.

I looked away. I wasn't sure I'd be back.

"You don't have to decide now," he said, recognizing I wasn't going to speak. "Knock, knock."

I had to smile. Same old Katz.

"Who's there?" I said.

"Orange."

"Orange who?"

"Orange you glad it's almost Halloween?"

I laughed, and he slapped my shoulder, enjoying his joke more than most people would.

We headed for the exit, and I stopped. Katz had contacts with police, and he'd always come through in the past.

"Hey, I got something maybe you can help me with."

He stopped. "What do you need, Jake Man?"

"I got a missing person."

"A missing person, eh?"

"Yeah, a young woman. The client is the sister. Would you make a call and see if someone matching the MP's description has been arrested, or if they've found a Jane Doe with her particulars? And if you can, maybe run blue Honda Civics?"

He didn't hesitate. "All right, send me a picture, details, all that. I'll get back to you soon."

"Same number?"

"Same number."

"Thank you."

Another pause.

"Jake," he began, "what's done is done and all that, but I'm sorry how things ended between us."

A knot of sadness the size of a baseball settled next to my heart.

"I gotta go," I said.

I didn't mean to be an asshole, but I couldn't relive the past or hear that A.A. held the answers to my problems. I'd heard that fable one too many times.

15

I ate more Tylenol and waited for the bus, admiring a mural painted on a building across the street. It depicted the cartoon version of a tramp, stick resting on his shoulder, a small bundle tied on the end for belongings. Script above the man said *It's a long tramp* and next to him were distances, in kilometres, to various towns and cities in the province.

The ride to Hy's would take close to an hour, and more than once I contemplated renting a car. But I couldn't spend the money, so I resigned myself to the bus, reliving the meeting. It was difficult to clarify what I'd felt, some combination of scared, awkward, and anxious.

Seeing Katz made me feel like the new kid again.

Snippets of film swirled together, and it was impossible to determine where one memory ended and another began. Finally, one took off, and I went with it.

I was thirteen when a teacher noticed my dirty clothes and how withdrawn I'd become. They referred me to the guidance counsellor, Max Legace, who I remember thinking did not live up to his gruff appearance. He was bald and overweight, with a perpetually serious expression, but gentle and kind, the type of person that genuinely cared.

Legace told me he had the impression that I was neglected. I'd lied, said I wasn't, and wouldn't answer questions about my home life. We'd mostly talk about comics. He tried to contact my mom, too, but after a week she hadn't returned his calls, so he came by our apartment.

I opened the door and there he stood. "Mr. Legace?"

"Hi, Jake. Can I come in?"

I didn't know what to say, so I stepped to the side, revealing a small two-bedroom apartment. A flowered sofa and a matching chair. The faux wood of the coffee table, nicked and cracked in the middle, would have been in style a generation earlier. A mirror poorly hid a fist-sized hole in the wall. The kitchen had an old white Formica with four stacking stools around it. A mass of dishes overflowed in the sink. Caked-on food particles spattered each dish, and fruit flies hovered over a browning banana on the counter.

"Is your mom home?" he asked.

"Uh ... she's out."

"Do you know when she's due back?"

"Well, that's the thing. She comes and goes."

"When's the last time you saw her?"

"My mom's all right, she just works a lot," I said, trying to sound honest, like it was no big deal.

"Jake," Legace said, "I need to know something, and it's important you tell me the truth. Can you do that?"

I hesitated. "I think so."

"When was the last time your mom was home?"

I rubbed my head, blew out a slow breath. "A couple days."

"All right," he said. "You mind if I use your phone?"

I nodded to the cordless phone on the wall, and Legace picked it up, dialing as he walked into the other room. He talked for five minutes, then returned and hung up.

"Why don't you grab a suitcase and pack your things?" he said.

"What–why?"

"It's illegal for you to stay here on your own. It's also illegal for you to skip school."

I understood his words but didn't know how to act on them. "Suitcase? I don't have a suitcase."

"How about a backpack?"

I shook my head. Legace found garbage bags under the sink, and I loaded one with clothes, the two books I owned, toiletries, and, of course, my calendar. Kneeling on the worn carpet, I tossed items in, barely looking at them. The packing made it real, and tears hung on the edges of my eyes like icicles. I fought them with anger.

"This is bullshit! I don't know where she is. She's not a bad person. She's at work."

Legace sagged and sat down next to me on the floor.

"I know this is difficult, but we have to make sure you're safe. Young people need support, buddy, and we need to find your mom. Until we do that, you can't stay here alone."

I straightened myself, quietly nodded, and the anger subsided. "Okay."

That was the last time I lived with my mom.

At Hy's, I showed Bannerman's and Sadie's pictures to servers and a bartender. The bartender didn't remember them, but one of the servers did. Her name was Becca, mid-thirties and pretty in a girl-next-door way. She said Bannerman and Sadie had made out half the night, drank wine like it was free, and left together. Bannerman tipped well, and Becca hadn't seen them since.

I thanked her for her time and left.

***

I walked into Sport Sphere a hair before three.

"Hi ..." Krista greeted me. "Jake, right?"

"That's right. Is Bannerman in?"

I wanted to catch him unawares this time, so I hadn't called ahead.

Krista left, and a moment later out came Bannerman, runway walking toward me.

He shook my hand. "Jake, good to see you. Come on back."

We got to his office and sat down.

"Have you found Sadie?" he said.

"No, that's why I'm here."

"How can I help?"

The heat must have been on, and his office was too warm, stifling. I could have taken my coat off, but something prevented me from doing so.

"I've been to Hy's and talked to a bartender and the servers. I showed them Sadie's picture. And yours. The bartender doesn't remember shit, but one server has a memory like a steel trap, and she was happy to describe your make-out session in vivid detail. So, you can help by being honest with me."

Bannerman's disposition changed from laid-back and confident to urgent and grave. He closed the blinds, shut the office door, and sat. His lantern jaw stiffened. "I apologize for not telling you that Sadie and I were seeing each other. It's against our policy for managers and above to be romantically involved in a position below them. In fact, managers are strongly encouraged not to date anyone in the Sport Sphere family. As a leader here, it's incumbent upon me to set the tone."

I looked at him. "I appreciate that, but unless you want me raising all kinds of hell, you're going to be honest from this point on."

He nodded. "I can do that."

"Are the two of you still dating?"

He shook his head. "No."

"How long were you together?"

"Roughly two months."

"Was it serious or casual?"

Bannerman rested his elbows on the desk and leaned forward. "Casual."

"Until six months ago, Sadie was a member at a church called Watershed Moments. The church is huge. Lots of members, lots of money. Did she ever mention her time there? What it was like? Why she left?"

He squinted, thinking, and I was impressed at the level of focus he seemed to give his answer. I'd begun to sweat.

"When I was a kid," he said, launching into a story, "my family was religious. I grew up in Claremore. You heard of it?"

"No. It's in Oklahoma?"

"That's right. Let me tell you, you never been to church till you been to church in the South. Believe me," he said, pausing. "I also grew up with people from the Cherokee Nation. One of my best friends was a kid named Will Haynie. He taught me at a young age that the physical world can't be separated from the spiritual one. To that end, I won't attend church anymore. Haven't set foot in one in years. Me? I like to be outside. Let the elements touch me. Even in this harsh climate." Bannerman smiled, letting his story sink in. "Sadie didn't tell me why she left Watershed Moments. She just said it was a terrible place run by terrible people. Recently, she's embraced the natural world in a more balanced way. Or, I should say, she's working on it. She still has challenges."

"You're talking about her drug use?"

He nodded, and the serious demeanour returned. "I care about Sadie, and I've been driving around every night, stopping in at places she used to frequent. Calling hotels. Hospitals. I've been to them all. I don't know where she is."

Bannerman turned his head, and for a second, I thought he was going to continue. He didn't.

"How bad is Sadie?" I asked him, and as the words left my mouth, I realized it was a stupid question.

"Bad?" he said, not liking it, either. "She's not bad. Nothing about her is bad. People cope in their own ways. I think Sadie's coping."

"With what?"

He shrugged. "Life. Coping with life."

My take was that he knew Sadie had been through something at the church, and that it had to do with those notebooks Remple had found, but he was keeping her secret, or maybe he didn't understand the severity of it.

"Thank you," I said.

He nodded, stood, and it seemed like a good time to go.

"I'm here if you need me," he said as I got to the door. "But please call next time."

I walked out as a bead of sweat slid from my forehead down my cheek and landed on my shirt. It bled into the fabric, gobbled up by the porous material. That happens to people sometimes, too. They are swallowed whole and vanish.

16

As I waited for the bus, my phone vibrated. It was Katz.

"Knock, knock!" he bellowed before I could say hello.

"Who's there?" I played along.

"Wooden shoe."

"Wooden shoe who?"

"Wooden shoe like to hear another knock-knock joke?"

He howled, and I smiled, but my mind was preoccupied. Katz recognized it and got down to business.

"No bodies. None that match the approximate age, race, and sex of your MP. No arrests, either."

"All right. Thank you," I said.

"Call me if you need anything else."

I hung up without responding.

Something bothered me, a detail I'd missed. I played the last hour over, trying to figure it out, yet the answer never came. My story connected to Sadie somehow, but it was hidden in the murky water of my mind.

***

I'd been drunk everywhere, while doing everything. Driving, attending concerts, sporting events, and school. While shopping, picking up groceries, fishing, biking, lifting weights, and running. While shoveling, preparing food, reading, cleaning, talking on the phone, texting, and writing. While having sex, buying insurance, eating at a restaurant, in sports bars, dance clubs, gay bars, strip clubs, and on the corner.

And I'd been drunk with my mom.

Growing up, my mom worked as a cashier on the ten-to-six shift at the Dollar Store on Cavalier Drive. There was a time when we were drinking buddies, after I'd aged out of juvie and the foster system. As the years passed, we drank together less.

I walked into her apartment just before supper, and she stood at the counter, refilling her glass. With her hair cut in a bob, she didn't look fifty-six, but we had celebrated the milestone weeks earlier. She wore a tattered pair of blue jeans, a white Winnipeg Jets T-shirt, and checkered slippers.

"Hey, what're you doing?" I said.

"Je-sus," she barked, placing a hand on her heart. "You startled me."

"Sorry. I brought dinner."

I hugged her and plunked a paper bag on the counter.

"What're we having?" she asked.

"A rotisserie chicken, potato wedges, and a salad. Classic fare."

My mom retrieved a knife from a drawer and passed it to me. I took the knife, opened the container, and began carving. She sat at the kitchen table and lit a cigarette, inhaling long and hard, like it had been a day. "You want a drink?"

"No, thanks."

She looked at me like I thought I was better than her, or maybe it was in my head. Then she finished her drink.

"Preppy ..." she said, confirming what I thought.

Whenever someone didn't accept a cigarette or drink, my mom called them preppy, like they had personally offended her, said no because she was the one asking the question.

We chatted, but my thoughts drifted to Sadie.

"Jake ... what're you thinking about?" Mom said, her eyes sparkling with the glossiness of alcohol. "You're a space cadet."

I prepared two plates of food, carried them to the table. "Just work."

"Tell me about it."

"Missing woman. Twenty-three years old, and she was a member at this church that seems to be involved. She's been missing three days now."

"I never trusted the church, or religion for that matter," Mom said, extending the word never and pointing her wine glass at me to emphasize her point. "Too much faith is worse than too little. You mark my words, Jake. Those people lie."

"Yeah, maybe you're right. People need something to believe in, though, don't they? Look at Dad."

"What about him?" she said, challenging me.

"A little faith might have been helpful, that's all."

She paused, looked as if she'd respond, but something stopped her.

"Don't you ever think about him?" I asked her.

"Of course," she said quietly. "Do you?"

"Yeah ... I have a conversation with him."

Mom leaned in, interested now. "What do you talk about?"

"Different things. It depends how I'm feeling." I took a bite of chicken, chewed and swallowed, then continued against my better judgment. "If I'm angry, then the conversation goes that way. I tell him to fuck off and that he ruined our lives. We fight, and I punch him in the face."

The corners of my mom's mouth sagged, and her cheeks vibrated ever so slightly.

"Other times, I tell him I love him and ask why he left us. He says that he 'had to.' He apologizes, hugs me, and tells me he loves us both."

Tears slid down Mom's cheeks, sullying her makeup.

"Weird, isn't it?"

"No," she said, wiping her face. "It's beautiful. I still remember the day I met him."

I'd heard the tale a million times, and even though I could deliver it verbatim, I let her talk.

"August thirteenth, 1981. I remember the date because it's the day the Jets signed their number one pick, Dale Hawerchuk. I stood at the intersection of Portage and Main, shoulder to shoulder with thousands of people in the heat."

She laughed, recalling the memory.

"Your dad walked right up to me and said, 'I need to ask you something.' He plucked a smoke from behind his ear, taking his time about it. He was such a good-looking man. Wild, dark brown hair that draped over his ears. A thick moustache trimmed neatly, and that smile. When he was ready, he finally said, 'Will you engage in a one-week love affair with me?' That's the line he used. Can you believe it?"

I nodded, listening.

"He said, 'One week, that's all I ask. At the end of the week, we can reassess the situation. If one of us has doubts, then we can opt out. If things are good, we can opt in.'"

I played along. "And what'd you say?"

"I needed a minute to think about it, but there was something different about your dad. He had kind eyes. I said, 'Let's do it.'"

My mom's energy and fondness of the past inspired me to ask a question I'd wanted to pose to her for months, maybe years, but always balked at when the opportunity arose.

"Do you think Dad's alive?"

She tilted her head, and a thoughtful look appeared on her face. "No, I don't think so. You?"

I shook my head no, then leaned across and hugged her. It hurt to see my mom torn up like this, imagining my dad lying lifeless in a ditch or dead in a crack house. My mom still loved him, and I loved my mom more than words could describe. If my dad ever came home, I wasn't sure if I'd punch him in the face or hug him. That wasn't true, though. I did know.

I'd hug him.

17

The leaves lay nearly two feet thick along the curb, and bare trees hung over the street like tattered umbrellas. From my seat, I watched the city go by, people getting in the Halloween spirit. A giant goblin stood on the front stoop of one house. Carved pumpkins smiled maniacally in the yard of another. Ghosts haunted every window of an apartment building.

Ugly memories bumped up against regret. Specifically, the St. James Group Home for Boys. I didn't say much during those first weeks. I did my chores, went to school, and minded my business. I guess you could say I had one foot in the door, one foot out, waiting for my mom to return. Foolish, looking back, but I thought she'd clean herself up and I'd move in with her again.

The memory faded, and the nagging feeling I'd missed something became whole.

I called Nia.

When she answered, I stood up and moved to the back of the bus, where I'd have a little space.

"Hey," she said. "Any news?"

"No. The reason I'm calling is to ask if you know if Sadie spoke to anyone, like a therapist, psychologist, or guidance counsellor."

There was a silent moment of expectation as I gave her the time she needed.

Finally, she said, "I ... I don't know. I can't remember her doing anything like that. You need to understand, mental health issues were swept under the rug, and the church never would have supported talking to an outsider. I guess it's possible Sadie spoke to someone on her own, but she never told me about it."

I disconnected and dialed Arkell Lightfoot.

It rang five times before Arkell picked up, breathing heavily.

"He-llo," she said, turning the greeting into two words.

"Hi, this is Jake Joelsen. You got a minute?"

"I'm in the middle of destroying my legs. But for you ..." she said, and I heard liquid flowing as she drank. "I got a minute."

"Do you know if Sadie ever spoke to a therapist, psychologist, or guidance counsellor?"

"Not a psychologist or therapist that I'm aware of, but there was Mr. Pardy."

A pang of excitement filled me. "Who's he?"

"Oh, the way you asked, I thought you knew. All good, though. Pardy was our high school guidance counsellor. There was a little area outside his office where we used to hang out."

Two women got on the bus, talking loudly, and a man near the front played a tune I could not decipher on a violin. I turned the volume up on the phone.

"What was Pardy like?" I asked.

Arkell blew out a breath, animated, like always. She had a bubbliness I liked. "Shit, what can I tell you about Pardy? Well, for starters, Sadie would meet with him a couple of times a week."

"What'd they talk about?"

"Mostly her family, I think. The church. All that."

"What was your take on him? I know you were a teenager, but I mean now, looking back, what's your impression? Was he a decent guy?"

"My impression? I guess he seemed like one of those teachers who wants to be friends with students. That type. I don't think his intentions were bad, and his methods were all right. Getting close to the line, but nothing inappropriate, at least not in front of me."

"Did Sadie mention if he ever tried anything ..."

"Sexual?"

"Yeah."

"She didn't mention it."

"Did he try anything like that with you?"

"No, never, and I met with him one-on-one like every week for a while. He would talk about his own life, how he was divorced, or if he'd had a date, home renos–personal stuff most adults don't share. I think he got remarried at some point."

"How old was Pardy?"

"When we knew him? That was like ... ten years ago. He was probably mid-fifties."

I paused.

"You're going to track him down, aren't you?" she said.

I smiled to myself. "No comment."

"Promise to keep me posted, okay?"

"Will do."

***

I searched David Pardy AND Winnipeg on my phone and called six D. Pardys until I found him.

"Hello," he answered.

"Hi, is David there?"

"Speaking."

"My name's Jake Joelsen, and I'm a private investigator. I've been hired to find a young woman named Sadie Rowe. Was she a former stu–"

"Sadie's missing? For how long?"

I ignored his questions. "I'd like to speak with you. The sooner the better. Can we set up a time to meet?"

He provided an address in St. Vital. I grabbed a transfer, got off the bus, and caught another one heading east.

Pardy had a two-storey house in a middle-class neighbourhood called Dakota. Double garage. Christmas lights. Manicured shrubs. Like many people close to retirement, his house looked well cared for. He was probably one of those pricks who used scissors to snip the unruly pieces of grass on their lawn.

Pardy answered my knock, snapping his fingers. "Jake, right?"

I nodded.

I'd say he was five ten and weighed a hundred and seventy-five pounds, with a scruffy beard and longish hair. He wore slippers, joggers, and a thin sweater.

"Come in," he said, and waved a hand to welcome me into his home.

"You want coffee? I just ground some beans."

I walked in. "Sure, thanks."

"Don't mention it," he said.

His wife, a woman around his age, arrived, introduced herself as Lisa, and Pardy relayed the order. Two coffees. Sugar and milk for him, black for me.

Then he spent three minutes telling me about the beans. Where they were from (Guatemala), how he got them (he knew a guy), and the grinding process (he used the TIMEMORE Chestnut C2 MAX).

When he'd finished the bean speech, we headed for the living room, where Pardy lowered himself onto the sofa and crossed his legs.

A wall-to-wall bookshelf overflowed with hundreds, maybe thousands, of titles. Classics, bestsellers, and professional textbooks, it was quite the collection.

Pardy observed me as I inspected the books from my seat, a satisfied smile on his face. He seemed comfortable, the sort of person happy with what they'd accomplished, someone who now lived a life of leisure.

Lisa dropped off the coffees, and I took a sip. It tasted great, and that pissed me off.

"It's good, right?" he said.

I nodded, soaked in the sea of books one more time. "Are you retired?"

He paused, then said, "Yes, I retired at the end of June 2017. Now it's just coffee and books, traveling south in the winter, and the cabin in the summer." Pardy sipped his coffee, his right foot making tiny circles, legs still crossed. His smile widened.

I picked up my coffee so my hands were occupied, then leaned back.

"Sadie's missing," I said, careful not to let my dislike of the man enter my tone.

"Credentials, please," he asked.

"I don't have a license right now."

"Oh?" Pardy said. "Why not?"

"A legal matter."

He drank more coffee as he thought about it but didn't ask a follow-up question.

"So how can I help?" he said.

I'd explained to him on the phone who I was, and what I'd been hired to do, so I went right to the heart of it. "Are you still in contact with Sadie?"

He smiled, proud. "Yes."

My body reacted, pins and needles in my hands and feet.

"When was the last time you spoke with her?"

He contemplated that. Pardy only answered questions once he'd dramatically scrunched his face, turned his head to the side, and touched his chin. He was like that thinking-man statue in the flesh.

"I spoke to Sadie on ..." he said, and checked his phone. "October fifteenth."

The day she disappeared.

I placed the mug on the table and leaned forward. My instincts screamed to toss him around, but I remembered what Katz had shared at the meeting yesterday: *All we can do is take care of our side of the street*. We can't control people.

"What did you talk about?" I asked, my voice steady.

"I won't break confidentiality."

"Was she panicked? Did she sound sick or hurt? Anything like that?"

Pardy uncrossed his legs. "How might one sound sick? I mean, humans are a sick species, am I right? She sounded like she always does. Brilliant. Passionate. Lonely." He considered his words carefully. "I'm in contact with several former students, and you must understand that in my position, I connected with young people in an intimate manner–and I don't mean intimate in the way a layman might interpret the word. There's a closeness to the therapy I provided, and that closeness doesn't fade just because they've graduated high school."

"I'm not implying that you've been inappropriate," I said, "but I'm in a time-sensitive situation here. Sadie's been missing since the fifteenth. If you know where she is, spit it out."

Seconds ticked by loudly, then he said, "I gave her access to our cabin."

"You what?" I froze for a moment, hardly believing what he'd said. "Where's your cabin?"

"Granite Lake, Ontario."

"Did you ask why she wanted to use your cabin?"

Pardy repeated the face scrunch, tapped his chin. This time he even narrowed his eyes. "I assumed she wanted it for some R and R, or perhaps a romantic tryst. I didn't ask."

I stared at him, unblinking, but I didn't squish my face or touch my chin. In fact, I didn't move at all. Pardy broke eye contact almost right away, looked out the kitchen windows on the other side of the room. He recrossed his legs, picked up the mug, and held it in his hands. He bounced one foot.

When he couldn't take it, he said, "Do you have another question?"

"How did Sadie get the keys to the cabin?" I said, maintaining the hard gaze. "Did you see her?"

"I thought you'd drifted off," he said. "No, I didn't see her. We were out–concert at the Pantages Theatre–so I left the keys for her in the mailbox."

"Do you have a camera that shows the front entrance?"

"No."

"Do you have paper?"

A look of confusion fluttered across his face. "How come?"

"Because you're going to draw me directions to your cabin."

Pardy retrieved a notebook, drew a detailed map, including highway numbers, approximate distances, and landmarks along the way to Granite Lake. Ten minutes later, I ran out of his house, leaving the arrogant prick sitting on his sofa, drinking Guatemalan coffee.

18

Katz said to call anytime if I needed anything, so I rang him as I ran down the street from Pardy's place. He wasn't answering, so I ordered an Uber from St. Vital Mall, and twenty minutes later I was on the way to Katz's farm, where I knew he'd be tending to his babies. He had two acres fifteen minutes west on the Trans-Canada Highway around St. Francis Xavier.

The driver looked over his shoulder at me. "You know where you're going?"

"It's close."

I directed him to a dirt road, and we followed it for a kilometre before a patch of trees let me know the house was nearby. I told him to slow down and pull into a long driveway that eventually brought us to Katz's place. I paid the man and walked around the house to the backyard.

The sun sets early in October, and in another hour it would be dark. Katz was across the yard, and I watched as he stopped every so often to tend to a hive, wrapping each box. A silver cannister on the ground sent puffs of smoke into the air. Katz was shirtless, and the elaborate Geisha tattoo on his back shone in the moonlight. He wore army pants, boots, and a backwards cap, but no mask or gloves to protect himself from bees that swarmed him. He walked calmly through the smoke toward me.

"How're your babies?" I said.

"Oh, they're good. I'm just prepping them for winter."

I strained to hear him over the buzzing.

"Let's walk," he said.

I followed him farther into the yard, to a shed where two chairs and a table sat underneath an awning. Katz tossed me a bottle of water from a cooler. The cold bottle sent a chill down my spine, and I pulled up the hood of my sweater and sat. The temperature was 8 degrees Celsius, but would drop soon, reaching an overnight low of 3 or 4.

I put the bottle down, unopened.

Katz drank deeply. "So, how goes the battle?"

"I need your help."

I rushed through the story, providing details I hadn't mentioned to him earlier. I described Nia, Sadie, and the text message that Nia had received. I relayed the information I got from Pardy as Katz wiped his brow with a T-shirt before putting it on. He didn't seem cold. I added that I needed to get to Granite Lake as soon as possible, and I needed to borrow his vehicle because I'd sold mine.

We were surrounded by trees, sitting beneath a slate-grey sky barely visible. You couldn't hear anything that wasn't supposed to be there. Crickets. Birds. Wind. Trees flapping themselves silly.

Katz finished his water. "How about I drive?"

***

Katz's F-150 roared down the Trans-Canada Highway heading east into Ontario. The scenery turned from tabletop flat to rocky, rolling land with thick bush stretching for miles. The rumble of engines and the stops and starts of traffic lights, the busyness and congestion of city life, disappeared. What remained was the peaceful, quiet serenity of the wild.

Katz gripped the wheel tightly but didn't say anything as the first snowflakes of the season fell, bloated and slow.

I had a soft spot in my heart for this drive, and it reminded me of being a kid, looking out the window as the trees blurred by. My parents and I drove this highway several times on our way to Falcon Lake. On the drive, my dad used to tell me to look for bears. I never saw one, but I'd spend hours focusing on the open spots in the forest, the areas in between. *That's where they'll be*, he'd say.

That's where I'd like to live–in the quiet moments of life, the halcyon days, the calm pastures of a non-glamourous outback.

Maybe someday.

The snowflakes became flecks of moisture on the windshield,

and Katz turned on the wipers. We sat quietly, staring out into the thickly wooded trees, when I noticed movement. Fifty yards in, a black bear wandered aimlessly in the dwindling light. Its snout tap-tapped the ground, sniffing, searching for something more. I hoped he'd find it.

***

We arrived at Granite Lake just after eight. Katz parked in a small lot a short distance from the highway at a place called Pickle Pete's, and I brought up a map of the area on my phone. We went back and forth, figuring the best way to walk to the cabin, making sure we didn't startle Sadie with our headlights. Pardy's instructions matched what we saw on the map. He had explained them well with clear labels and surprisingly accurate scale.

The exterior lights on the cabin were off, but a Honda Civic was parked in the driveway. Sadie's blue Honda Civic. I saw the glow of a television flicker and flash in the front window.

We spent five minutes discussing the layout of the cabin, forming a loose plan.

"You ready?" Katz whispered.

I nodded my approval.

The moon provided enough light to vaguely see the water in the distance as we moved to the front of the cabin and up the stairs. We had considered a few options for the initial point of contact, and decided knocking was the best way. Sadie was hiding out, obviously scared. Why feed into that fear by going in hard?

At the same time, she didn't know us, and I kicked myself for not bringing Nia. Without her here to confirm my story, Sadie might think we were looking to cause her harm before I had the chance to explain that Nia had hired me to find her. We waited and, hearing no movement, Katz crept to the back.

I knocked, my flashlight ready to click on in case she ran.

She didn't answer, so I walked down the steps to the front window and peered inside. My eyes adjusted to the shadowy darkness, and I saw one large, open space, including a couch, two chairs, and a flat-screen TV on the wall. Behind this, at the back of the space, I could see a full kitchen. There were four doorways from the great room, what I guessed were three bedrooms and a bathroom.

A wave of adrenaline spiked my blood, a hyper-focus, as I saw the silhouette of someone lying on the couch, watching a Will Ferrell movie.

Or so I thought.

The figure abruptly launched themself off the couch and sprinted into one of the bedrooms.

I knew from Pardy that there was a deck and staircase that led toward the water. I felt confident Katz had that part of the property covered. There were neighbours on both sides of the cabin, but trees and darkness made those in-between sections difficult to navigate.

I waited a beat until I heard a window raise in the bedroom alongside the cabin, then bolted that way and saw the open window but not Sadie. I scanned the trees with the flashlight, waving it back and forth.

"Jake?"

It was Katz, coming toward me from the rear of the property.

"Yeah?" I said.

"You got her?"

"No."

I jumped, grabbed the frame with both hands, and pulled myself up, staring into an empty bedroom.

That's when the engine of the Civic came alive, followed by the loud crunching of gravel as the vehicle reversed and sped away. We got to the driveway in time to watch its taillights turn the corner and disappear.

***

It was a fifteen-minute walk, and by the time we reached Katz's truck, Sadie would be long gone. Instead, we turned on lights and searched the cabin. The dressers in the largest bedroom were full of clothing we assumed belonged to the Pardys. The other two bedrooms had few personal items, and the dressers contained blankets, pillows, and additional clothing.

The fridge held milk, bottled water, and sandwich meat that said *Packaged on October 15*. The cupboards held a box of cereal, bread, and canned ravioli. Fresh wrappers, scraps of food, and used paper plates had been left in the kitchen garbage. Towels on the rack in the bathroom were damp from use. I wondered if Pardy had called Sadie to let her know we were on the way. It was unlikely or she would have left before we arrived.

"Fuck ... she must have gone into the bedroom and opened the window to make me think she went out that way, then ran right out the front door," I said, discouraged by my mistake. "I should have stayed with the car."

"Woulda, coulda, shoulda," Katz said. Then he dropped to his knees and inspected the coffee table in front of the TV. He craned his neck and eyeballed it from the side. Katz ran a finger along the surface.

"Residue," he said, holding up his finger. "I got a guy who might be able to help. A cop." Katz paused and glanced at the watch on his wrist. "Let's get on the road."

***

It was after midnight when we stopped at an all-night diner called Brogan's on the edge of the city. I ate an omelet, and Katz had a burger and fries. We sat on stools at the counter, reminding me of ones I might find at the wood in a bar. This place wasn't licensed, and for that I was grateful.

We ate, not saying much, as I dwelled on the conversation I was about to have with Nia.

Sorry, we found your sister, but I fucked it up and she's gone again. Where? I have no idea.

Katz pushed his plate away, finished, and retrieved a newspaper from a corner table while I settled our tab, leaving thirty on twenty-five. The rain had stopped and outside, surrounded by two semi-trucks with trailers and a black night so clear you could see stars, I made the call. It was late, but Nia answered, her voice thick with sleep.

"Jake? It's like ... What time is it?"

"Almost one."

"Is everything okay?"

"Lots has happened since we last spoke," I said. "I tracked down a guidance counsellor that knew Sadie in high school, a man called David Pardy."

"Pardy?" she said, her sleepy voice becoming more awake.

"Yeah, did you know him?"

"No ... but I vaguely remember him."

"Sadie called Pardy on the fifteenth. He gave her the keys to his cabin on Granite Lake, which is in Ontario, just past the Manitoba border."

"What?" she said, fully alert now. "She's alive? I thought–I honestly thought she was ..."

"It's not all good news. I'm on my way back from there now, and I saw her, but–"

"Whoa, whoa, whoa, hold up." Her voice hardened. "Saw her? What does that mean, *saw*?"

How do you tell someone you found the person they hired you to find, only to lose them again?

"She got to her car and took off before we could speak with her," I said. "My guess is she thought we were the people who are after her. She's scared."

Nia said, "Who's we?"

"What's that?"

"You said 'before we could speak with her.' Who's we?"

"I brought a friend of mine, a guy I used to work for. He's an investigat–"

"Why didn't you bring me?" Nia shouted. "If she had seen me, she wouldn't have run."

"You don't know that."

"Yes, I do–she's my sister! Of course, she's going to run when two strange men show up in the middle of the night. I can't believe this. I–you found her, she's alive, and you fucked it up."

"I'm sorry," I said, "but this is good news. She's alive. I'll find her again."

A long moment passed, and when it became clear that Nia wasn't going to say anything, I described how Katz knew a cop who could help and asked if she was okay with the police assisting in the investigation. She said she was fine with it now, and maybe they wouldn't fuck up as bad as I had.

Nia hung up and I felt awful. I looked up and my eyes landed on a constellation, or maybe I just thought it was. Either way, the shape of the stars looked like a gun, and it was pointed directly at me.

19

Saturday, October 19 (four days missing)

The next morning, I got off the bus on Main Street, walked down Pioneer Avenue, and hung a right on Israel Asper Way. In front of the Canadian Museum for Human Rights, I stopped and smoked a cigarette, wondering how much the place had cost to build. Gargantuan in size, beige rock formed the massive base, leading to the upper part of the building, which was windowed in sheets of glass and rose to a single point. The museum's summit is visible from miles around, its full size and shape not fully realized unless one walks in the front doors. Even driving by will leave you with a lack of appreciation for the bulk.

I pulled out my phone and read that they broke dirt in December of 2008, and the museum opened in 2014, total expenditure in the neighbourhood of $350 million.

Jesus.

I'm all for human rights, but that amount of money used in other ways could have done a lot of good. Food, clothes, winter jackets, shoes and boots, and housing for thousands of people. Or maybe improve infrastructure, lower property taxes, or plug a couple potholes. I hit one the other day I didn't think I'd climb out of.

I know it doesn't work that way when you're dealing with public and private money, but still, $350 mil? It's excessive.

I met Katz's guy outside of The Original Pancake House at The Forks. He was a white guy, mid-forties and average height, who puffed on a thin cigar like a pro. He wore his hair in a fade shaved close, with a thin face, sharp brown eyes, and a straight nose. He was fit, and he reminded me of a retired soccer player. Likable is the first word that came to mind.

"You Duke?"

"That I am."

I walked up, and we shook hands.

"So," he said, "what's the good word?"

Smoke rings drifted in my direction, and I lit one, too. "No good words. What's the haps with you?"

"Living the dream, man. Living the dream."

I laughed, we finished our cancer sticks, and went in.

"I got us a top," Duke said, and I followed him to a table in the far end of the space, away from the other patrons.

I looked at the half-empty mug of coffee and Duke's red-rimmed eyes. "You on an all-nighter?"

"Something like that."

We sat down and a server stopped in, placed menus in front of us, and freshened up Duke's coffee.

"You want coffee, honey?" she asked me.

"Please."

She poured and departed, promising to return soon and take our orders.

"Are you a drug cop?" I asked.

"Nah, Organized Crime. Same shitbirds, different pile. I was a rookie when I worked with Katz. A kid, really. Too much testosterone and not enough brains, man. Katz did me a solid on more than one occasion. Saved my ass ..." He took a sip of coffee, momentarily lost in a memory. "I can tell Katz likes you."

"I've known him for a long time. Did he tell you I worked for him?"

"Yeah, he told me that. And he mentioned your pops. I lost my old man, too, when I was young, younger than you were, and that shit is emotional. The things you remember ..." Duke waved his hands as he spoke, animated. "My pops was the biggest basketball fan, taught me the game. Gave me a love for it that I still got." He paused, then added, "Bottom line, Katz asked me to give you what you need."

I trusted Katz, meaning I had to trust Duke. In a way, Katz had vouched for me. He trusted me not to make him look bad.

Duke told me his team was the Mavs and talked about his time on the force, his rise to detective. I shared the SparkNotes version of my dad's story, then my own, and it surprised me that Duke hadn't mentioned that Katz had fired my drunk ass. Maybe he didn't know.

We ordered food, and Duke rubbed his eyes, a gesture meant to clear his head and wipe away the exhaustion. "So ... how old is your MP?"

"Twenty-three. She was a member at this church called Watershed Moments. They call it the 'Church of Spiritual Enlightenment,' and I met the top man there, a minister called Brad Walton. Guy is close to sixty. He's calm, strikes me as smart, a man at peace with himself. That type of confidence."

"What denomination is this place?"

"I don't know, but you need to interview before becoming a member. And people of colour? Forget it."

Duke nodded as I spoke, following along.

"But I found a guy who left the church a year ago. He's twenty years old. This guy says he sold drugs to Sadie, but that's not the worst part. Walton, and some of the other men, are pimping out teenage girls."

Duke looked like I'd poured cold water on him. He blew out his breath and leaned back. "Does this twenty-year-old who left the church have proof?"

"His dad was one of the church's founding members. When his dad died, he stumbled onto some notebooks recording each encounter."

"Encounter?"

"Who had sex with who. When. Cash exchanged. Other details. It was all in the notebooks."

"And let me guess, these notebooks have been lost?"

"The guy burned them."

"People ..." Duke said, shaking his head like he'd seen it all. "If they aren't fucking up, then they're about to."

My mistake at the cabin blew through my mind like the breeze off a landfill on a scorching summer day, smelling of rot. I pushed it away.

"And it's always normal things," Duke continued. "Good things that they fuck with. Faith. Family. Relationships. We need these things to be well, and without them, we turn to internet sex sites and bar hookups, drugs and alcohol, gangs, or other fucked-up shit that's even worse. But this thing you're telling me about with the church, it's about control."

That sounded like Remple's theory that the notebooks represented power. I chewed on it, contemplating how Walton had been so businesslike, so professional. There was nothing, not one indication, that he had trafficked young girls. Even now, part of me thought it was crazy to think he was capable of that.

"You're probably right," I said, still trapped in thoughts of Brad Walton and Carl and Muriel Rowe.

Duke smiled. "I know I'm right."

The food arrived and we dug in.

In between mouthfuls, Duke said, "So what do you need from me?"

"Had you heard of Brad Walton before today? Has Watershed Moments been on your radar?"

"Nah, man, not at all. Let me reach out to the DEU and Sex Crimes, see what they know." Duke shoveled another load in. "What drug was this guy selling to Sadie?"

"Meth." I took a bite of my omelet. "And her co-worker says she was doing coke."

"Coke is bad, but it ain't meth. Worse than heroin in a lot of ways, especially when it's laced with fentanyl. I've been hearing a lot about it lately. ODs are way up." Duke looked through the window. "Zombies walking them streets. Dead already, they just don't know it."

"Why would a preacher draw attention to himself by selling underage girls?" I said, taking a bite. "I understand the obvious reasons, but it's just so careless. So stupid."

Duke shifted his gaze back inside. "Well, money for one. I'm sure he was getting paid. And arrogance, man. He must think he's above the law. And you know, he's not on the corner pimping. This sounds organized." Duke hesitated, then started again. "I'm sure he's told himself a story, like you said, that he's a businessman or some shit. That's another thing us humans love, telling stories. We're a story-telling species, man."

I agreed. What other reason could there be, other than you thought you were entitled, better than everyone else, and didn't need to follow the law and morals of the society you lived in?

"There's something going on with Muriel Rowe," I said. "During the meeting, she never said a word, but she wanted to. I'm going to take another run at her, see if I can't get more information."

Duke took a minute, stabbed three potatoes with his fork, ate them, and wiped his mouth.

"How many former members of the church do I need before you'd take this to the deputy chief?" I asked.

"We've got a young DA who loves this shit. He'll jump all over it, but he's a stickler for dotting them i's and crossing them t's. That means we need ironclad testimony from solid people." Finished, Duke added, "One former member is good, two is better. I need a second witness before I involve the DC. When you have that, let me know. And if you want me to tag along on anything, give me a shout."

Duke slid a card across the table.

Duke Jansen the card read.

"In the meantime," he continued, "I'm going to run Brad Walton and see what I can find. I already checked morgues and recent arrests for Sadie, and she wasn't there. I'm sure Katz told you that."

I nodded, and Duke made notes in a small notebook until his phone rang.

"Hello," Duke answered. "Yup ... yup ... done." He hung up. "I gotta roll, man. I'll give you a shout when I know more and vice versa."

I settled the tab, leaving fifty on forty, paying for Duke's breakfast along with my own. We left, and the A.A. meeting crossed my mind again, Katz's story about stealing the flag from the golf course. The idea of amends made sense, but I wasn't sure it was possible for me. How could I make up for something that let a murderer go free?

20

It was approaching noon, and all I could think about was getting drunk, so impaired that I couldn't function. I didn't know where to go or what to do to get rid of the urge, so I went to a meeting in the basement of a run-down church on Whytewold Road in the heart of Sunny St. James. The air was wet, like the walls held water, and the people looked worn out but cheerful.

I listened to an elderly man who said he'd been sober for twenty-one years, but that he'd drank at seven-year intervals, so the longest he'd ever had was seven years. He presently had three days sober, just like me.

After the meeting, I picked up a sandwich from Safeway and ate it on the bus on the way to the Millennium Library on Donald Street. I'd sat too long and needed to stretch my legs, so I got off early, walked down Broadway to Main, past Union Station and The Forks, where the Red and Assiniboine Rivers converge. I took the scenic route to the infamous juncture of Portage and Main and spent a minute admiring the Bank of Montreal building. Six columns lined the exterior, and I didn't know the history or particulars of the building, but I appreciated the simple design. I noticed brief inscriptions above the name of the institution and what must have been important dates of the establishment written in Roman numerals, tiny details I hadn't seen before.

I continued west on Portage Avenue, took a left on Donald, and walked into the library just after 2 p.m. I passed through security and began the trek up three flights of stairs. High ceilings hovered over stacks and stacks of books, and wide, tall windows brought in plenty of natural light. I gazed across the open space, and as I arrived on the third floor, thoughts of Logan Bergel entered my mind.

I pushed them away and approached the Micro Media Services

desk. A woman named Rose showed me to a cubicle with a desktop computer with access to newspapers from around the world dating back to 1960.

If you wanted an article older than that, then it would be on microfilm, and you needed to use a device next to the desktop computer. It looked like a microwave, and there was a reel underneath where you could feed the film.

I spent the next two hours reading.

First, I searched for articles that included the words Watershed Moments and found two, that was it. Someone had died in a car accident on St. Mary's close to Gauthier Road, "across from Watershed Moments," and the second one described an outdoor concert on the church's property that drew the ire of people living on the closest streets. Both were short and told me very little.

Most of the time was spent reading about Christian fundamentalism, which was where I suspected Watershed fit. It seemed like every religion, political party, and philosophy included a sect of people with an unwavering belief system that had gone too far.

After reading about several churches with extreme beliefs, I settled on the Fundamentalist Church of Jesus Christ of Latter-day Saints to examine closer. I read that most Mormon churches had stopped the practice of polygamy decades earlier, yet there were groups independent of the LDS that continued the tradition.

The word polygamy cut through my soul like a Samurai blade, followed by an image of the women in the doorway calling Henry Formenton for supper.

Jesus, is Formenton a polygamist?

I packed up and left the library, hoping I was wrong.

***

On the sidewalk in front of the library, I dialed the Rowes, holding my breath. If Carl answered, I'd introduce myself as an employee of the local MLA's office, conducting a survey with women between the ages of fifty and sixty. Then I'd ask if there was anyone in the household within that group. Carl might not let me speak to Muriel, but I'd try. I hoped it worked better than my last plan had at Watershed Moments.

Two rings and Muriel answered, bypassing the need to lie.

"Hi, Muriel," I said, then quickly added, "before I say anything, is Carl at home?"

There was a pause. "No."

"Okay, this is Jake Joelsen. You met me two days ago at–"

"I remember."

"I could tell you were upset the other night."

"I can't have this conversation."

"I need your help. I–"

The line went dead. I stood amidst the sidewalk traffic, wanting to call back but knowing she wouldn't answer if I forced it. My phone vibrated, revealing a different number than the one I'd just called.

"Hello," I answered.

"Why?" she said firmly, not at all like the delicate flower I thought she must be.

"You're on a different phone?"

Silence.

"Hello," I said.

"Yes. It's a different phone. I know you're not a lawyer," she said. "You're some kind of investigator. Brad knows who you are, too. But the question is, why? Why did you arrange that meeting? What do you want?"

"I have more questions about Watershed that I'd like to ask you without Brad Walton and your husband."

"Okay ..." She hesitated again, but less than before. "Does it involve my daughters?"

Before the call, my plan had been to say as little as possible, but I'd left it open to come clean, if necessary, to be honest, and to explain that I was searching for Sadie. In that scenario, Muriel might tell Carl, and Carl would tell Walton. Nia would take heat from her parents, but other than that, what was the harm? I didn't care if Walton knew I was investigating the church. The look-alikes told me to stop, but I'd never liked being told what to do, and that would never change.

"Yes," I said, "it involves them."

"There is an alarm system here, and cameras. They record the opening and closing of doors, and movement." I gave her time to organize her thoughts and come to terms that she was going against her husband. "Carl checks the videos daily."

Even though I'd never met Sadie, something about her mom reminded me of her. It was how Nia described Sadie as a champion of human rights, and how Bergel said she'd camped out on the lawn of government buildings in protest of the closure of emergency rooms. I sensed that same fighting spirit in Muriel, hidden by a deep sadness.

"I appreciate you telling me those things," I said. "The why I'm calling has to do with my job. Nia hired me to find Sadie. No one's heard from her since the fifteenth."

Muriel made a noise I'd describe as a hiccup, a short burst of air, almost a click.

"Are there signs of foul play?" she said, her voice full of worry.

"No. I found her last night, but she drove away before I could talk with her."

"Thank you for being honest." There was a pause, and a patter of optimism fluttered in my chest.

"I've spoken to a former member of the church who is willing to go on record about abuse he says happened there. The details, I'll keep private, but I want to build a case against Brad Walton. I–"

"You want names of people who've left the church?"

"Yes," I said. "People who left abruptly, under conditions that were strange. Maybe there were rumours of something unethical, or illegal."

I pictured Muriel on the other end of the line, traveling back in time, racking her brain. I also saw her weighing the pros and cons of sharing a name with me. What would it cost her?

"There are two people who I can recall leaving the church that way. The names are Tracy Remple, who you already know about, and Delilah Moore."

"One sec ..." I said, and wrote the second name in my phone. "Is it Delilah, spelled D-E-L-I-L-A-H?"

"Yes, I think so."

"Okay, one more question, and it's a doozy," I said. "Is polygamy practiced at Watershed Moments?"

A kid like fifteen years old bumped into my shoulder, hard, and I struggled to keep my balance as I stood on the sidewalk. He wore a Raptors hat, a sweater two or three sizes too big for him, and high-top sneakers with pants that only a belt could save. He gawked at me, like "you got a problem?"

I let it go, and he tossed a middle finger my way.

"My goodness ..." Muriel said.

She hadn't said it with scorn, more like surprise.

"I've done some reading, and I thought I'd ask," I said, watching the kid who bumped into me bop down the sidewalk.

"Polygamy is being phased out. It's not mandatory at Watershed, and my husband doesn't have multiple wives, but, and I say this so that you hear me loud and clear, some families apply pressure on the next generation. So, it still happens. It used to happen more ..." She trailed off like there was more to say.

"Was Sadie married? Was she in one of these polygamous marriages?"

"No, but ... we were pressured hard when she was young. Carl and I wouldn't allow it."

Fucking Nia, I thought. She knew about this–how could she not?–and had withheld it from me. What else was she hiding?

"Please," Muriel added, sounding desperate for the first time. "Find her."

I nodded, shook my head, and broke one of my cardinal rules: Never make promises you can't guarantee.

"I will," I said, wanting to take it back as soon as I'd said it. "I'll bring her home safely."

21

I was surprised by how many Delilah Moores there were, located across the world; the most famous was a Black soul singer who had a bunch of hit songs in the early seventies. When I focused the search to *Delilah Moore AND Winnipeg*, I found a likely candidate straight away. She was a hairdresser at a place called Winslow's Hair Design on Harrow Street, in between Taylor Avenue and Pembina Highway.

I went to Winslow's site and clicked on Stylists. In each picture, the subject wore a black top and was captured from the shoulders up. The pictures were organized three across, and you could read a brief biography of each person as you scrolled. Moore was in her forties, listed as a Senior Stylist. Her dyed blonde hair showed dark roots, and she'd parted it off-centre. She had brown eyes and a small nose and smiled widely, which caused natural creases to form on either side of her mouth. Her T-shirt fitted her shoulders tightly, and Moore appeared to be athletic and in decent shape. She was cute.

I located a phone number and called.

"Hello," a man answered.

"Hi, I'd like to make an appointment with Delilah."

"Okay, let me see here ..." the man said, clearly checking a schedule. "When would you like to come in?"

"Well, I have a last-minute event this weekend. Is she in today?"

"She is, but she's completely booked. The absolute earliest I can do is Tuesday, and that's for a thirty-minute appointment only. What kind of service are you looking for?"

I almost asked "Service? How many kinds are there?" Instead, I said, "Unfortunately, it has to be today. Thanks for trying."

"No problem. Have yourself a good day."

"You, too."

I hung up and studied Moore's picture for a long time, wondering when she'd left Watershed, and why. I sat back, alone in my apartment, and harkened to a memory I placed in October of 2004. I had been living in the group home on Olive Street for close to a year when Bergel scrambled into the room we shared, reached into his pants, jerked out a clear freezer bag, and dropped it in my lap as I lay in bed reading a wrestling magazine.

"Here, take it!" he shouted. "Quick, put it somewhere! Perry's coming!"

Mick Perry was the assistant coordinator of the home and could have been the biggest stickler for rules I'd ever met. Veiny arms grew from a thin and wiry frame, and his hangdog face looked like it had been electronically stretched in an app. His nose extended too long, and jack-o'-lantern eyes drilled into you when you met them. A Jay Leno chin jutted out like a bear trap. He hadn't been hard on me, but Perry and Bergel butted heads daily. They argued about missing curfew, messiness, swearing, and poor grades due to shoddy attendance.

Perry kept saying "the chickens will come home to roost" and "it takes two to tango." We were teenagers, so we made fun of him, and plus, Perry was only twenty-five. What the hell did he know about life? Guy was a major try-hard.

Perry had also homed in on Bergel's potential drug dealing, and he wasn't wrong. Bergel sold weed and mushrooms, but the bag on my lap, underneath the page showing Goldberg standing over Randy Orton, was not weed or shrooms. The bag had been folded in half, and the powder reminded me of sugar on those white mini donuts.

"The fuck you waiting for?" Bergel said. "Hurry!"

I grabbed the bag, stood, and surveyed my options, settling on a LeBron James bobblehead, one of those figurines of a pro athlete with a huge head that shook. The base had broken days earlier when another kid, Taylor Winstone, threw it at the wall in anger after he bet big the Cards would beat the Red Sox in the World Series.

The bobblehead was eight inches tall and maybe three or four in diameter. I removed the bottom, crammed the bag inside, and reconnected the base as best I could so that it looked like it should. A second later, Perry hightailed it into the room as Bergel lay on his bed, and I stood there, staring at the ceiling.

"Where is it, Bergel? I know it's here," Perry said.

"Huh?" Bergel responded, playing dumb.

"Don't give me that goofy look of yours. I know you have a bag of drugs in here. Where is it?"

"I don't know what you're talking about," Bergel said.

Perry placed his hands on his hips, fed up. "Get over here!"

"Me?" Bergel said, continuing the innocent act.

"Yes, you! Get over here and empty your pockets."

Perry inspected Bergel's pockets, patted him down, checked his wallet, and even made him take off his socks.

Then Perry turned his attention to me. "Where is it?"

I looked away, aloof.

Perry clapped his hands. "Wakey, wakey, Jake! Where did Bergel hide the drugs?"

I didn't have time to plan, think, or coordinate a story, so I hesitated. Bergel tilted his head toward me, not enough for Perry to notice, but I sure did. The look said "you better say the right thing."

Most of the boys smoked cigarettes and weed, and many had tried shrooms. I'd done my fair share of both, but not cocaine. Coke was movie-type shit that bikers sold, and people got addicted to cocaine. It was serious business.

I could tell Perry where the bag was and score points with him, but Bergel would become an enemy. Or I could lie and make a friend. Bergel was seventeen, two years older than me, and he could probably kick my ass, but I wasn't afraid of him. Truth be told, I thought it took balls to sell drugs.

"Perry," I said, "you're barking up the wrong tree. I've never seen Bergel with drugs, and we're roommates. If anyone would have seen something like that, it would be me."

Perry looked perplexed.

"Oh, come on, you two! I know you're lying. And you know

how I know? Your lips are moving! I'm not done with you," Perry shouted at Bergel, turned, and blustered out of the room, slamming the door.

Bergel slapped me on the back. "Jake, you fuckin' beauty, I owe you big time, man." He undid the bottom of the bobblehead, pulled out the bag, and put the figurine back together. "As a thank you, I'm going to give you a freebie."

He bopped and bounced, fully energized, excited to show me the ropes. I watched him pluck a Blockbuster membership card from his wallet along with a twenty, crack open the seal of the bag, and pour a small mound of powder onto the dresser. He carved two white caterpillars, then rolled the bill into a funnel.

"You do it like this," he said. "Watch and learn."

He breathed out, bent at the waist, and inhaled one of the lines. The powder quietly disappeared, and he held out the bill to me.

"You're up, Holmes."

"Do I plug a nostril?" I asked him.

"You can if it's easier. Up to you."

I did, breathed out and bent down, inhaling.

The drug entered my brain, and I became superhuman. I cured cancer and saved the oceans. I solved conflicts between warring nations and found solutions to global warming. I balanced budgets, leapt tall buildings, and my penis grew two inches. I solved mysteries and ended racism. I could not believe something like this existed.

I was home.

22

I met Duke an hour later in the parkade across from Winslow's. He sat in a beat-to-shit Volkswagen Rabbit. The window was down, smoke billowing out.

I walked to the driver's side and patted the roof. "How the hell does this thing run?"

"Don't you be disrespecting the Rabbit. She doesn't look like much, but she's faithful. Got over three hundred K on her."

"I'm surprised it's not four hundred."

He laughed and I got in, riding shotgun.

"She's in there?" Duke said, pointing at Winslow's.

"Yeah."

"My girl in Drug Enforcement says that Watershed Moments is not on their radar. Ditto for Sex Crimes. Neither unit has heard of them."

I lit a cigarette and hand-cranked the window down. "Really?"

"Really."

Duke tossed his butt out the window and squeezed the steering wheel. Then he picked up his phone, found a picture of Dustin Bannerman, and pointed at the screen.

"This fucker's a piece of work, I'm afraid. He was born and raised in Claremore, Oklahoma, but the incident happened in a bar in Dallas when he was twenty. I guess some guy made fun of him earlier in the night, and here's the best part. Apparently, it had to do with Bannerman's hair."

"His hair?"

"His fucking hair." Duke laughed. "The guy called him a fag for having long hair. They fought inside, but only Bannerman got tossed. I guess he waited for the guy and jumped him later that night when the bar let out, sucker punched him. Punch hit 'em just right, or wrong, I guess. Killed the guy."

"Nooooo!"

"I shit you not."

"He moved to Canada when he was twenty-two, after serving two years for manslaughter. First, he lived in BC and worked at a timber mill just outside of Prince George. Then he worked on a rig north of Edmonton in Fort McMurray. From there, he lived in Saskatoon, where he studied business and accounting at the University of Saskatchewan. He graduated in 2005. He's a ghost from '05 until he joined Sport Sphere in 2016."

I blew smoke. "Record in Canada?"

"No, Sandy says Bannerman's clean up here, at least as far as the system goes."

I kept my eyes fixed on Winslow's, waiting for the door to open and for Moore to stroll out.

"This morning, I read about religious extremism," I said, "trying to better understand Watershed Moments. There's a church called the Fundamentalist Church of Jesus Christ of Latter-day Saints, a branch of Mormonism, that sounds like what might be going on in Watershed."

Duke glanced at me. "What do you mean?"

I took a drag. "The LDS church practiced polygamy out in the open for a long time until the late 1800s. Some of the men wanted to re-establish the tradition of polygamy, so they decided to separate from the more mainstream version of Mormonism and start FLDS. These groups still practice it."

"Polygamy?" Duke shook his head and answered his own question. "More than one wife."

I nodded.

"Christ, I can barely keep one happy," he said. "You married?"

"No," I said.

"You got a woman?"

"No."

"You're a good-looking man, and a man needs a woman. Or another man." Duke turned to me again. "You gay?"

"No," I said. I'd answered the question from people who didn't know me a few times over the years. It didn't bother me.

"I'm not prejudice. Gay, straight, bi, tri, you do you, but I do know a man needs someone, someone to reel in their base urges. Men are hardwired toward certain desires, and those aren't all good." Duke nodded to himself. "Get yourself a woman. Or a man."

Duke laughed loudly, and so did I. He slapped me on the shoulder, like he'd delivered a real zinger.

"So," Duke said, "where is this FLDS church? The original one, I mean."

"On the Arizona-Utah border. But there are communities elsewhere."

"And they do that shit publicly? The po-lyg-a-my," he added, emphasizing each syllable.

"It's not that simple. They own land, a lot of it. And they have money in legitimate businesses. The marriages, they aren't what we'd consider legal. They're only legal within the church, not with the state. It's the same here. But it hardly matters to members of the church, especially the women in these arrangements. For all intents and purposes, they're married."

"And you think Watershed Moments is a Mormon church affiliated with these Americans?"

"No, I think they are an independent, borrowing from more than one faith. But I think polygamy is going on. I didn't tell you this, but I followed a man from the church to his home and knocked on the front door. That's how I got the name of the kid who left Watershed. During my conversation with this guy, two women called him for supper. At the time, I thought one was his wife and the other one a sister, or one of the wife's friends, whatever. But something felt off. There was an intimacy between the three of them. I don't know, it just felt wrong. Muriel Rowe confirmed that Brad Walton pressured the Rowes to force Sadie into one of these polygamous marriages, but they didn't allow it. As much as I want to smack Carl Rowe, it seems he had his daughter's best interest in mind on that one."

"What if Muriel was lying?" Duke said. "What if Sadie was–is–married?"

"She might have lied, but I don't know, it felt honest."

Duke paused a moment and turned to me.

"There's something we need to discuss," he said, his mood shifting. "How come you never told me you pleaded guilty to aggravated assault? And that you were shit-faced out of your mind when it happened?"

Fuck.

"You didn't need to know," I said.

"I didn't need to know you broke the guy's jaw? Come on, man, you're smarter than that."

That morning, I'd decided not to tell him about my legal woes. That might've been a mistake.

"You're right," I said, "and I'm sorry. I wanted your help, so I omitted details from my past."

"*Omitted* is one way to put it."

"The judge suspended sentencing for two weeks so I can earn enough money to help my mom while I'm inside. My mom is–she needs my help. I have ten days left."

"And have you made enough money?"

"Not even close."

"I'm sorry to hear about your mom. Family shit is hard." He paused. "But I also heard you're a drunk. Are you solid now, man, with the booze and all that?"

My chance to be honest and tell Duke about A.A. It might have been the right thing to do, but I let the opportunity pass like a warm breeze on a summer day. Here one second, gone the next. I chose middle ground.

"I have been known to drink too much," I said.

"Shit, that's a prerequisite for this line of work."

At 5:45, Moore walked out wearing a black coat, purse slung over a shoulder. She got into a mint-looking cherry-red Impala. Duke followed from a distance, just a casual nobody out for a quiet drive. We followed her onto Harrow heading north. She turned left on Grant up to Wilton, turned right, and right again on Scotland Avenue, stopping in front of a two-storey.

The house was the opposite of the car. Front deck beat to shit. Paint peeling in random patches. A crack in the foundation.

Cheap Halloween decorations dominated the front of the house, taped to the windows and hanging from the eaves troughs. We parked four houses away, and Duke cut the engine. "Let's go. And roll up the window. I don't want the Rabbit turned to shit by the elements."

Duke knocked twice, we waited a beat, and when the door opened, Moore scooted onto the porch like she was late. There was zip in her step. She wore a work shirt without a jacket, and in person she looked older than the picture on Winslow's site. She smiled widely, though, looking happy, and said, "Hi."

"Hey, what's the good word?" Duke said, showing her his badge that hung on a chain around his neck.

Moore's happiness faded, and I could see the wheels in her head begin to turn.

I'm in trouble. Do I run? Do I stay? Do I run? Do I stay? Do I run? Do I stay?

Her brain worked overtime, and Duke read her mind.

"You should know," Duke said, "I've never lost a foot chase. I'm seven and oh. I'll run your ass down without breaking a sweat."

She stayed put.

"Good decision," Duke added. "Can we enter your home?"

Moore pondered the question, then said, "Sure."

Once inside, Duke said, "Is anyone else in the home?"

"No."

"Do you have ID?" he asked her next.

"Yes." Moore turned to a purse that sat on a small table.

"Woah, hold up," Duke said quickly.

She stopped.

"Slowly ..." Duke added.

We watched as Moore opened the purse, took out a wallet, and located her license. She passed it to Duke, who read, "Delilah Moore," then added, "That's some name. All right, I'm going to pat you down. Anything on you I should know about? Needles? Sharp objects? Weapons? Drugs?"

"No," she scoffed. "Of course not."

Duke patted her down, then placed his hands on his hips and

three-sixtied a clean home. No random trash, dishes, beer bottles, or ashtrays.

"Take a seat," Duke said.

She sat on the couch. We remained standing.

"My name is Duke, and this is Jake. We are in the middle of something and need your help."

"I don't understand. How would I help you?"

"You were a member of Watershed Moments–" Duke said.

"You must be mistaken," Moore interrupted.

"I'm not mistaken." Duke smiled like there was no way she'd pull one over on him.

"I understand your hesitancy to talk about that time in your life," I said. "A man called Tracy Remple, another former member, told me what happens to people at that place–to young women, that is. We're looking for a woman now. Her name is Sadie, and she's twenty-three. We think Brad Walton forced her into the sex trade when she was a teenager."

Her face took on a shadow of something bleak. "Twenty-three?"

I showed Moore a picture of Sadie on my phone.

"That's her," Duke said.

Moore nodded, closed her eyes, and took a deep breath, overemphasizing the inhaling and exhaling in a Zen-like manner.

Duke was short on patience. "If you–"

"I want to help," she said, eyes closed in concentration. "Just give me a minute."

We waited.

Moore opened her eyes. She took deliberate breaths, folded one leg over the other, and looked away. "The same thing–what happened to Sadie–happened to me. I was just a girl, really. Fifteen."

My god, I thought. *Fifteen ...*

"Were you one of Walton's wives?" I asked her.

Moore looked up, astonished. "You know about that?"

"I suspected it. Why'd you leave?"

"The last straw for me was when Walton moved into drugs."

***

Delilah Moore filled a glass with tap water and took a long pull, the way you might drain a glass of liquor after a tough day.

She said, "My family moved from Utah in 1995 with Brad Walton and around fifty other people. There was a power struggle, and when the church splintered, the more intense men sought greener pastures up north, after reading about the success of other megachurches in Manitoba. The plan had always been to settle outside of the city, where there would be the space and freedom to establish their church.

"My dad wasn't one of the founding members, but he was part of what I'd call the inner circle. I married Walton in late '96 in front of a congregation of three hundred people. I got ... Well, it was terrible, but I was also lucky." She was on a roll and when someone gets on one of those in a confession, which this was, you let them go.

"Around 2000, I started doing little things, nothing major at first. I'd leave ingredients out of recipes, or add something that was not called for so the food tasted awful. I didn't do it all the time, but I kept Walton wondering. I fell down the stairs, cut myself while chopping vegetables. I'd misplace things, forget people's names. I started a fire in the laundry room. I damaged a vacuum. Dozens of mistakes over a year and a half, and I did it all on purpose. I wanted Walton to think I was crazy. I'd take the verbal abuse and the odd slap, all while planning my next move.

Moore peered off into the distance as she recalled a memory.

"One morning, I saw two men delivering toilet paper and other supplies to the church. I packed a suitcase and asked them if they could drive me to a hotel. They agreed. Didn't even ask questions. As far as I know, Walton's never looked for me. I think he wrote it off as a mental break and decided I was expendable, or at least not worth the trouble. I'd already given him two kids, so ..."

Two kids ...?

"Why stay here? In the city?" I said. "Why not move?"

Moore shrugged. "Where would I go? Back to Utah? I don't

know those people anymore, and the ones I know were involved in what I was trying to get away from. And my kids are here. At the time, when I got out, I accepted that I wouldn't be able to see them for a long stretch, but I hoped that we could reconnect when they were teenagers."

"And have you?"

She nodded. "Yes."

"You said earlier that Brad Walton was involved in drugs," Duke said. "What did you mean?"

"He was moving meth," Moore said. "I'm sure he still is."

Duke and I exchanged a glance.

"Who supplies him with product?" I asked.

Moore shrugged. "I don't know."

"Would you testify in court against Walton," Duke said.

Moore's body hardened, but her eyes showed strength.

"Yes," she said, "with a big smile on my face."

23

Sunday, October 20 (five days missing)

Tracy Remple lived in a small bungalow on St. John's Avenue in the North End. There was barely six feet between houses, a patch of backyard, and a chain fence that backed onto an alley. I'd considered asking Duke to come with me, but this was a one-on-one conversation without police, for now.

I knocked, and Remple opened the door with a muscular rottweiler on a leash. The animal was contained energy, its back legs ready to spring from a muscled torso, an arched back built for power.

I planned to ask Remple to go to the police with his knowledge of the notebooks, the sex crimes perpetrated against underage members of Watershed Moments. I felt like it would be enough for Duke to acquire a warrant to scour the church with a fine-tooth comb.

If Remple refused, I could always rough him up. I didn't use violence often anymore, but I'd do it when the ends justified the means. I saw myself throwing a hard right to the solar plexus, a fist to the nose, and Remple agreeing to speak to the police, blood dripping from his chin.

But then I'm sure a halfway-decent lawyer would have anything he said excluded from court.

No, this wasn't the time to get physical. I'd tell him about Delilah Moore and appeal to his sense of right and wrong.

Remple waited a second, then said, "We're on our way to the park."

I walked down the steps without answering, giving him room to exit the house and lock the door. We walked down St. John's to Parr Street, then Church Avenue until we got to a large field next to Sinclair Park Community Center. I might have been imagining it, but the dog's head seemed to look my way every twenty or thirty feet, sizing me up.

On the field, Remple tossed a tennis ball, and they settled into a game. The dog's speed and strength were impressive. It retrieved the ball efficiently, placing it in front of its owner, who'd scratch its head and pat its side affectionately. Every so often, Remple gave the dog a treat.

"What do you want, Jake?" Remple asked after the second round of fetch.

"You remember my name. Wasn't sure you would."

Remple tossed the ball again, and the dog took off.

"Yeah, well ..." he said. "I don't usually forget people who show up on site and ask questions about Watershed Moments."

I stood ten feet away, giving him space. "I shouldn't have done that. In hindsight, I could have tried to get your number or email."

"Doesn't matter. I don't blame you. You've got a job to do."

The dog returned with the ball but kept it in its mouth, staring at me.

"Nice animal," I said.

"Yes, she is."

"What's her name?"

"Bullet."

Jesus, a dog named after something that was designed to kill.

"I need to make a request," I said, maintaining the soft approach, hoping it would yield results. I also didn't want to find out how accurate the dog's name was.

"Okay ..." Remple said.

"I'd like you to meet a police officer, a detective, and tell him what you told me about the notebooks."

The dog growled and I took a step back.

"Here, girl," he said. Bullet kept her eyes on me but trotted toward Remple, who knelt and patted the dog's side, holding her collar. "Talking with a detective seems so ... I don't know if I can do that."

"It's an opportunity to make up for the past. For selling drugs and keeping the abuse a secret. It might prevent someone from being hurt in the future, so no one else needs to get married when they're fifteen or sixteen years old."

Remple turned, surprised, then caught himself.

"That's right, I know about the polygamy," I said.

He stood, his hand around the leash, and looked off into the distance. The sun hung in the sky like a disco ball, above rail-thin, empty branches. The leaves were scattered on the ground in a cacophony of orange, yellow, and red. It was a beautiful fall day.

"Shit." He turned to me. "I just can't do what you're asking. I can't relive it. Talking about ..."

And that's when I lost my composure.

Days of uncomfortable sobriety, encountering Brad Walton, the talk of meth, and my upcoming stint in prison was too much for me.

"I'm going to prison soon," I began, my voice layered with calm menace, "but if you don't help me, I'm going to follow you around for the next nine days."

Bullet vibrated, a guttural noise, like an engine warming up. *Fuck it. If this dog comes at me, I'll run or fight, but I'm not leaving unless it's with Remple.*

"I'll take pictures of you and post them on social media," I said, "with captions describing that you used to use to sell meth, and that you've covered up sex crimes. I'll be on the job site, at the table next to you when you're on a date, and in the bathroom when you're taking a shit. I won't stop until you help me, and if you manage to last the nine days until I go inside, then I'll continue when I get out."

Bullet pounced, and Remple strained to hold her back. I squared off stupidly, ready to fight a dog.

"Easy, girl," Remple said. "Easy."

It took a second, but he got the animal under control.

"You'd actually do that? Follow me around? Post all that stuff?"

"Yes. How much damage do you think I can do in nine days?"

He must have seen conviction in my eyes, or maybe he wanted to do the right thing and just needed a little nudge.

"I wasn't a hundred percent honest with you the other day," he said.

"What do you mean?"

"I told you I destroyed the notebooks. I didn't."

A raw breeze blew across the park and I shivered.

"Are you fucking with me?" I said.

"No, I have them."

"Where?"

"They're in a safe place."

"Okay," I said, getting worked up again. "You need to–"

"I know," Remple said as Bullet finally sat by his side. "I know. I'll do it. Give me a minute to bring Bullet home, and we'll go together."

"All right," I said.

Neither of us spoke on the walk back to his house. I waited in the entrance as Remple kenneled Bullet and packed the notebooks. I worried he'd skip out the back but decided to trust him.

Five minutes later, he was ready, carrying a gym bag and a heavy burden.

***

Foster-care abuse is notoriously difficult to study, so it's impossible to get accurate statistics about the percentage of children that are abused. Most experts believe it's between 20 and 25 percent. I'd experienced all kinds.

The Pimentals were name-callers.

The Hills got physical, a smack here, a punch there.

The Joneses were the worst.

Their go-to punishment was withholding food. Gary also liked to beat his kids with his belt, which he wore around his waist like a registered lethal weapon. He had a small paunch from drinking beer and eyes set close together on a stupid-looking face. His trick was to pull the belt from his pants in one swift motion, like a magician yanking the tablecloth off a table while keeping the dishes intact. His wife, Patsy, was mean, nasty, and generally incompetent, all out of anything that resembled a conscience. Her psychological and emotional abuse wore on me as much as Gary's beatings.

I coped by taking pride in my ability to survive, to never back down. I'd move my mind elsewhere during and never talk about it after. One day, I stole a pair of bolt cutters and cut the lock off the fridge. Gary walked in after work to find me sitting at the kitchen table destroying a turkey and Swiss on rye. Three pieces of bread, two layers of meat, and cheese a quarter-inch thick. I purposefully left mayo on one cheek just to fuck with him, to rub it in.

Gary looked at the fridge and saw the ruined lock, the chain coiled on the floor like a robotic snake. He always pulled the belt from his pants with his left hand, brandishing it like a sword.

"One moment and I'll be right with you," I told Gary between mouthfuls. "I have another couple bites."

Soon after that beating, I decided I didn't want to live like that anymore. Considering many types of revenge, ranging from petty theft to murder, I settled on one I thought fit the crimes committed against me. I concocted the perfect sort of revenge, a blend of sadism and comedy. The idea had been cooking for a while, and I had all the ingredients, but the idea required patience. I had to conduct strict research prior to pulling it off. It would be my Picasso, the perfect "fuck you," the move that might finally get me out of the system. I called it the Sticky Situation.

Gary's routine looked like this:

6:00 to 6:15 a.m. - shit

6:15 to 6:25 a.m. - shower

6:25 to 6:40 a.m. - shave

I knew this because I kept track of the times in a spiral notebook for two weeks. That's right, I woke up early every morning to record the time Gary took a shit, the precise moment he showered, and as close to possible, the moment the razor touched Gary's beard.

That morning, I crept into the bathroom at 5:55 a.m. and painted a layer of industrial glue onto the toilet seat. Gary walked in at 6 a.m., dropped trou, and sat. Half-asleep, it took him seven or eight minutes to realize that something was off. His ass cheeks likely felt weird, a mild burning sensation that was getting worse. Did Gary stand up, check the seat, and see what was going on back there? Of course not. Like any lazy fuck, he couldn't be bothered.

The door slowly swung open at 6:15 a.m. and I stood there, grinning. "Hi, Gary."

"Hey, close the door, you little shit."

I was in shape at sixteen, but I didn't have much meat on my bones. I'd liken the physique to a wolf near the end of the coldest stretch of winter. I wasn't thin, I was voracious.

"The door remains open."

I brought my left hand around to reveal a wallet. Gary's wallet. I opened it, took out the cash, about eighty bucks, and tossed the wallet on the floor. Gary launched himself at me, then screamed, realizing he was glued to the toilet seat.

"The fuck ...?" he cried.

"It's PARFIX Cyanoacrylate Adhesive. Your ass is glued to the seat."

He tried to free himself, bouncing up and down, grimacing.

"Don't bother. That shit dries in five minutes or less. You'll be there for a while. Wake the missus if you want, but she won't be able to get you off. I guess she can call the paramedics, though. Going to be embarrassing." I brought my right arm into view and showed him the aluminum baseball bat. "I figure I owe you."

Gary panicked. "No please, no please, no please!"

"I'm not an unreasonable person, so I'm going to let you choose a knee."

"Come on, Jake. I'm sorry. I'm so fucking sorry."

"Sorry? For what? For not letting me eat? For the beatings? For calling me a dirty little shit? For calling me worthless?"

"For ... for ..."

"You have to say it, Gary."

"For the belt ... for the chain on the fridge ... for the insults ..."

"What else?"

"For ... for ... for ... being mean."

I paused, letting Gary think that he'd convinced me to change my plan. "Thank you for apologizing. Now choose a knee. Left or right?"

"What! I apologized! I'm sorry!"

"Left or right? Or I'll do both."

"Oh fuck oh fuck oh fuck oh fuck!"

Gary slowly tapped his right knee.

"Do you want to keep that one or lose it?"

Gary whimpered. "Keep."

I smashed Gary's right knee like Thor swinging that big ol' hammer of his, feeling the knee implode. The screaming woke Patsy, who arrived in time to see Gary lean over and puke.

I said "move" and Patsy stepped to the side. I picked up a garbage bag filled with my meagre belongings and walked out of the house, the Louisville Slugger balanced on my shoulder like Jose Batista. The violence bothered me for years, but it had to be done. You couldn't let people hurt you and get away with it, not if you were capable of doing something, and I was. This thing with Walton was like that for me. He had to pay.

24

Duke responded that he couldn't meet at the station and asked me to bring Remple to a bar at the Ellice Motor Inn, a drinking hole in St. James on the edge of downtown.

We rode in Remple's Chevy Avalanche, and I told him a little bit about Duke on the way, emphasizing that the notebooks were one piece of evidence in a larger investigation. I tried to put him at ease by showing him the case didn't rely on him, but I wasn't sure it worked.

We walked into the bar and Blake Shelton's "Boys 'Round Here" entered my eardrums like a curse. I blinked to get my bearings, my eyes adjusted, and I saw that it was busy, people pissing away the afternoon.

Hundreds of bottles behind the bar drew my gaze as anxiety spread along the back of my neck. It felt like spiders crawling on my skin. The positive effects of the meetings had worn off, and my willpower was fragile.

I approached the bar for a soft drink, and the woman at the stick regarded me with an awkward flirtatiousness. Her crispy, dirty-blonde hair was fried from too many dye jobs. Tons of makeup couldn't hide a bad complexion, and her jowls drooped like a basset hound's. She wore a tank top and blue jeans, a towel slung over her shoulder.

"What'll it be, young stud?" she asked me.

"Just a Coke Zero."

"Coke Zero?"

"Yup."

"You want something in that?"

Here was my chance.

I could ask for two fingers of CC and a draft, then tomorrow, when I was half dead, I could rationalize that I had to drink. Had to. It had been necessary to calm my nerves, right? Right? Right!

"Just Coke Zero," I said.

"All right, young stud. What about you?" she said to Remple.

He said he was fine, and I watched as the bartender took a glass and shot syrupy Coke into it. She plopped the glass on the bar. "Three dollars."

I picked up the glass and brought it to my nose. It reeked like booze. I smelled it again, thought about taking a sip, but stopped. I'd watched her pour the drink, and she didn't add alcohol, yet it smelled sweet and potent, and a voice inside my head said not to drink it.

We found an open table in the corner and sat, waiting for Duke. I placed my hands on my head, rested my elbows on my knees, and focused on not having a panic attack.

"You all right?" Remple said.

I sat up. "I'm fine."

A woman at the table beside us wore scrubs. Just got off a shift or on her way to one. I couldn't tell, it was that kind of place. I checked my phone.

"You shouldn't text and drink," someone said.

I looked up and Duke stood there. He wore street clothes, his badge dangling on a chain around his neck.

"It's Coke Zero."

I still hadn't taken a sip.

"Turning over a new leaf?" he said.

"Maybe."

I shook Duke's hand, and he moved the chair close to Remple, the legs scraping loudly on the floor.

"What's the haps?" I said.

Duke sat down and ignored my question. He looked at Remple. "Where are the notebooks?"

This was a different version of the man I'd met yesterday, the one from breakfast, Winslow's, and the conversation with Delilah Moore.

This man was lethal.

Spend any time around cops, and you learn they can be your

best friend, but when a situation gets real, they flip a switch, removing all humour from their person.

Remple opened the gym bag, pulled out a ratty Hilroy notebook, and passed it to Duke. The bag held at least four more that I could see. Two yellow, one blue, and one green.

Duke opened the notebook and read for a solid minute. No one spoke. A Garth Brooks tune played on the house speakers.

"This is good," Duke said. "But it's all initials. You'll need to corroborate each name."

"I can do that," Remple said.

"So, what now?" I asked. "Do we have enough for a warrant?"

"That's the question, isn't it? It depends what else this guy knows. I get the sense you're holding out on me," Duke said.

I sat back, surprised.

"I gave you the notebooks," Remple said. "Isn't that enough?"

"You've got to know more." Duke glared at Remple. "Jake says you sold drugs. Tell me about that, and I want details. Who did you sell for? Was it Walton? Give me something, man. Give me something good or else ..."

Duke's voice rose at the end. Part singsong, part threat.

"I've got nothing," Remple said, and looked to me for help.

"I don't believe you," Duke said, and smiled. "Let me tell you a little story. Maybe it'll jog your memory." Duke moved his chair until his knees touched Remple's. "I've got five kids, a mortgage, and a wife that likes to shop."

"You have five kids?" I said.

"Yup. Three in university and two in high school. Jay, Landon, Dom, Brittany, and Serena."

"Have you ever heard of birth control?" I said.

"I love kids, man. They're my whole life," Duke said, and looked at Remple. "Handling assholes like you is a means to put food on the table. That's it, that's all. The more criminals we put behind bars, the better chance I have of moving up. If I move up, I get paid. It's all about that scratch when it comes to work. So, I don't give a fuck about you, or that you want to do good now, like it excuses the terrible shit you did before. It doesn't. I want justice for the victims, and I want to move up. That's it. And the only way those things happen is by putting Brad Walton in prison and shutting down that church."

Remple was caught off guard by the intensity of Duke's words. He looked at me again for support.

"Don't look at him. You got yourself into this mess. If you want out of it, give me something good," Duke said. "Think about the victims, the people Walton and those men assaulted. What did they get? A lifetime of misery. You fucking owe them."

Remple bit his lower lip, and I felt sorry for him.

"Give me something," Duke spat through gritted teeth. "Now."

"I-I sold ... I sold drugs ... I sold drugs for ... I sold drugs for the church," Remple finally said, the words squeaking out.

Duke's eyes widened. "I can't hear you. Louder."

"I sold drugs for the church," Remple repeated.

Just like Delilah Moore had said.

"Where'd they get the product?" Duke said, pushing hard.

"Walton cooks in the basement of the church. There's a lab there ..."

Duke smacked the table, turned to me. "That's what I'm talking about!"

"Jesus. Why didn't you mention this earlier?" I said to Remple.

He shrugged. "I don't want to get involved."

"Well, you're involved now, son." Duke said, dropping the notebook in the bag with the others. He scooped up his phone, tapped the screen, and held it to his ear. "Warrant, here we come."

25

Duke had the affidavit written before he'd met with Remple, and he said it wouldn't take long for him to amend it, adding the information about the notebooks and the lab. I had to keep busy as I waited to hear from Duke about the warrant, so I bussed to the Y for a workout.

I started with six sets of curls with a hundred pound barbell, then alternating curls with forty-fives. I followed that by doing a hundred close-grip push-ups, triceps extensions, and a hundred sit-ups. I worked fast, with little time in between sets, and drank water like it was my only friend. Maybe it was.

Sweat leaked from every pore, and it felt good, but my mind moved quickly, and instead of thinking about the warrant, I obsessed about the conversation I needed to have with Nia.

Why didn't you tell me about the polygamy? Why did you withhold?

Had Nia been one of Walton's wives? She'd placed her trust in me to find Sadie and made a financial commitment. I needed to honour that, but I needed answers, too.

I showered in the change room, dressed, and left the Y around 3 p.m. In my apartment, I read the Free Press on my phone, promising myself I'd call Nia at 5. When my phone vibrated, it was Arkell Lightfoot.

"Hello."

"Jake, it's Arkell."

"What's up?"

"I'm not sure. It might be nothing ... Maybe I'm wrong. But, no, well ..."

"What happened?"

"I tried to leave work, and this guy got out of a car and walked toward me. I'm in my head now, because all I can think is that he was coming for me. He didn't really do anything. He just ... walked."

"Where are you now?"

"In the gym."

"Okay, that's good. What did this guy look like?"

"Like he'd walked out of 1950. He wore a white short-sleeve shirt tucked into black dress pants and a red tie. He had flat hair, like it was glued to his head."

My stomach dropped.

"Stay in the gym," I said.

I began collecting my keys and wallet.

"Wait, hold up. You know this guy?"

"Maybe ... I'm on my way."

I left my apartment, locked the door, and ran down the hall.

***

I walked into the lot of Rupert's but didn't see the Cadillac or Arkell as two Navigators pulled in. They stopped abruptly, and all three look-alikes got out–two from the first vehicle, one from the second.

"You're in my way there, boys," I said, feigning humour as I tried to get around them.

The back window of the second SUV opened to reveal Brad Walton's ugly mug.

"Get in."

I turned from Walton to the three men, marveling at the synchronicity of them. They looked almost identical, standing there silently, ready for whatever Walton had in mind.

"I'm not going anywhere with you," I said.

Look-alike One slid a hand behind his back.

"What do you want?" I asked Walton.

"I want to show you something. No harm will come to you. The only thing you'll lose is time."

Look-alike One kept his hand where it was until I nodded okay.

Look-alike Two patted me down, and the trio escorted me into the second vehicle with Walton. One rode shotgun, while Two and Three got in the first SUV.

I sat beside Walton on a leather bench, studying him. Even in the luxury ride, his knees almost touched his chest.

The first Navigator pulled away and we followed.

I motioned toward the gym. "You lift?"

Walton shook his head, not to answer my question, but in response to the wisecrack.

I looked at One riding up front. "How about you? What'd you bench?"

No answer.

Walton looked like he'd smelled something rank. The confused corners of his mouth couldn't decide, should we go up or down? He didn't appreciate the remarks.

"I don't lift," he said. "I don't need to."

The Navigators weaved through traffic at a comfortable gait, and I respected the efficiency of the driver. He didn't seem to be in a hurry, but the energy in the vehicle vibrated with expectation, and I couldn't get a read on it. The radio played low gospel music. I felt like I was that character in the movie on the way to a magnanimous death, murdered in a field beyond city limits.

The traffic thinned as we left the city and got on the Perimeter Highway, then went south on St. Mary's. I looked over and saw Walton reading from a lined paper as the song rose to its climax, a palpable pulse. Tracy Remple came to mind, and the notebooks he'd found when his dad passed away. I saw Walton taking advantage of a sixteen-year-old Sadie, and I wanted to reach over and throttle him.

The song ended and another one began.

"Volume," Walton said, and One turned the dial way up.

Walton's head bobbed, but he continued reading as the singer's voice reverberated through the vehicle, pensive and unafraid. We drove through St. Adolphe, pulled onto Gauthier Road, then drove the nameless stretch bringing us to the Watershed Moments property. The gate opened, and the drivers brought both vehicles to the back of the church. The first SUV pulled up close, and the look-alikes got out.

The driver parked our SUV, and One opened Walton's door.

Two and Three surveyed the open area beyond the fence. One spoke into an earpiece and shouted "Clear!" as the driver helped Walton from the vehicle. They worked with focus and precision.

Walton adjusted his suit, smiled, and stepped through the gauntlet and open door into the church. One followed him, then the drivers and I, while Two and Three brought up the rear. I felt something at my side and knew the unmistakable shape of a firearm.

We entered directly into a narrow hallway that led backstage to an area reminding me of a high school drama room. There were podiums, mobile lights, chairs, a rack of clothing, temporary walls, and a curtain at the far end of the stage. A din of voices grew louder, and I heard the crowd cheering, clapping hands, and chanting.

We got closer, and I realized what they were saying. My heart sank.

"Wal-ton! Wal-ton! Wal-ton!" they droned in unison.

Is this for real?

Walton didn't break stride and walked onstage to aplomb as the curtains parted. He raised his arms, welcomed by a screaming mass of people I'd estimate to be several thousand strong.

"Stop," the man with the gun said. He pulled me back, so I stopped, we all did, settling in to watch. I looked out at the sea of people, mesmerized.

My earlier visit to Watershed Moments had left a bad taste in my mouth. Walton had been dismissive, Carl Rowe angry, and Muriel Rowe had filled the room with sadness. It bothered me, but I understood their reactions. This? This was impossible to explain. How can you accurately describe thousands of people screaming the name of a racist minister, a criminal, and a polygamist?

Fixated, I watched.

Walton subdued the crowd like an animal trainer gently quelling an unruly tiger, slowly bringing them to their seats. He smiled, shook his head like he had an important thought, and said, "I'm always amazed at the love and support of my fellows. We are the saved."

He let that sink in with his revelers.

"We are the great revivalists," he added. "We are the missionaries, the only true followers of Jesus Christ!"

The crowd went wild, hooting and hollering "amen," slapping high fives, and hugging each other.

"Men," Walton continued, "your strength is in dominance."

More cheers.

"Women, obedience is freedom."

Loud cries of passion. Words of agreement.

"But the Devil is among us," Walton said, slowing it down. "In the dark races. In the whorish fiends, and the divorcées, the rock and roll music, and the popular culture. The mud people want you to become like them. Undisciplined, willing to succumb to the pleasures of the flesh. That's how the Devil works–he exposes human weakness. And to combat that evil, we must be even more intensely committed to the cause. Pray with me."

Two of the look-alikes entered stage left, picked up an eight foot cross from the back of the stage, and held it behind Walton as the house lights dimmed. Walton extended his arms, as if crucified, and thrust his head back. A floor panel sank, and he descended beneath the stage, lit from below like someone telling a ghost story. Walton was gone, but the cross remained, and with most people's attention focused on Walton's descent into the subterranean, the look-alikes must have cracked a vial or two of fake blood. It leaked down the cross and spread like a disease. When the revelers noticed the bleeding cross, an audible hum echoed through the room as people pointed, covered their mouths in disbelief, a confirmation of faith.

I watched, stunned, and a minute later, Walton appeared at my side. He had spoken for less than five minutes but to say he'd made an impact would've been a gross understatement. He was potent, a harbinger of conviction.

We reversed the process of our arrival, exiting the back of the church as another speaker took the stage and the celebration continued. I was in the Navigator again, seated beside Walton.

"Does Arkell Lightfoot know where Sadie is?" he said.

"No, she doesn't."

"Would you tell me if she knew?"

"Probably not. But she doesn't know, and neither do I, so it's a moot point." I couldn't help myself. "Why do you want to find Sadie?"

Walton maintained a sealed expression, firm. The pre-performance spark had been replaced with this more affable version.

"I need to speak with her," he said, revealing nothing.

He nodded to One, and the guy passed a manila envelope to Walton. He opened the envelope and removed a piece of paper.

"Jake Joelsen. Thirty years old. Newhaven Apartments. Apartment R. You work as a private investigator–self-employed. Arrested," he said, and looked at me, "on April twentieth, 2019. Pleaded guilty to aggravated assault on October fifteenth, 2019. Sentence suspended until October twenty-ninth. Should I continue?"

"No," I said, turning away from the window. "You know a little about me, but I know about you, too. You moved here in '95 from Utah and grew the congregation from fifty or so true believers to what it is today. You're a polygamist. Oh, and you sell drugs."

Walton leered at me, taking his time. "It's good you think you know me, then we understand each other. You've been hired by Nia to find Sadie, but you'll terminate your contract with her immediately and stop investigating my church. No more tracking down former members, no talking to current members, and no coming to the property. You are persona non grata. Do you understand?"

I nodded.

"I'm not sure you are grasping the full scope of what I'm saying to you," he added, "so here it is in plain English. Stop, or there will be consequences."

Walton returned the paper to the envelope, handed it to One, and a minute later, we arrived at Rupert's. The locks on the door clicked open, and I stepped out of the vehicle.

"Jake," Walton said, "you can't compete with the Lord Almighty. And he's on my side."

I closed the door, my head floating on my shoulders like a balloon filled with fear and worry and anger.

26

It had been over an hour since I'd spoken to Arkell on the phone, and I wondered if she'd still be inside the gym. I passed Seung without a word and found Arkell on a bench doing overhead dumbbell presses with thirty-fives.

"I wasn't sure you'd still be here," I said.

She glanced my way and took the gargantuan headphones off, leaving them on her shoulders. "Hey, what's up?" She drank deeply from her four-litre jug filled with the lightly coloured red liquid. "I was able to train a new client, and I got a second workout in."

She sounded pleased with herself. I sat down on a bench, rattled, thinking about Walton. She didn't need to know about the speech I'd witnessed at the church, but she deserved to know she was in danger.

"There are some scary people looking for Sadie," I said, "and they know who you are. They might try to speak with you."

"About what?"

"About Sadie, and if you know where she is."

"I don't."

"I know, and that's what I told them, but they may want to ask you themselves."

Arkell opened her mouth to speak but froze, a statuesque picture of anatomical perfection.

"You can't hurt steel," she finally said, flexing her bicep, looking for a cheap laugh.

Fear makes you say and do silly things.

"However impressive your physique is, and I assure you it's impressive, unfortunately, it is possible to hurt steel," I said. "I don't think they mean you harm but be careful. Leave the gym with someone. Don't go for a walk on your own at night. Pay close attention to your surroundings. Lock your doors."

"I'll do that."

She took a sip of the red stuff, smiled, and said, "Provincials are coming up, and I'm the defending champion. You should come by. Have you ever been to a bodybuilding or fitness competition?"

"No," I said, wondering what that would be like. If Rupert's represented the scene, then it would be something else. Interesting, to say the least. "I'll think about it."

"All right, Tom," she joked. "Text me if you need tickets. I'll comp you."

"I just might do that. Call me if you hear from Sadie."

"All right," she said, and readied for a set.

***

The look-alikes had threatened me three days ago, and now Walton had done the same. I was scared, but not enough to quit. I'd been hired to do a job, and I'd do it, consequences be damned.

I called Duke. He had secured warrants for Watershed Moments and Brad Walton's home, both scheduled for 7 p.m., two hours from then. I asked if I could be a part of one of the searches, and Duke laughed so loud the phone vibrated. I wished him luck and ended the call.

I drank a protein shake and finished reading the Free Press while the idea of walking to my office for a double vodka hovered in the background. I updated my notes, watched an episode of *Seinfeld*, and busied myself with more paperwork. I'd spent sixty-one hours in five days looking for Sadie, earning just over six thousand dollars. This meant, with the sale of my truck, I was at $26,000, a good chunk of change, but it wasn't enough. I needed that money from Bergel.

A knock summoned me to the door, and I checked the peephole.

Nia.

I opened the door and tried not to let my surprise show.

She wore black tights, a snug turtleneck sweater, and a three-quarter-length coat with the collar up. Her straightened hair was parted just off-centre, and large hoop earrings dangled seductively.

"I'm sorry," she said. "For what I said the last time we spoke. That wasn't fair of me. Let me buy you supper as an apology."

I held my phone, checked the time, and shrugged internally. I wanted to be ready to move, if necessary, but I couldn't sit there anymore.

"Okay," I said, "but I'm waiting for a call, and I might need to leave abruptly."

"You?" Nia said, a smile underneath an expression of exaggerated shock. "Abrupt? Never ..."

"Shut up," I joked, grabbed my coat, and we headed out to hail a cab.

It had rained earlier, and the streetlights shone with an emerald hue. The driver had the vehicle too cold, but I didn't ask him to turn the heat on. Instead, I accepted it and checked my phone, but Duke hadn't texted.

We settled into the ride and Nia talked about work, how an update to their system had been causing everyone in the office fits. I revealed I'd been to two meetings, and she raised her eyebrows, impressed.

"Do you like the meetings?" she asked.

"I don't think I'd use the word *like*, but they aren't bad, either. I'm not sure how I feel about them," I said. "It's a lot ..."

I told her about how I'd reconnected with Katz, described our history and how I'd worked for him. The conversation balanced with long stretches where neither of us spoke. During a moment of quiet, the Scotiabank building loomed large, lights still on, staring at us like the eyes of a giant robot. We moved through downtown, and the city changed as we went over the Provencher Bridge. Tiny Ma and Pa shops lined both sides of the street amid recently renewed condos, organic food stores, and Starbucks. St. Boniface had enough of the old to make it feel uniquely French, a neighbourhood from a bygone era, but gentrification had reared its head, and it wouldn't be long before Amazon put those shops out of business.

Inside Le Garage, blues legends painted on massive canvases lined the walls, and tall tables and chairs flanked a classy bar, which made the place feel a combination of elegant and rock 'n' roll. Posters advertised that *Live Music Played Regularly*. We got a booth, I ordered a Coke Zero, and Nia asked for water with lemon. She excused herself to the bathroom, and I checked my phone again. Nada. I brought up Duke's number and was about to hit send but stopped myself. He'd call when he could.

Nia returned, picked up a menu. "Can I ask you something?"

"That depends." I smiled. "What's the question?"

Nia laughed. "If I tell you, then I've asked the question."

"But I don't have to answer."

"That's true."

I gently smacked her arm with a menu. "Ask your question."

She laughed some more, and said, "All right, tough guy. Why are you a private investigator?"

"That's your question?"

She nodded. "You're smart. Organized. Good looking. A bit pretty, but in a rugged sorta way."

"Good looking," I confirmed.

"You could do something else," she continued. "Get a trade, sell houses, I don't know. Go back to school. Something more stable. More mature."

"Hard question," I said to buy time until I could concoct a decent response. I shrugged. "It's a living, and I like what I do. It's an important job, I mean, no more than any other, but it's what I do."

It wasn't the best response, thin and flaky, but that didn't make it wrong.

"Every job is equally important," I added.

"Oh, come on, you can't believe that," Nia said, fire behind the words. "You can't tell me some people aren't more capable than others, that some people aren't more fit to do certain jobs than others–better jobs–more important jobs. A mechanic and a surgeon are not equal."

"I couldn't disagree more."

"You think they should be paid the same?"

"No, but they should get equal respect from society, and they don't. One's deemed more valuable than the other and that's not right."

"Agree to disagree," Nia said, not breaking stride. "One saves lives, the other fixes cars."

"I agree there's nothing more important than health, but if your car is broken and you're healthy, then a mechanic is pretty damn important and a doctor, well, he's probably useless. I'm just saying we place certain professions on pedestals, and that's bullshit."

We were mid-argument, but it felt okay. There was no animosity.

The server returned with our drinks, and I took a sip.

"Do you know what happened to your dad?" she said, catching me off guard.

I stiffened, then relaxed. "No, we don't know."

"We?"

"My mom and I," I said. "Since we're getting all personal here, have you ever met your biological parents?"

"No."

"Have you looked for them?"

"No."

"Why not?"

The server arrived, and Nia asked for another few minutes.

"I'm worried it will hurt," she said when the server was out of earshot. "Have you looked for your dad?"

"Not in years."

She pondered that and read her menu as I checked my phone again. The server returned and we ordered food. Le Burger American for me with fries, and something called a Buttercup Burger for her with fries.

"When I was a kid," Nia said, "I mean young, like six and seven years old, I thought my childhood was normal. I was happy, even looked forward to Sunday School. Sure, we prayed at meals, but we only went to church on Sundays. I'd say it started to change for me when I turned ten. I'm not sure when it changed for Sadie."

I debated telling her I'd spoken to her mom again but decided against it.

"What happened when you were ten?" I asked.

"Confirmation classes began–Tuesday and Thursday evenings. There was a lesson each time, like school, only instead of learning how to do an equation or how to write a proper sentence, we learned why people who belonged to Watershed Moments were superior, what the role of the woman was, things like that. I was one of only six people of colour in the congregation."

"Who taught these classes?" I said.

"Members of the church. Always men. There were videos, assignments, report cards."

"Report cards? *Your racism is strong, but your sexism needs work.*"

Nia laughed. "Something like that. I stopped with the classes when I turned fourteen. I remember because I was in grade nine at Hedges Junior High in Mrs. McKellar's class. Sadie was younger, so my parents wouldn't let her quit. Picked her up and physically carried her into the church a couple of times. She'd lie on the floor, screaming. She'd throw books, pens, anything she could get her hands on. She'd smack other kids. My parents were so embarrassed."

I shook my head, thinking I wasn't the only one who'd had a messed-up childhood.

"You have to remember," she said, "I was young. I knew the teachings were different, but I still went to real school, so I had kids in my class who were Black, Indian, Indigenous. I didn't feel completely isolated. When you're ten years old, or even as a teenager, you don't always know what's right and wrong. You just know what feels normal to you."

"I have moments like that. Looking back, they seem crazy."

"But they also made you who you are."

I nodded and Nia continued.

"In some ways, I liked being adopted. It made me unique, and I liked the attention. Our family would get double takes in public and at school events. I was in the spotlight. I think that made me want to be successful. I was a top student in high school–class president, starter on the varsity basketball team, valedictorian. I got a scholarship to Western. Graduated from there with honours."

"Wow," I said, impressed. "So, how'd you end up with Logan Bergel?"

"Dating app."

I laughed out loud.

She smacked my arm, laughing, too. "I'm busy. I don't have time to date. Online saves months of preliminary getting-to-know-you bullshit. He presents well, at first. I didn't know anything about the club until much later."

"He still wants to be with you," I said.

"I know," she said, but didn't elaborate.

Nia suddenly reached across the table and placed her hands on mine. We sat like that for a while, not saying anything, just accepting the moment and enjoying it for what it was until the food arrived.

"Looks good," I said, but I wasn't sure Nia heard me. She was deep in thought.

I glanced at the dark screen of my phone, then dug in.

***

We ate quietly, smiling at each other every so often, and I wasn't sure if that constituted flirting or something else. I had questions, but I didn't want to ruin the moment.

Finally, Nia wiped her mouth, and said, "Do you believe people can change?"

I took a bite, swallowed, and considered how best to explain what I felt. What I believed. I went short and simple.

"Change isn't possible for most people," I said.

"What do you mean?"

"I think it takes a major event for someone to change. Even then, the change is minimal. People exist on a spectrum, and they can only move so far along the axis. That's just the way human beings are. Nature trumps nurture. You don't wake up one day and become a different person. It doesn't work like that. A tragedy can change someone, absolutely, but that type of change is usually forced upon you."

"Fair enough, but I disagree. It takes time and effort, but people can change." She hesitated, locating the words. "Do you think you'll find Sadie?"

"Yes."

"What will we do then?"

"I don't know. It depends how she is."

I felt wobbled by the conversation, and I wanted to kiss her. Katz told me once that it was fear holding me back from committing. I didn't know if that was true, but I knew I felt embarrassed to be thirty years old with only a slew of casual relationships and one-night stands under my belt.

We went outside so I could smoke, and the chilled air rose up from the ground around us. Nia peered through the glass window at the small dance floor inside. "Jake, let's go in. I wanna dance."

The band played "Harvest Moon" by Neil Young and we danced, gently swaying to the soft rhythm, our bodies touching in that comfortable way only couples know. Neither of us spoke. The light from the stage caused unusual shadows to form on the floor beneath our feet, odd shapes that morphed into ghosts on the hardwood.

For the first time, maybe ever, I fantasized about a house in the suburbs, a nice lawn, and a backyard for the kids to run around in. I'd be on the barbecue and Nia would be watering plants. We'd smile at each other and gaze at our children, marveling at what we'd created.

***

We didn't say much in the cab, studying the buildings downtown and passersby on foot. I saw couples holding hands and wondered if they cared about each other, or if they were temporary companions, something to do to fill the time. I saw glass monoliths, the headquarters of financial institutions, and couldn't decide if they should be admired or burned to the ground.

The cab pulled to the curb in front of my building, and Nia exhaled like she had something to say.

"What?" I said.

"That was nice."

"Nice?"

"Yeah, nice. I enjoyed myself."

"Well, I had a terrible time."

"Fuck off," she said, and smacked my shoulder.

I leaned in, kissed her against my better judgment, and she placed a hand behind my head at the base of my neck, scratching my scalp with her nails. I paid the driver, then we banged and crashed our way inside and tumbled onto the couch. Nia straddled me, and I felt myself harden beneath her. She snapped her hips back and forth, and I clutched her along the rib cage, rolled her onto her back, and fumbled with her pants as she kicked them to the floor. I undid my jeans and slipped off her underwear. She pulled mine down as I opened a condom.

I pressed Nia's leg up and steadied myself with the other arm as she threw her head back, exposed her neck, and I licked her jugular. At some point, we fell onto the floor. When she came underneath me, I finally relaxed, thankful I'd achieved that feat. I was done a second later.

I stayed on top of Nia for thirty or forty seconds, sweating and breathing deeply. The entire scene was chaotic, passionate, and ended abruptly with a roar and a quiver and a sigh.

"That," I said, rolling off Nia, "was nice."

We laughed until our eyes watered.

***

Rain tapped the windowpane in repetitive beats. Despite remaining sober, I felt like a sack of hammers, tired and dehydrated. My body was still trying to adapt to sobriety. I slipped out of bed and walked naked to the fridge, filled a glass with water from the tap, and drank it standing in the kitchen. Then I crept back to the bedroom and slipped back into bed.

"What's up?" she said, surprising me. "You're tossing and turning."

I lay on my back, stared at the ceiling, and looked for the right words. I'd always been short in these situations. It wasn't purposeful, I just couldn't massage the truth.

"Yesterday, I spoke to your mom, and she directed me to a woman, older than Sadie, who left Watershed years ago. I also spoke to Tracy Remple–"

"Tracy? I–How is he?"

Nia rolled onto her side, propped up on an elbow.

"He's okay," I said. "Works as a plumber. He's got residual damage from his time at the church. He's also got evidence against some of the leaders, including Walton. He's part of the reason we got a warrant to search the church."

She sat up.

"A warrant?"

"Yeah."

Nia looked across the room. "Walton's going to be pissed."

"He's already pissed. But that's not what worries me. Duke was executing the warrant last night at seven, and he said he'd call and let me know how it went. He hasn't called."

"Shit ..." she said, stopping short. "Wait, when did you see Walton again?"

"Yesterday. He forced me into his vehicle and brought me to some kind of performance at the church."

Nia ran a hand through her hair, and I waited a beat, trying to know how to ask my next question. When I couldn't think of anything, I just came out with it.

"Why didn't you tell me about the polygamy?"

"This again?" Nia raised her hands in frustration. "Why didn't you tell me about Remple before now, huh?"

"That's not the same. My job is to find Sadie. I do a hundred things in a day. I can't report back to you with every one of them. You'll get a report at the end of it."

"The end of it?"

"You know what I mean."

Nia shook her head. Coldness radiated off her, like she had so much to say but held it in.

"Yeah, I know exactly what you mean. I didn't tell you about the polygamy because it's fucking embarrassing. You happy now?" She flung the covers off and began getting dressed. "Sadie is my sister. I hired you to find her and to keep me up-to-date. I'm paying you to do those things. Paying you well above your normal rate, might I add. So do your job."

I had nothing to offer her.

27

Monday, October 21 (six days missing)

I had been awake since Nia left at five, so I answered partway through the first ring when Duke called at six.

"It's all fucked," he said.

I stood so fast that the chair crashed into the drywall behind the kitchen table.

"What? Why?" I said, my heart plummeting off a cliff.

"They knew we were coming," Duke said.

"Tell me what happened."

"I was with the team at the church, and Walton was there. He was sitting in his office, doing paperwork, and you should've seen his smile. I knew something was off, man. I knew it, you know, but what could I do? I grabbed him by the arm and led him out of the room, down the hall, and to the stairs.

"It was a six-person tactical team, me, and Walton. At the bottom of the stairs was an open room with a concrete floor, small when you consider the footprint of the church. Maybe twenty by forty feet, with two hallways leading in opposite directions. We approached the northern entrance with caution. Remple said this was where we'd find the lab, and that there would be five people working twenty-four seven.

"It was eerily quiet as we approached, but I caught a whiff of something chemical. Ammonia, maybe. I stayed with the pack and followed the path of the hallway. It was wider than the staircase, with medical fluorescents that I became more aware of the closer we got to the lab. The lighting bothered me–not sure why–and a sinking feeling put me on high alert. Was this a trap? Were we marching to our deaths? One gunman opening up on us as we entered the room would be catastrophic." Duke stopped.

"Fuck me, it's an ambush, I thought. But with Walton by my side? That didn't make sense."

"Was it ..." I said stiffly, wincing, "an ambush?"

"No. We went in and I waited for automatic fire, the white light of an explosion and the shrill cries of the dying. None of that happened, but it was a death of sorts, man.

"I looked at Walton. I mean I just fucking bore into him, you know, staring holes, and I swear he laughed. Other officers said later he didn't, but I heard it, man, and I saw it. So, I clocked him. I clocked him good, you know, just fucking pounded him. Busted nose. Blood everywhere. I don't remember much else, only a vacant room scrubbed so hard you could almost see the chemical vapours of cleaning products hovering above our heads. Shit ..."

The dark street outside my apartment was lifeless. I stepped out onto the balcony and lit a cigarette.

"We still have Remple's testimony, and the notebooks. We have Delilah Moore, too," I said.

"Oh, I know. And that's all good. I guess I wanted that home run, you know? I wanted to be the man. The he-ro," Duke said slowly, the way he liked to do.

"What about Walton's house?" I said. "Anything there?"

"Complete miss," Duke said. "Strike out."

My brain was a wet noodle, flopping around from one random thought to the next, trying to understand how it had happened.

How did Walton get the room scrubbed clean? Why had he stayed at the church?

Focus, Jake. Focus.

A long silence led me to a scary question: What if Walton had a cop on his payroll?

"I'll call you right back," I said, and hung up.

I guessed Watershed Moments had a congregation of around five thousand people. Quick searches revealed Winnipeg has a population of about eight hundred thousand and fourteen hundred police officers, not including around six hundred more people working for the Winnipeg Police Service in civilian capacities.

My Manitoba math told me that if the ratios remained, there would be ten or twelve members of the church working with or for the WPS.

I needed those names. I dialed Duke.

"I got something I'd like you to do, and it's a big ask," I said.

"How big?"

"Can you get a list of members from the church and cross-check them next to members of the WPS?"

Duke whistled, a polished and smooth whirr. He was good at it, and the sound reverberated through the phone and into my head like a shock.

"You're right, that is a big ask," he said.

"I know."

"I can't see how I'd be able to get the list from Watershed. No judge would subpoena those documents now. Not after the search went tits up." Duke paused and I could hear him scratch the stubble on his cheeks. "I tell you what: If you can get me that list, I'll take a look at it. But if you're saying what I think you are, then this thing just got a whole lot more complicated."

He was right, it did.

We said goodbye and I went to work, trying to figure out how to get that list.

***

I searched Watershed Moments AND members, Watershed Moments AND congregation, Watershed Moments AND annual report, and came up with very little. One report was of the financial variety and showed the church's annual budget was close to twenty million, but names were few and far between. I wondered if Tracy Remple might be able to get an older list, but he was so young, it didn't seem likely he'd keep a list. For what purpose? I could talk to Delilah Moore, but she'd been out for much longer. She could give me names and the people would most likely still be members, but how many would that be? I couldn't see it amounting to more than fifty people.

Then there was Henry Formenton.

I did another search, found Formenton's work number, and learned he sold batteries at a place called The Battery Baron. I called, but he didn't pick up, so I left a message.

I filled the kettle, hit the button, and prepared a mug with a tea bag. Then I sat at the table and read my notes through twice, convinced a police officer had let Walton know about the warrant.

Maybe Walton had more influence than I knew. He wanted to find Sadie, and that meant she had information he needed, or she had stolen something. My guess, Sadie had lifted drugs from Walton. But when, and how?

***

I used an app to generate a list of less-known hotels, motels, and bed-and-breakfasts, hoping Sadie was still local, hiding out. The list was long, but shorter than I thought it would be. I knew most of the streets, looked up the ones I didn't know, and organized the hotels by general neighbourhood. Next, I mapped out my route. I finished and texted Katz.

You around?

Seconds later, my phone lit up.

Yup just dicking around at home

No punctuation, but a purple vegetable emoji arrived next, then a smiling face, tears of laughter flying from the eyes.

What a guy.

I texted him my plan. He had experience, could read people like a book, and he was good company. I asked:

You want in?

The tiny bubbles calibrated.

Absofuckinglutely b there in 20

***

Seventeen minutes later, I sat next to Katz, his truck rumbling down Osborne Avenue, heading south. I was armed with a picture of Sadie, listening to the local news on the radio.

A bus driver had been assaulted on the job, and a group of fifteen-year-olds had robbed a liquor store, speeding off in a stolen SUV. A string of early morning fires had stretched Winnipeg Fire Paramedic Service thin, and when an emotional man who'd lost his grocery store in one of the blazes was interviewed, he sobbed, answering in starts and stops. Depressing shit, and I fell into a sour mood.

This fucking city.

Katz looked over at me suspiciously and I met his eyes. He wore the same bright jacket and red shoes, a different BoSox shirt, and blue jeans. He was one happy-go-lucky motherfucker, and I didn't understand it. How could you hear stories of violence, robbery, and loss, and maintain a smile?

The urge to drink arrived, and I visualized a never-ending, chaotic night. The gumminess of hard alcohol spilt on the floor, the taste of aspirin as the cocaine drip tickled my throat, and I even caught a whiff of perfume. Was it vanilla?

"How goes the battle?" Katz said.

I sent angry glares out the window, breathing slowly, trying not to say something stupid.

A sleazy rain pounded the street at a sideways angle. Not snow, exactly, but not rain, either. Sleet might've been a more accurate descriptor. I wore winter gear–black toque, mitts, and jacket–and blue Levi's with a brown sweater that I'd paid twelve bucks for at Walmart.

I don't know why, but that made me feel better, that I could live a cheap, sustainable life. Even if everything went to hell and I was a total failure, I could survive.

"You awake?" Katz added. "How're you doing, Jake Man?"

I turned to him. "I'm all right."

Katz smiled and said, "Yeah?"

Happy-go-lucky, I thought again, affectionately.

"Yeah," I said.

Katz had this way about him, where he could be nonchalant about things I considered life-and-death. He didn't rattle, stress, or overreact. Yet, the nonchalance wasn't patronizing, and he could be serious when necessary.

"Are you thinking about drinking?" he said.

I opened and closed my hands. "I'd kill for a beer, but it's not that. It's this city. It's destroying itself. Buildings are falling apart. The roads are brutal. You need a 4x4 just to drive down the street. The weather is awful, the crime rate sky-high. Theft, assault, and worse. You know there were three car jackings on the same day last week? It's the unemployment, the sadness I see. So much poverty. The schools are bad. Downtown is unsafe. Should I continue?"

Katz drove on, not saying a word, and it took several minutes for him to respond.

"I can't say you're entirely wrong, but you just listed all the bad stuff. You can do that with anything," he said. "Winnipeg's got all the amenities of a city but feels like a big town, and it's affordable. There are hundreds of lakes within a two-hour drive. All the fishing and snowmobiling a person can handle. There's a vibrant arts scene, music, dance, theatre, you name it. And Folklorama is one of the biggest cultural festivals in the world. If you're a sports fan, we have the Jets, Moose, Bombers, Goldeyes, and Valour FC. I think most schools are fine. Some are even good, maybe great. And if you're not involved in a certain lifestyle, then it's relatively safe. No, we aren't Toronto or Vancouver, but we have something here. Something quietly good."

Katz stopped, took a turn, and we approached the first place on my list. He pulled into the lot, parked, and shut the engine off. He looked at me.

"My wife's dying," he said, and my stomach dropped, not sure if I'd heard him right.

"What ... Naomi?" I said, startled.

"She's got leukemia. Been sick for a year and treatments haven't worked. She's close now ... to the end."

If I wasn't the most selfish prick in the world, I was in the running. I was so fixated on myself that it hadn't occurred to me that Katz might be hurting.

"Katz," I said, "I had no idea. I'm an asshole."

"You didn't know. We've barely spoken the last couple years. And you're not an asshole, you're human." He took a sip of coffee and returned the to-go mug to the console. "Listen, the only thing I can do for Naomi now is be there for her. Put a hand on her back. Rub her feet. Read books to her."

It would take an incredible amount of love and commitment to provide that kind of support. I wasn't sure I had it in me.

"I'm sorry to burden you with my moods," I said, a quiver in my voice. I cleared my throat. "I'm just having a bad day. I want to drink."

"Did you?"

"Not today."

"Then don't sweat it. You're golden."

I couldn't see how my situation was golden. He must have seen it in my expression.

"You're angry?" he said.

"Yeah."

"Do you react often to your anger?"

I nodded.

"Someone once told me," Katz added, "that reacting with emotion is a surefire way to do or say something you'll regret."

"I feel like a loser," I said, the words pouring out. "I don't want to be like my parents is a mantra of mine, yet look where I am ..."

Katz smiled. "Don't be so hard on yourself. No one ends up in A.A. cause they're doing well. It's one of the last stops on the line. There's no point beating yourself up. I'm sure you've done enough of that already." He paused. "Did you know Winnipeg's the second coldest city in the world with a population greater than six hundred thousand people?"

I laughed. "What's the first?"

"Ulaanbaatar."

I paused. "Mongolia?"

"That's right, nicely done. There's hope for you yet, young grasshopper," he said. "There's hope for you yet."

***

We showed the picture to desk clerks, custodians, hotel patrons, and servers in restaurants at each hotel. I asked to speak with managers, leaving my number with them, including instructions to call me if they saw Sadie no matter the time of day.

Katz hung back, added a question here and there, provided his thoughts after we'd spoken with someone.

Four hours in, we'd been to fifteen places and had next to nothing to show for our troubles, but I hadn't thought about drinking and I considered that a win.

Katz dropped me off at my apartment, and I walked to a church that I knew had hourly meetings in the basement. I came in late, as a kid like twenty years old with tattoos on his face told his story. He'd joined a gang at thirteen, killed an opposing gangbanger while drunk at seventeen, and he'd been out of prison for almost a week.

Next, a middle-aged man told the group that he'd reconnected with his son. It had taken years and lots of hard work, but he did it one day at a time.

"You work the program," he said, "and good things happen."

Yeah, until they don't.

28

Tuesday, October 22 (one week missing)

I awoke from a nightmare, sweaty and disoriented. In the dream, I'd been walking on the shoulder of a highway, hitchhiking, my shirtless torso so tanned I blended into the wheat fields swaying behind me. Heat bounced off the pavement and I carried nothing. An SUV pulled up and stopped, blocking my way. Men exited the vehicle. Hard men with sandpaper complexions, holding archaic axes, knives, and other blunt weapons.

I didn't run, nor did I panic. I didn't speak, and I accepted my fate.

In the ditch next to the highway, they hacked me to pieces. My blood and body matter splattered on the grass, blond wheat blowing gently in the distance.

I opened my eyes as the memory blended into the realization that someone was knocking on my door. I checked the clock.

1:04 a.m.

No one had buzzed from the lobby, and I wasn't expecting Nia. I threw on a pair of jeans, approached the door, and stood to the side.

"Who is it?"

"Logan. Open up."

Bergel?

I opened the door.

Bergel stood there, and he'd brought Tight Shirt from the strip joint.

"You gotta minute?" Bergel said.

They walked into my apartment, despite not having been invited in, leaving wet imprints on the carpet. Worry and fear lurked in the panels of my mind.

Bergel looked around, slowly nodding to himself, and my apartment registered to me at that moment as pathetic, the sad domicile of a drunk. Bergel looked like he thought the same thing.

He pointed at the bedroom. "Is this where you fucked her?"

I didn't answer.

"You and me," Bergel said calmly, "are going to fight."

***

Logan Bergel was nineteen when he killed Pete Argyreos on May 20, 2006. Argyreos was five years his senior, and I was seventeen when I lied in court on January 28, 2007, to keep him out of prison. I'll never forget either date.

I'd told myself that Argyreos wasn't an innocent victim, that if you're in the world of drugs and crime, you deserve what you get. But it was me who'd testified in court, under oath, on behalf of Bergel. That had been all me.

The Argyreos family owned a string of convenience stores, and his dad was an important man in the community. The media presented Bergel as an at-risk youth living in a group home with a criminal past, poor marks, and a drug problem. Argyreos was described as a young person with potential who had gotten into drugs almost by accident, like it wasn't his fault. The stories weren't all wrong, but each one lacked nuance.

Neither the *Free Press* nor *Sun* mentioned how Bergel arrived in the care of the province, and they did not report the circuitous business dealings of the Argyreos family as they rose from new immigrants to pillars of the business community. There was corruption and abuse in both stories, as there so often is.

Bergel came to me one night near the middle of May 2006, prior to the murder. I had spent a year in juvie for the assault of Gary Jones and had been placed in another group home until I turned eighteen and aged out. Bergel found me skateboarding at the Forks skate park, smoking J's and drinking beers amidst a group of twelve or fifteen teenagers. He came as a friend, the way he always did, with manic energy and a smile. But he didn't come alone, and when he waved me over, I noticed that the guys with him were overdressed in long sleeves and baggy sweaters.

Bergel and I shot the shit for a minute, then he got down to brass tacks.

"Jake, my man, I need a favour from you."

"Okay ..."

"You know what I do to make money, right?"

"Yeah."

"And you know that I'm not the only person who sells dope around here?"

"Of course," I said.

"Okay, that's my man. I need you to go to a ten o'clock movie on May twentieth. And if ..." he said, emphasizing the word. "If the police bring you in, show them the movie stubs and tell them I was with you from nine to one in the morning, okay?"

Bergel had treated me with kindness in the group home during a time when I didn't have anything. He'd bought me clothes, a phone, and food. He'd been generous, but this felt like something I didn't want to be a part of.

"Why?" I asked.

"I got this girl, a real smokeshow. Ass on her that won't quit. Tits out to here," he said, holding his hands in front of his chest, "but she's got a man, and I know him. He's in the same line of work as me. You hear what I'm saying?"

His frantic speech and jumpiness put me on edge, and he could tell. Bergel put his arm around my shoulder.

"And we have business dealings," he continued. "If he was to find out ... it'd be bad for business. This girl and me, we schedule our romantic trysts in advance. Easier not to get caught. You understand?"

It still didn't sound right, and I knew if he needed an alibi in case police came around, he was going to commit a crime. But not murder. I figured a break-and-enter or armed robbery, although neither fit Bergel's MO. He liked people, a "relationship guy" he used to call himself. He liked to sell, and he was good at it.

"I understand," I said, "but I don't want to do it."

He laughed, and in hindsight, it felt like the prequel to violence. He removed his arm from my shoulder and stood tall, hovering.

"What about all the shit I did for you? The shit I bought you? The protection? Did any of the boys fuck with you at Olive Street?"

I didn't say anything.

"Did they?" he said, hammering me with the words.

"No ..."

"And why do you think that is? Because you're so scary and tough? No, it was because of me. I put the word out that no one could touch you or they'd have a problem with me. And did Perry ever give you shit? No, he didn't. Not at all. And why do you think that is? Because of me," he said. "That job you got now, at the lumberyard? The one that got you out of juvie and into a new group? That was me, too. I took care of you, and now I need a solid. You owe me."

Bergel readjusted his feet and dropped the hardness. His voice was quieter now, compassionate.

"Listen, I wouldn't ask if this wasn't important to me," he said. "People like us, we're from nothing, and we need to take care of each other because no one else cares. Where's your dad? Where's your mom? Gone, that's where. They never loved you. I do. You and me? We're brothers till the end."

Everything he said was true, more or less. Maybe he was right. Maybe I did owe him.

"Okay," I said. "I'll do it. But how will it work? Are you coming with me to the movie?"

He smiled, then explained to me the details of the plan.

***

I was picked up in Bergel's truck by a guy I'd never met. He introduced himself as Remy, and the first thing I noticed was that he wore one of Bergel's hooded sweaters. The weather was cool, so it made sense to wear a sweater. I wore one, too.

The next thing that struck me as weird was Remy pulling his hood up before we entered the theatre, and he kept it on for the duration of the movie. Again, some people wear their hoods up. It's not that unusual. After the movie, we went to Wendy's for a bite to eat, then Remy drove me back to the group home.

The police brought me in three days later. I told them Bergel and I had gone to a movie on the 20th, then grabbed food and cruised around in his truck, listening to music and hanging out until 1 a.m. I guess the Crown thought it was a good case, even though I had provided an alibi, because they charged Bergel with first-degree murder.

The slow wheels of justice turned, and eight months later, I sat on the stand in a courtroom, with the Crown attorney, John Renaud, looking at me like I was a bug. He was about five foot seven and had dark hair that was greying above the ears. His eyes were wide and bright, his mouth a thin pink line. He pulled at each of his cufflinks.

"Mr. Joelsen, I understand you know the accused."

"Yes."

"How do you know each other?"

"We grew up together in a group home."

"This is the St. James Home for Boys on Olive Street?"

"Yes."

Renaud asked me about Bergel's moral character, and I described him as a stand-up guy. He asked about our relationship, and I said he was like an older brother. He also asked me about the night Pete Argyreos died.

"We've heard on three accounts that Pete Argyreos supplied Logan Bergel with cocaine for the means of distribution," Renaud said. "And we've heard that Logan threatened Pete in Wiggly's Pizza around eleven thirty on April thirtieth. Witnesses heard Logan say he was going to quote, 'teach that bitch a lesson.' End quote. We have heard an account that the deceased refused to continue supplying drugs to Mr. Bergel after finding someone willing to take a smaller percentage. More importantly, we have Logan's DNA and fingerprints in the victim's home."

Renaud paused and then his voice picked up steam.

"However, you claim you were with him at a movie on May

twentieth. And yes, you have provided two ticket stubs. How convenient. And yes, we've all watched the security video from the theatre, where you enter and purchase tickets with a man who looks like Logan Bergel. But he's got the hood of his sweater pulled tight and we never see his face. It could be anyone." Renaud paused for effect, then continued his speech. "I'm going to ask you two questions as clearly as I know how to ask a person." Renaud paused, making me wait. "Did Logan Bergel ask you to lie and say you were with him on the evening of May twentieth?"

"No."

"Were you with Logan Bergel on the night Pete Argyreos was murdered?"

The room shrank and then expanded. The whole sensation repeated itself. The judge's mahogany desk moved to within an inch of my nose, and I could smell his coffee breath lapping at my cheek.

Everyone in the room eyeballed me–jury, attorneys, gallery, judge. Sweat pooled on the upper part of my forehead.

"Tell the truth," someone whispered.

I closed my eyes, opened them, and the words spilled out. "Yes, Logan was with me. We watched *The Proposition*, with Ray Winstone and Guy Pearce."

The courtroom went silent.

Bergel's lawyer, a woman called Kelly Carmichael, approached the bench. She was mid-forties, and what people used to call big-boned. But she was in shape, a former college basketball star at the U of M. Her dark hair was long and coarse and wavy, and for some reason, that's what I see when I think about her.

A bailiff wheeled in a TV on a stand, and Renaud stood up, flabbergasted.

"Objection, your Honour. We've watched this video ten times. We know what's on it."

"Respectively," Carmichael said. "I don't think we do know what's on it. Your Honour, I'm presenting new evidence today."

The judge considered both comments, then said, "I'll allow it."

Carmichael pressed play on the VCR, and the black-and-white

video played. It showed Remy and me from behind, paying for tickets at the movies, buying popcorn, and walking into the hallway with the theatres. There was a brief cut, and the video played again, only this time images had been enlarged. Carmichael hit pause.

"There," she said, pointing to the screen. She wheeled the TV so it was in front of the jury, then turned it so it was facing me. "Mr. Joelsen, what do you see on the back of Logan's left calf?"

I squinted in disbelief. "It's a ... a tattoo."

"Correct," Carmichael said. "And what is the design of the tattoo?"

"It's a cross."

I knew Bergel had the tattoo, but this was the first time I had seen it on the video. Jesus, they must have put a fake on Remy.

"Correct again," Carmichael said, and retrieved two large pictures, walking them to the judge. Then she clicked a button on the remote and an enlarged image of the tattoo on Bergel's leg appeared on the screen. "This photo was taken this morning. It shows the defendant's leg, and the very same tattoo we've now seen in the video."

There were audible gasps from the Argyreos family in the crowd. The judge's face tightened, and Renaud turned so red I thought his head might blow up.

A week later, we sat in the basement of a house on Ness Avenue, celebrating. It was toward the end of the night that I learned Bergel had killed Argyreos.

Nothing that could be presented in a courtroom, though. It was a look across the room. He raised his glass to me, smiled, and shrugged. That's it, a shrug, and I knew I'd helped a murderer escape prison.

***

I looked at Bergel, then Tight Shirt.

"Are you fucking kidding me?" I said, dumbfounded.

"You and me are going to fight," Bergel repeated.

"I'm not fighting you."

Bergel turned to me, and I saw the younger version, the person who'd come to me at the skate park, asking–no, demanding–that I help him beat a murder charge.

"I'm not in the game the way I was, that's true. I quit selling drugs years ago. I just needed a change. But I have people all over the place, and it so happens that one of my former customers tends bar. Where do you think he works?" he said, and bounced side to side. "That's right, Le Garage. He saw Nia there with someone and thought it was strange because he thought we were together. He sent me a picture. Guess who's in that picture?"

"She said you two were done."

"Doesn't matter." Bergel shook his head. "Outside ... on the street ... now."

This can't be for real.

My fear turned to anger as I threw on a sweater and runners, and followed Bergel out to the street, readying myself as quickly as I could. We squared off, an old Dodge half-ton truck on one side of the street, with Tight Shirt standing flexed and wide on the other. Streetlights cast shadows on a makeshift ring, and it was loud, rain smacking the pavement.

I outweighed Bergel, but he had five inches reach on me, peppering jabs off my nose until I moved in close and slammed his back against the Dodge and tried to elbow his face. He blocked the strike and threw a right that glanced off my shoulder as I ducked, turned, and repositioned my feet, then fired a left hook that clipped his chin. He buckled and dropped.

Sheets of pre-snow rain cascaded through the sky to the ground. I attempted to jump on top of him, but on the wet street he rolled and shrugged me off. My left shoe gave way, and I fell, crashing to the ground.

We took turns trying to get up, but neither of us managed it, throwing fists and elbows, anything to land a blow. Bergel tossed me hard across the street onto the lawn, but I jumped up, finally able to stand without him hanging on me. He approached and we squared off again.

I felt a cut on my left eyebrow and a mouse formed under my right eye. His nose bled, red and swollen.

What happened next happened fast.

We both charged, and our bodies came together in a tornado of fists, blood, rain, and sweat. We went toe to toe, throwing wildly.

Left, right. Left, right. Left, right. Over and over.

I reached back to the sky and pivoted, my back leg shifting weight and springing forward, using the momentum to throw an overhand right. Bergel spun and rotated his torso, screaming as he hit me with a body shot.

The punches connected simultaneously.

My haymaker struck him on the temple, and his got me in the liver. My knees bowed and my ears rang, corrupting my ability to think. The pain was incredible.

I stumbled into a tree, scratched at the bark, and strained to keep myself upright. Through bleary eyes, I saw water kick up from his shoes as he skidded across the grass, crashing into the side door of the Dodge. He slouched over the side mirror on wobbly legs, the mirror broke, and he fell to the ground. Spitting blood, he rose to his feet.

I doubled over and held my side, making sure I looked wounded, playing possum. When Bergel got within striking distance, I put everything I had into a kick that connected with the outside of his left leg. He shrieked and stumbled but remained on his feet. Tight Shirt grabbed me by the sweater, pushed me back, and blasted me in the face with a hard right. I collapsed, and he kicked me twice in the ribs.

"No!" Bergel shouted.

Tight Shirt stopped and looked for an explanation.

"No ..." Bergel repeated.

The rain came hard, pelting us with drops that stung. I got to my knees and water dripped down my face, hair, and clothes. Time moved slowly, then sped up.

"Have you found Sadie?" Bergel asked, breathing hard.

"I found her ... for a minute. She's in the wind again."

"My offer remains ..." he said between gasps. "You find her ...

let me know ... and ten grand." He spit blood on the street, touched a finger to his nose, and tried to put weight on the leg I'd kicked. He couldn't do it. "Stay away from Nia."

Bergel turned and limped to the vehicle as Tight Shirt followed him like a puppy.

What a fucking shitshow.

29

It took two attempts to sit up and another three tries before I could swing my legs over the side of the bed, stand, and shuffle to the bathroom. I looked at myself in the mirror. A few days of growth in my beard, mussed hair, and an eye rimmed black and blue. I had scrapes and bruises on both cheeks, and my chin had been rubbed raw, along with random cuts on my back and shoulders.

The worst pain, though, came from the body shot that Bergel had delivered, and the kicks from Tight Shirt. My ribs ached and a wave of nausea hit. I held on until the feeling passed, then ate two Tylenol, washing them down with tap water. I showered, debated shaving and decided against it, grabbed my shit and left.

***

I got to Sport Sphere hyper-focused, with bad intentions on my mind. Inside, Krista welcomed me for a third time.

"Hi, again. How can I help you?" she said.

I approached. "Is Bannerman in?"

She noticed my face, eyes wide. "What happened to your face?"

"I box. Sparring got out of control."

"I'd say. You look like you went twelve rounds."

I tried to smile but could only manage a half-ass grin. "Is Bannerman around?"

She furrowed her brow, and with a slight shake of the head, said, "I'm sorry, he went on holidays."

"What?" I said, taken aback.

Krista stiffened. "He took some time off. Said he's going out of town."

"When?"

Krista looked frazzled, like it had been a morning. "Yesterday."

I looked away, making sense of it. "Do you have his number?"

"I'm sorry," Krista said, looking nervous. "I can't give you his number."

"Krista," I said, my voice becoming urgent. "I need to see Bannerman."

She opened her mouth to speak, then reconsidered. "I ... well, it's just ... there have been other people here asking about Dustin."

"When?"

"I really don't want to get involved."

"What did they look like?"

She hesitated. "I'd rather not say."

I softened, realizing how scared she was, and rightfully so. "I can have the police here, and they can obtain the video from your security cameras. They'll watch it, and then they'll tell me what the person or people look like. That might take days, hours at least, and I need this information now."

Krista whispered, "What if they come back?"

"I can't promise you that they won't, but it's unlikely."

She stared at me, and I held her gaze. She was around the same age as Sadie.

"Three of them came in," she said.

Fuck...

"Three guys that looked the same?"

She nodded.

"When were they here?"

"Yesterday afternoon. Bannerman had already left."

"Thank you," I said. "One more question, and this one's a favour. What's Bannerman's address?"

"No offence, but I'm not doing that. I've said too much already. I'm not getting fired over this."

I noticed Jason Parilla watching us talk. He caught my eye and motioned for me to meet him outside with a less-than-subtle tilt of the head, mouthing the words "Tim Hortons."

I answered Krista with a terse "I understand" and left.

I walked down the street to Tims, ordered a black coffee, and sat down at a table. When Parilla walked in, he looked conspicuous, a man made for covert missions he was not. He noticed me but continued to the till. He ordered a sandwich and an orange juice, waited for his food, and when it was ready, the guy passed it to him in a to-go bag. Parilla walked toward me like I wasn't there, and I thought he was going to walk right by, when at the last second, his arm came up and he left a yellow Post-it note on the table. Then he walked out.

I read the note:

Bannerman

1103 Oak Street

A phone number was underneath.

***

The cab sailed down Portage Avenue, onto the St. James Bridge, and into River Heights, an older neighbourhood famous for ancient trees a hundred feet tall that grow on either side of the street, forming a ceiling above. The houses are close together, well cared for, and most streets have back lanes.

The cabbie dropped me on Academy, and I jogged down the sidewalk to Oak Street. Bannerman's house had a camera facing the front walk, and blue A.P.I. Alarm stickers let me know the house was protected 24/7 around the clock, but I couldn't worry about that now.

I knocked on the front door, waited, knocked again, and got impatient. The gate to the backyard was unlocked, so I entered and peeked through the garage window for vehicles. The garage was empty, but I noticed a second camera on the corner of the roof at the far end of the house.

I walked back to the front and tried the door. Finding it locked, I searched for a key under planters and a welcome mat, then returned to the back and did the same. No key, and the patio door was locked. The house was eerily quiet, and this left me with competing thoughts.

Either Bannerman was dead inside the house, or he had left,

on the run from Walton's men.

I needed to get inside, to confirm he wasn't hurt or in need of help. If he was dead, well, there wouldn't be much I could do, but at least I'd know.

The patio door had a long pane of glass that I could smash, but that would be noisy. A better option was to kick in the front door. Both options would trip the alarm, but I'd have at least five minutes. Most alarms used a two-hit system. If a window, door, or garage entrance was breached, a hit registered with the alarm company, who then called the homeowner to see what was going on. If the homeowner didn't answer, a second hit was required before the police were dispatched. Once inside, I'd probably set off a motion detector–hit two– but unless a squad car cruised down Oak at that precise moment, I'd have time to conduct a quick search. I was already on camera, but there was nothing I could do about that.

I ran to the front, assessed the door, and kicked it just under the knob. The frame cracked, and I pounded it four more times until the door swung open and an ear-piercing twang vibrated through the house. I walked in, closed the door as best I could, and surveyed the details of the house in a hurry. Living room. Kitchen. Bathroom. Nothing out of the ordinary.

Upstairs, I peeked in each bedroom until I got to the master.

Drawers were left open, and the walk-in closet was a mess. I noticed an open spot underneath a rack of clothes about the size and shape of a small suitcase. That's all I needed to know. I trotted back downstairs and went out the way I'd come in.

Bannerman was alive, but he was gone.

30

Henry Formenton called me back as I waited for another cab.

"Hey," he said. "What's up?"

I told him I needed a list of all the members of Watershed Moments.

"Impossible," he said. "I don't know anyone with access to those records, and even if I did, that person would never in a million years give them to me. What do you want with the list?"

"I can't tell you that."

"Then goodbye."

"Okay," I said, realizing I had to give him something. "I'll tell you why I want the records, if you tell me about the polygamy at Watershed."

"Are you kidding me?"

"No, I'm not. I thought it was strange when the two women called you for supper. Then I did a little research and asked questions. It didn't take long to piece it together."

A lighter snapped to life and I heard dry paper burning. Formenton exhaled. "Outsiders always judge. How do you know it doesn't work? That it's not a superior way to live?"

"Let's just say I'm skeptical."

More paper burned, longer this time, and I could feel the smoke as he sent it into the atmosphere. "Men don't have to marry multiple women. It's not a rule that's enforced or anything, but in some families, it's expected. Listen, I've said too much, and you've made your point. Why do you need the list?"

"I want to run the names through a database and see if any of them are cops."

A loud scoff, then he said, "Shit–I don't need a list for that, and I don't need a computer, either. Everyone knows who's on the force. You got a pen?"

"No," I said. "Text them to me."

Formenton provided six names, all men. I thanked him for his time, excited, but knowing a list would be better. Six seemed low, although the more I thought about it, that fit. I couldn't see Watershed men marrying female police officers, and women accounted for around 20 percent of the WPS. If I expected ten names, removing women dropped it to eight. So, six wasn't that low, and it gave us a place to begin.

***

From my office on Osborne, I walked to a sub shop and ordered a turkey on rye, cringing as I took a booth near the window. I lifted my shirt to inspect the damage. The ribs on the left side of my body were the colour of a plum, but I hadn't thought about drinking yet today, and that was a moral victory.

I texted the names from Formenton to Duke, and he said he knew four of the six, two of them well. He said those two were good cops, solid people, and he questioned if they were even members of Watershed Moments. I told him they were, and he called to tell me heartfelt anecdotes involving both. Duke said he'd run their names, though, along with the others, just to be sure, but he didn't like doing it.

The sandwich arrived and I ate it, contemplating what I could sell. I had a good leather couch, chair, and a decent fifty-five-inch television, but electronics lost value as soon as you plugged them in. I read two marketplace websites, and it seemed like the best I could do for the TV was two hundred bucks. The couch and chair might sell together for eight hundred, maybe a grand.

I posted it all.

Then I got up, tossed my wrapper, and left the shop.

***

At the Millennium Library, I wrote an apology to Cory Francis, and the boneyard of crumpled paper next to the table showed my distaste for the task. I must have written ten first sentences.

Dear Asshole,
I sincerely apologize for breaking your jaw.

Cory,
Go fuck yourself.

Dear Cory,
You are a piece of shit.

Finally, after seven or eight of those, I got something resembling progress:

Cory,
I'm sorry I hurt you.

That was as strong an opening as I could muster. What followed made me sick to write, a series of platitudes meant to reduce my sentence. I prided myself on never being fake like this, but if pretending allowed me to take care of my mom, I'd do it.

I decided to call Nia and ask her to pay for the work I'd done, but I couldn't hit send because it felt like I was quitting, and that didn't sit right with me. Plus, Bergel's threat lingered in my mind. My phone vibrated with a text from Duke.

Come on by the station. Ask for me at the desk.

From the library it was a short walk to police HQ and Duke's office. In the lobby, I moved through security and told a guy at the desk, who looked at me with suspicious eyes, that I wanted to speak with Detective Jansen. The guy had to be a retired cop, and I was pretty sure he hadn't smiled in at least a week. He asked who I was, and I gave my name. He made the call, motioned to the next person in line, and dismissed me without a word.

Three minutes later, Duke strolled across the expanse of the room, shook my hand, and brought me up the stairs to floor three. His office held pictures of his kids, wife, and commemorations. He took a seat behind the computer.

"Pull that chair and bring it over here," he said.

I picked up the chair on the other side of the desk and placed it beside his so I could see the screen of the monitor.

"Listen," Duke began, "you're a civilian and we're looking into cops. These people are my own, and if they ever caught wind I'd looked at them, even so much as a quick read of their files, I'd be answering a bunch of hard questions. You hear me?"

"I do, and if there was another way, I'd try it, but this is it. I know Walton's got someone working for him. I think it's a cop."

"You might be right ..."

"What have you found?"

Duke handled the mouse, bringing up three pictures on the screen, each opened in a separate window.

"Jack Palmera, Mike Ridgewood, and Brian Patterson. Nothing in their files connected to Brad Walton or Watershed Moments. Palmera and Ridgewood are both in cars, meaning they're on general patrol. Patterson is part of Air one helicopter police."

Two new pictures popped up as Duke licked his lips and continued.

"Steve Harstone and Barry Hendrix are detectives, and I know them. They've been in various departments, including Major Crimes and Organized Crime. They haven't, to the best of my knowledge, worked a case involving other members of Watershed Moments, or done anything shady at all, for that matter. Nothing I can see that would benefit Walton or Watershed. And I know them." He paused, second-guessing what he'd said. "Can you ever really know someone? Probably not. But these aren't the ones. Now, the last one is different."

"How so?"

"I can't open his file."

"What do you mean?" I said.

Duke talked with his hands, like he was reaching for the information as he spoke. "For the others, each file includes a personal history–date and location of birth, when they graduated from the academy, their postings, previous assignments–and if they are a detective or higher, you can see what cases they've worked. Al Monsoon's in the system, but none of that shit I mentioned is visible."

"What is he, undercover?"

"I don't know," Duke said, scratching his chin. "But I'm going to find out."

We heard footsteps in the hallway, and both of us looked up. A door closed and the steps faded.

"Listen to me," Duke said. "I'm not saying you're right, but if you are, and if it's one of these six people, it's Monsoon." Duke paused. "A staff sergeant I know says Monsoon works out of Station two."

"All right, so we track him down and ask him what he's working."

Duke's vacant stare told me I wouldn't like what came next. "You're not asking him anything."

"What?" I sat up. "Why not?"

Duke looked up at me. "A guy like this, there's no way he's answering any questions from you. And it would only make him wise that we're onto him."

Angry ghosts appeared in my head, and I felt twelve years old again, unwanted and stupid.

"You can't be serious," I said.

"It's the only way. And I'm not asking, I'm telling you. Stay away from Monsoon. I'll talk to him, but I need to talk to a couple people first. This isn't just a move, it's my career."

"Fuck!" I said.

"Keep your voice down," Duke said, standing up. "I understand what you're feeling, but you need to relax. Investigations take time. If we go out there without all the information, we'll make a mistake that we can't rightly afford to make. This is the best way."

He placed a hand on my shoulder, and I looked into his eyes. They were the colour of dark mahogany.

"I'm on your side," Duke said. "We'll nail Walton, but it happens by the book."

I nodded, left the office, and walked down the hallway to the staircase, taking stairs two at a time, knowing I wasn't going to listen.

31

It was almost supper time, and I had been sitting across the street from Station 2 in a Pizza Hut for the better part of an hour, nursing a Coke Zero. I had a booth next to the window, and I could hear the wind spiraling and whipping against the glass. It sounded like I was in a tunnel, and I watched branches bend in the fray, keeping an eye on the front door of the station. Monsoon was forty years old, but I knew little else about him, other than in his police picture he had a shaved head and a lean face bordering on too thin.

He came lumbering out twenty minutes later, dressed like an outdoorsman, with thick Wrangler blue jeans and a Cabela's hooded sweater. He walked like a praying mantis, long and methodical. I jogged across the street as he sat on a bench, removed a tin of chewing tobacco from a back pocket, and plugged a wad in his lower lip, something it looked like he could do in his sleep. He sent a stream of saliva cascading through the air, and it landed on the pavement, staining it brownish black.

"Monsoon?" I said.

He assessed me with sleepy eyes. "Who's asking?"

"My name's Jake Joelsen. I'd like to talk to you about Watershed Moments."

Why bother fucking around? Get to the point, right?

He paused, doubling down on the hard stare. "You police?"

I was about to speak, but he cut me off.

"If I had to guess, I'd say you're private." He smiled. "Yeah, that's it, and you're on a case. You got my name from someone, and now you're doing your best tough-guy routine."

"How far would you go for Brad Walton?" I said.

Monsoon hocked another loogie and it hit the ground inches from my boots. "That depends."

"On what?"

"On what he wants me to do."

"Let's pretend he wants you to give him the details of an impending warrant, the where and when of a search and seize."

He shook his head and leaned back. "Not my style."

"Then why is your file blocked?"

Monsoon paused. "You must have someone on the force accessing files. You can bet I'll be looking into that."

"I got someone," I said, "and if you've given Walton any police-related information, we're coming for you."

"I don't know what you're talking about, but I'm going to fill you in on something you should have been told a long time ago, but I expect you weren't. Your posture when you approach people and your facial expressions reveal too much." He made a series of strange, exaggerated faces, mocking me.

"And ..." he said as he stood and repositioned his body, "you walk like you're carrying suitcases. You might be tough. Yeah, I think you are," he said to himself. "But that don't mean shit. There's always tougher."

"You think you know me," I said, "but you don't, and I don't know you. I don't know if you're a good person and a decent cop, or a corrupt scumbag. Then again, what does 'good' even mean?"

Monsoon met my stare and smiled. "You're right about that. Good and bad ... most people aren't smart enough to comprehend them."

I nodded. "Did you give Brad Walton information relating to a search and seize of Watershed Moments?"

Monsoon removed the chewing tobacco with the index finger on his right hand, flung it onto the grass, and spit one more rope of saliva.

"Nope, I did no such thing." He walked toward the station. "I'll catch you on the flip side, JJ. Got work to do."

The door closed, and although I didn't like it, I believed him.

***

I called Duke but he didn't answer, so I sent a text, asking him to call me. I was in my apartment, pacing, my mind too revved up to relax. I emailed the letter to Bancroft, and he called a minute later. He sounded impressed when I said I'd been to meetings and had a week sober, then recommended I shave for sentencing and told me to bring my "A game." When I asked what that meant, he said, "It means you don't fuck up."

Now that I understood. Fucking up was my forte.

Bancroft said, "I wasn't going to tell you this, but I spoke to the Crown. They've agreed to recommend eighteen months, with another eighteen months probation, and mandatory anger management classes, as well as continuing with A.A. An apology is also a condition of the agreement. It sounds like you're well on your way. How much money have you mustered up?"

"Twenty-six," I said. "Twenty-seven if I can sell my couch, chair, and TV."

"Twenty-seven, that's impressive. You must be working."

"Yeah, the case is ongoing."

"Will you wrap up the job before the twenty-ninth?"

"I hope so."

"All right, it's probably good you have something to occupy your mind, and it helps with money. I caution you, though. Be up front with the client, and if you can't finish the job, send the files to someone you trust who can take over. You don't want this thing causing stress the day you go in."

"I understand, and I've been honest with them. If I can't finish it, I'll pass it off."

"Good, that's good. You're close, Jake. Well done."

"Thanks, Roger. I'll see you on the twenty-ninth."

I hung up, placed the phone on the counter, and went to work making tea. The phone vibrated, Duke's name on the screen. I stopped and answered it, eager to tell him about Monsoon even though he would be angry because I hadn't listened to him. He'd get over it.

"Hello," I said.

"You mobile?" Duke said, getting right to it.

"Not really. What's up?"

"Tracy Remple is dead."

His voice was thick, like it took effort to force the words out of his mouth.

I didn't move. "How?"

"Stabbed. Looks like a robbery gone bad."

I saw an image of Remple in the bar at the Ellice Motor Inn, defeated, as Duke questioned him until he broke.

"Where did it happen?" I said. "When?"

"This morning. He was out for a walk, at least, that's what it looks like."

"Where's his dog?"

"Dog?"

"He's got a rottweiler. Bullet."

"I'll check, but there was no dog or leash, none of that on scene. One second," Duke said, and took another call.

You'd have to be nothing short of psychotic to go after Remple with only a knife if he was with Bullet, and why would he go for a morning walk without his dog? It didn't make sense.

Duke came back on the line.

"Moore ..." he said. "Moore's been shot."

I didn't scream, but something inside me spasmed, like a record skipping. "Shot?"

"Yeah," he said. "I ... I can't believe it. She's in the hospital."

For maybe five seconds, I stood there, mouth frozen in an O, fixated on the wall.

How could ... Why?

"This is my fault. Walton did this," I said, speaking as I worked out the details. "He told me to stop. I didn't."

"Don't you blame yourself, not for one fucking second," Duke said, his voice firm. "You didn't have anything to do with this."

Duke's concern resonated with me. He cared, and for that I was grateful. I asked where Moore was being treated, and Duke told me Grace Hospital. I called a cab and waited, my guilt molting into anger.

***

Duke met me at the reception desk of the Emergency Department. I ran toward him, and he put his arms up, like "stop." Behind him were two constables and a man wearing the formal blues of upper management.

"What happened?" I said.

"She got shot in her car at a red light. Witnesses say it was road rage. Black Dodge Ram. Passenger window rolled down, and she was hit twice from close range."

"Could witnesses describe the shooter or driver?"

Duke exhaled slowly. "Not really. It was dark. She was hit both times in the chest."

I stepped to the side and Duke moved with me, shuffling.

"You can't go back there," he said.

I glanced over Duke's shoulder at the constables, then back to Duke.

"Get out of my way," I said.

"I can't do that."

"Can't or won't?"

We danced back and forth until the constables took notice. So did the man in dress blues, and as he moved to stand next to Duke, it became clear I couldn't get by without really forcing my way in. I let it go. For the moment.

"How is she?" I said.

Duke looked at the man beside him. "This is Deputy Chief of Investigations, Don Gleeson."

Gleeson had a slight hunchback, a stoop that made him even shorter than his natural five foot eight. His dyed black hair and a fresh shave embellished the pasty brightness of his skin. Small eyes and a sharp nose made him look like a condor or turkey vulture, a bird that tore meat from dead bones. His skin had ruddy marks, like tiny lakes on the prairies.

He extended his hand. "I know what you're going through, and we are on the same side. We want the same thing."

"And what's that?" I said, ignoring his hand.

"Walton."

I shook my head. This fucking guy. I hated it when people thought they knew me, or even worse, when they said "I know what you're going through." It was supposed to bring us together, show we had a common history or shared story, but these statements always came from people in positions of authority.

"You don't know me," I said, "so don't pretend to know what I want." I turned to Duke. "How is she?"

"She's in surgery, but the doctor says it's unlikely she lives through the night."

"Fuck ..." I said through gritted teeth. "What are you doing about this?"

Duke was irritated by the way I'd asked the question. "We got officers going door to door on Remple's street. The witnesses of the shooting are being questioned."

"What about video? Remple was knifed on a sidewalk, maybe there are exterior cameras, home security footage. And Walton–"

"What about him?" Gleeson said.

"Have you arrested him?" I finished, looking at Duke.

"We don't have enough evidence. Without Remple and Moore here to testify in court, their statements look like disgruntled complaints from people with grudges."

"What about the notebooks?"

"Hearsay," Gleeson answered. "First, they're in shorthand, a code that's indecipherable. Second, at trial, Walton's lawyer would claim Remple made the notebooks himself. A jury needed to see and hear Remple explain what the notebooks are and where he found them. The jury needed to connect with his story."

"This is bullshit!" I said, getting loud, that step before I lost control.

"It's not," Duke said. "I agree Walton's involved here, but we have no proof."

I turned to go and stopped, remembering why I'd called Duke in the first place. "I spoke to Monsoon."

Duke's face became a sheet of drywall, blank and lifeless. "Are you fucking kidding me?"

Gleeson moved closer to Duke. "What's he talking about, Detective? I heard a name that I hope I misunderstood."

"Oh, you didn't tell him?" I said to Duke. "This is a game to you, isn't it? A promotion."

Duke pointed a finger at me. "Who the fuck are you to say that? I made this investigation happen."

"No, I gave you this investigation," I said, spittle flying from my mouth.

Duke shook his head. "Fucking drunks, man," he said to Gleeson. "They never take responsibility. It's always someone else's fault. You know, Jake, the only reason you aren't in prison right now is because a judge suspended your sentence for two weeks so you can look after your mom ... another loser, might I add."

I grabbed Duke by the lapels of his jacket and reared back to sock him, but the constables were quick, and they got there before I could. They wrestled me to the ground, my ribs lighting up like I'd been burned with a branding iron. I swore and spit and foamed at the mouth, thrashing. The cops kneeled on my back, and soon I ran out of gas, closed my eyes and lay there, my cheek flat against the cold floor, futility and shame running through me. I heard Duke's voice.

"Let him up."

"You sure?"

"I said let him up."

I scraped myself off the floor, still breathing hard, turned, and told both constables to go fuck themselves, which I seemed to be saying a lot lately.

Duke was breathing hard, too, agitated.

"I'm sorry," he said. "I shouldn't have said that."

"Fuck you," I said, brushing myself off, "at least now I know how you feel."

Although I appreciated what he'd done for me, he'd crossed a line.

The two constables stood side by side, and one guy rested his hands on his belt like a gunslinger. It took every ounce of self-control I could muster not to deck him.

That's when a doctor arrived and told us Delilah Moore was dead.

32

I bussed to the closest liquor store, and it dawned on me that I couldn't spend any money, not if I wanted to hit my goal. I rationalized that I deserved a couple drinks after everything that had happened–the search of Watershed that yielded fuck all, the fight with Bergel, and the murders of Tracy Remple and Delilah Moore.

The clerk behind the counter looked at the cuts and swelling on my face and rang me up like I was radioactive. He looked mortified.

I drank a beer on the bus, the album *Let's Go* by Rancid pounding in my headphones. Then I met my guy in the back lot of a restaurant on Main Street and picked up an eight ball of blow and five hits of MDMA. I dry-swallowed a pill as I got on another bus going south on Main.

Traces of the drug glowed in a halo of phosphorescence, a bright, shaky fuzz that surrounded each streetlight. Headlights blurred together, and I felt like the last man alive on an important mission as I reached the first bar on the list Nia gave me. Same places I'd been to days earlier.

Two nightclubs and a dive bar.

Questions.

Have you seen Sadie Rowe? Can you call me if you see her?

It must have been around 12:30 a.m. when the bus glided down Portage Avenue heading west, turning onto Broadway. The driver took a break outside a gas station, and I used the time to buy a pack of cigars, the thin, cheap ones wrapped individually in cellophane. I smoked one outside as I waited, staring at the stars, thinking. I pulled a baggie out of my pocket, did a bump in each nostril, and my worries disappeared.

I arrived at a pub called The Crooked Wig to people spilling out the door, and pushed my way to the front, holding my damaged ribs. I nodded to the bouncer, Matt, and he nodded back, then noticed the cuts and swelling on my face.

"What happened to you?"

"Church," I said, and Matt laughed. My response was truer than he'd ever know.

I paid the cover and accepted the stamp on the back of my hand. The ink looked like a scar. A current of self-destruction ran beneath my skin as Shay set me up with a double gin and tonic.

Images sped up, slowed down, and paused at random intervals, making it impossible to move through the bodies like a capable adult. Stumbling, I bumped into people and received dirty looks.

I leaned against a wall to the left of the stage, letting the guilt wash over me. The joint was two-thirds full and loud. A woman around twenty walked onstage with an acoustic guitar around her neck. She sat on a stool, adjusted the mic, and began singing. She didn't introduce herself. Her gravelly voice made me think of chain-smoking cigarettes and good hangovers, the kind that inspire action and provide purpose, not the kind that bring pain and suffering.

She sang:

"A woman like me is always around.

"Suffering crazy, ignorant but happy.

"Stolid and petty, attractive and ugly.

"Maybe that's why I sing."

I vaguely remembered another club, but I couldn't say which one or for how long I was there. I danced to house music so loud the inside of the speaker pulsated with each beat. I did shots and had conversations with random people. More bumps.

A white guy with a dramatic fade told me I had to get on board and join "the cause," but I couldn't remember what cause he felt so strongly about. An Indian woman described how the farmers in India were being persecuted, but I had no clue how or why.

The last memory I had was talking to a buxom brunette who told me I should be an actor. I think I agreed.

I asked everyone I talked to if they knew Sadie Rowe, Brad

Walton, and if they knew anything about Watershed Moments.

All it got me was blank stares.

33

Wednesday, October 23 (eight days missing)

I woke up fully dressed around 3 p.m., breathing heavily, sweating, and unsure where I was. It took a few seconds to recognize my apartment. The room smelled rank, and I scanned for the source, spying an ashtray that would have been full ten cigarettes ago. But that wasn't it. This was human. The sogginess of my clothes registered, and I realized I'd pissed the bed. I sat up, found my phone, and scrolled through my contacts.

Katz answered and after a brief conversation, said he'd be right over. He didn't hesitate when I told him I needed help, and thirty minutes later he knocked on my door. I stepped to the side, and he came in.

"It smells like shit in here," he said, then looked me up and down. "But you look great," he added, and smiled.

I would've laughed but I didn't want to throw up.

"You look awful," he said, serious this time.

We sat down at the kitchen table.

"If this is an A.A. pep talk," I said, "it sucks."

"It's not a pep talk, it's the truth. You look hurt. You look sick." Katz paused. "Are you okay?"

"I don't know. I'm hungover. I'm sore, but I can handle pain. It's ... my brain isn't right."

"What happened?"

"Remple and Moore are dead." I shook my head. "And it's my fault."

Katz stopped and I got the sense he was trying to determine if I was being honest. I'm sure he'd heard it all, every excuse, and I'd lied to him many times when I'd worked for him.

"How?" he asked.

"Officially, one's a robbery and the other a road rage incident, but it was Walton." Tears filled my eyes. "He told me to stop investigating Watershed, and I didn't listen."

Katz stood and walked to the fridge, doing a quick assessment of its contents. He looked in the freezer next.

"This'll work," he said, shutting the door.

He gathered up a cutting board, knife, two pans, and fired up the elements. He got potatoes, eggs, and then bacon from the freezer, and went to work chopping the potatoes into cubes, tossing them in a frying pan. He added vegetable oil and adjusted the element to medium-high, then defrosted bacon, pulled apart the strips, and set them in the second pan to fry.

I stood up. "Can I help?"

"Nah, sit down."

Next, he cracked eight eggs into a bowl and whipped them. When the potatoes had browned, he poured the eggs in. Then he removed the crispy bacon, broke it into bits, and added the pieces to the pan along with the eggs and potatoes.

"That's how you do it," he said. "A hearty scrambler."

We destroyed the food.

After eating, I felt a little better, emotionally stable-ish.

"I'm sorry for what happened to Remple and Moore," Katz began, "and I don't have the words to properly tell you how much I wish I could help. I think it's going to take a long time to make sense of it all. I'm not even sure it's possible. What I do know is that you won't heal if you're drunk all the time. Sobriety isn't easy, but there are things you can do to make it easier. There's not much point sharing them, though, if you don't want to change. Do you want to get sober?"

"I don't know," I said.

It was the truth.

"That's a problem."

"Why?"

"It's easy getting sober for a while. Any drunk can do it, but living the rest of your life sober, that is difficult. It's not rocket science, but it takes consistency and discipline. Living sober takes courage."

"What's the point of being sober if I have to give up everything I know and love?" I said.

"Everything you know and love got you where you are. I'm not saying you'll never have friends, or that you can't have fun or go on a date. I am saying those things should not be your priority right now if you want to get sober."

"You said earlier that there are things I can do ..."

"There are. You want to hear them?"

I nodded.

"Go to a meeting every day," Katz said. "That might change in the future, but right now you need to go every day."

"What else?"

"You can't associate with friends when they're drinking. To be honest, it might be good to distance yourself from them altogether."

I nodded. "I don't have any friends."

"Then that one's easy," he said. "And three, you can't go to places that serve alcohol. This is nonnegotiable. Bars, restaurants, licensed coffee houses, concerts, sporting events. None of them. If you do, you'll drink. Eventually. I guarantee it. Lastly, when you're ready, you need to do the steps."

"Listen, man," I said, "this is a lot for me to handle. I've been to a couple meetings, but ..."

"Let me ask you something. Why'd you go to that first meeting?" Katz said.

Why did I go?

Sure, there was my sentencing and Nia's ultimatum, but those weren't it.

"I ... I guess I was scared."

"Of what?"

"That I'm out of control. I just want this to stop."

"It won't stop on its own. In fact, it'll get worse."

I gave him a look.

"Let me tell you a story," he said. "I got hit by a car once. I was drunk and crossed when I didn't have the right of way. Spent three weeks in the hospital. I thought I'd hit rock bottom, so I started making promises. I'll quit drinking. I'll go to meetings. I'll do the steps. I'll be a better husband. I promise, I promise, I promise. When the hospital discharged me, you know what I did? I walked directly to a liquor store. I didn't even go home, never mind a meeting. I walked in, bought a forty, and got absolutely shit-faced. It wasn't until my first wife left me a week later that things got really bad. You see my point?"

"I do. Okay ..."

"Okay what?"

"I want to get sober."

"Then let's get you to a meeting."

We sat in Katz's F-150, listening to a talk radio station. I asked about Naomi, and he talked about her treatment, and how she mostly slept now. I couldn't stop sweating, nor could I shake the feeling of a looming threat, but by late afternoon I'd made it through another meeting.

PART 3

VIPASSANA

34

Duke texted to let me know he had contacted the RCMP and checked rural arrests, but the names Dustin Bannerman and Sadie Rowe did not appear in any recent citations or small-town jails. He didn't mention my behaviour the previous night at the hospital.

I dosed again after talking to Duke, waking to a call from a blocked number.

"Hello," I answered.

A hacking cough filled the line for a solid five seconds, followed by a throaty gathering of phlegm and a loud spit. "Is this–" a man said, and the cough returned briefly. He tried again. "Is this, uh, Jake? Jake Joelsen?"

"This is Jake." I rubbed my face, sitting up. "Who am I speaking with?"

"We met two days ago. I got–" he said, and started hacking, spitting, and swearing. "I got two people here."

The man sounded older. I'd met three or four men like that the other night on my hotel tour, men who, for whatever reasons, owned, managed, or worked the front desk on the night shift at roach motels to pay the bills. In fact, I saw myself in those men. A bad break here, the wrong decision there, and that's who I would–still could–have become.

I racked my brain but couldn't match his voice to a face.

He must have gotten impatient. "What, you forget? You came to my place and showed me a picture of a woman. She's here ... with a man."

I paused. "You sure?"

He cackled. "Does a one-legged duck swim in circles?"

I smiled. "Okay, I'll be right over. Where is *here*?"

"Whoa, hold up there, big shooter. This information isn't free." He sipped a drink, and I heard ice cubes rattle against the glass.

I knew the sound well. "It's going to cost you, oh, I don't know, maybe ... two hundred."

It wasn't worth haggling, but I had to or else he'd ask for even more when I arrived at the hotel, motel, or bed and breakfast. I guessed he was at a motel. Either way, the expense was going on Nia's tab.

"Fuck that," I said, fake angry. "One is the best I can do."

"One eighty," he countered.

"Nah, too much. One twenty."

"One sixty."

"One forty."

"One fifty."

I hesitated just enough to let him think I was debating. "Done. Where are you?"

"Name's Tony"–the ice cubes vibrated again–"and I'm at The Fairlane."

Tony, of course. Mid-seventies, grey brush cut, and a leathery, scarred-up face that resembled a hockey glove. He was an evening man at the front desk of one of the most dangerous motels in the city. Located downtown–not commerce-and-concerts downtown, but stabbed-and-mugged downtown. Incredible poverty downtown. Prostitution, drug deals, and homelessness downtown–The Fairlane's clientele made the average prison inmate look like a soft touch.

"Thank you for calling," I said. "Watch their room. If they leave, call me immediately. I'll be there in twenty."

"With the cash."

"With the cash," I confirmed.

"See you then."

He hacked up a lung and rasped "fuck" before hanging up without saying goodbye.

I ran across the lot of my building to a cab and told the driver to take me north.

***

It had started to rain, and a thin layer of fog hovered above the wet concrete. The cab sailed through it as I fought nausea and shakiness, and Katz's words came back to me: *Living sober takes courage*. I'd lived for years believing it took courage to hurt like this, being broke, feeling shame. I couldn't get rid of the feeling that I'd been so completely wrong. I also felt an immense pressure, like my life rested on my next move.

The driver pulled into the lot of The Fairlane and parked. I paid, closed the door of the cab, and approached the hotel. The façade included a pizza restaurant I wouldn't eat at if you paid me, and a dry cleaner reminiscent of a crack house. Tony greeted me in the lobby.

"You got that one fifty, Jake-O," he sang.

I passed him the cash.

"They're in room two oh eight. Second floor."

I nodded, running it through in my head. "How would you like to make another fifty?"

"Hundred," he said quickly.

"It's fifty or I find someone else." I pointed at the nightclub that ran alongside the building. "I bet there's people in there who'll do it for ten if you don't want to."

"All right, all right. Cheap fucker," Tony said. "I'll do it for fifty. Wait ... what am I doing?"

***

Tony stood in front of room 208, holding towels. There was an outside hallway that wrapped around the entire second floor, so we stood under the few stars you could see in the city. I hid in the doorway of the next room, away from the stairs.

I had to hand it to Tony, he was likable. Fearless, too. Something old-school about him, and he seemed unshakable, which made sense. I bet he'd seen some shit. Deskmen at fleabag motels usually had.

Tony knocked, and a moment later, Bannerman shouted "Who is it?" through the door.

"It's Tony from the desk. Got you fresh towels," Tony shouted back.

"We didn't order towels."

"Never said you did. It's a service we provide." There was a brief pause, then Tony added some spice to his voice. "Do you want them or not?"

You could hear the chain slide across the lock rail, and the door opened. Bannerman stepped out, took the stack of towels, and went back inside. Tony walked off like I'd told him to, and I heard the door close and the rattle of the chain.

Threatening Sadie and Bannerman, or approaching them with any kind of aggression, would only create a confrontation. They were obviously scared, on the run, and desperate. This needed to be different. I needed to be different.

I went downstairs into the lot, around the corner, and into an alley, dialing Duke as I walked.

"Jake," Duke answered by way of greeting.

"I'm sorry I said you don't care," I said. "I know that's not true."

A brief silence, then: "That's okay, man. I get it, and I'm sorry again for what I said about your mom. I had no right to say that."

"Thank you."

"Well, all right, then. Now that that's out of the way, why'd you call?"

I smiled, remembering why I enjoyed Duke so much. "One second."

A man stumbled toward me and asked for change. I said I didn't have any but gave him a smoke to send him on his way. When he was a good twenty feet to my rear, I continued.

"I found them," I said.

"No shit?"

"I got a call from a front desk guy who said they were at his place. I just got here, and I've seen Bannerman."

"Not Sadie?"

"No, but the guy who called described the girl Bannerman's with and it sounds like her."

Duke's voice picked up steam, the way it did when he was

following a lead. It had momentum. "If you're thinking about talking to them, don't. Wait until I get there."

I turned and checked the alley. The man I gave the smoke to was out of sight.

"I hear you," I said, "but bright lights and sirens aren't going to work. Let me talk to them first. Sadie and Bannerman need to trust us, otherwise they'll run, or worse."

Silence filled the line for a moment. "Okay. Quiet is better. No need for anything that could bring reporters or citizens with their cameras and shit. Know this, though, my man: We'll try it your way, but if they don't come quietly, then they'll come loudly. The cavalry's going to be on standby. You understand?"

"I'd expect nothing less."

"Where are you?"

"The Fairlane."

"I'm en route. Be there in fifteen."

***

I knocked on room 208 and stepped to the side, while Duke waited in the lobby. I did my best to stay under the awning and avoid the rain.

"Who is it?" Bannerman said.

"It's Jake Joelsen."

Neither one of us said anything for a long time. There was no other way out of the room, so I waited, listening to the rain slap the shingles of the roof. It sounded like hooves.

"What do you want?" Bannerman said.

"I want to help you ... and Sadie."

"Sadie isn't here."

"I understand you want to protect her," I said, thinking about lying on the stand for Logan Bergel, breaking Cory Francis's jaw, and all the drinking, drugs, and bad decisions I'd made over the years. I considered what Bannerman must be feeling. If he loved Sadie, then he would do whatever was necessary for her.

"I'm an alcoholic," I said.

I heard shuffling, then, "What?"

"You heard me. I drink. I use drugs. I joined A.A. a week ago, and had seven days sober but–"

"But ...?"

"But I fell off the wagon last night. I've lived one way so long, I don't even know how to stop." I stepped in front of the door. It was sticky with condensation. "Nia told me Sadie might need help."

"It's not her fault ..."

"I know, but the bottom line is that the two of you took something from Brad Walton. He wants it back."

"How do I know you haven't been hired by Walton? That he isn't out there with you right now?"

I turned and removed my phone from a pocket, entered the code, and found Nia's number. I dialed.

She answered right away. "Jake ..."

"You home?"

"Yes, why? What's going on?" she said, worried.

"It's good news," I said. "Good news."

Snow started to fall, and a thin layer covered everything. Big, wet flakes.

"I've found Sadie again," I said to Nia. "Bannerman, too. If I put you on speaker, will you talk to her? Convince her I'm here to help."

"Of course," she said, tears in her voice.

I just smiled and nodded.

"Sadie," I said through the door. "Nia wants to talk to you."

I put the phone on speaker and held it in front of the door, volume way up.

"Sadie?" Nia said. "You there?"

There was an obvious scuffle inside the room–raised voices, footsteps, jostling–then Sadie's voice: "I'm here ..."

It was like hearing the voice of a quiet classmate you'd watched across the room for months. When they finally spoke, their voice hit different notes than the ones you'd assigned them in your head. She sounded older than twenty-three.

"Are you okay?" Nia said, crying. "I love you."

"I love you, too."

A chain slid along its moor and there was a long pause. The waiting almost killed me. Finally, the door clicked open.

35

Sadie had lost weight, and the hooded sweater she wore hung on her shoulders like a windbreaker clinging to a hanger. She held a large tumbler of what looked like wine in her right hand and tore the phone from my hand with her left. Then she turned and stormed back inside. Bannerman replaced her at the entranceway. We held each other's gaze a moment, and I wondered if I could take him.

"Come in," he said, unsure, and stepped to the side.

Sadie had gone into the bathroom and shut the door. Bannerman sat at the small table. I removed my shoes and sat with him. He looked as bad as Sadie, like he hadn't slept in a million years.

"What are you doing here?" I said. "Why haven't you blown town?"

"We're working on it." He leaned back and ran a hand through that hair of his. "Walton's got resources. You put people on doors at the airport, another one or two at the entrance to security–we'd never get past them. Busses and trains require ID, so there'd be a record of where we went."

"Why didn't you take your car?"

"I had to ditch it yesterday. Too easy to follow and track," he said. "And every vehicle purchase leaves a trail. I've been trying to find someone willing to forgo the paperwork for cash, but it's not easy." He looked at the table, then his hands. "So, you asked why we're here? We're waiting on something."

"For fake passports?" I said.

Bannerman stood and grabbed two beers from a bucket of ice he had on the dresser. He plopped both cans down hard on the table.

"I found a guy online who provides a quality product that's good enough for a bus."

Passports meant if Walton's people checked, they wouldn't find the names Dustin Bannerman and Sadie Rowe. It made some sense, but I wasn't buying it.

He opened the beer and took a sip, noticing I hadn't touched mine. "Oh shit–I forgot you're an al–You want a coke?"

"No, thanks," I said, and passed the beer to Bannerman, where he let it rest next to his own.

Bits of ice glowed as they slid down the aluminum cans, and I imagined drinking one of them, gone in three gulps, the first heat of a buzz caressing me like a lover. I shook off the fantasy.

"Listen," I continued, "you could have flown out of here that first day, before Walton even knew what you'd done, but you didn't. You stole something, didn't you?"

He took a sip, inhaled a long, slow breath.

"What did you take?"

"Shit," he said. "I'm surprised you care this much."

"Care?" I asked.

"I thought you would have let it go by now."

I wasn't sure if caring had anything to do with it. Maybe it did, I didn't know. I just felt an unwavering desire to help my mom and hurt Walton.

"We took a million dollars," Bannerman said, sipping the beer.

"A million ...?" My mouth hung open. "Is it here?"

"Yes."

"You took a million dollars of drug money from Brad Walton?"

"Yes."

Pieces of the story continued to elude me. "How?"

Bannerman leaned forward and moved his beer to the side. He'd only had two sips. Normal drinkers baffled me.

"Sadie and I haven't been together long, and I never would have believed it could happen to me, but it did–love at first sight," he said. "When she told me about the church ... Walton needed to pay. It didn't take much work, a couple weeks recon to learn their routines. When they sold. To whom. On the night of the exchange, we let Walton make the sale and then took the cash by force."

"Sadie was there?"

He nodded. "It was a two-person job. I needed coverage. Problem is, she used my name."

"During the robbery?"

"Yeah ... to get my attention. An accident, but still, I told her to get out of town, didn't want to know where. That way I couldn't give her up if–"

"Why didn't you leave, too?"

"Walton only had my first name and my general physical description. We wore masks. I hoped they wouldn't find me."

"And then I started poking around."

"And then you started poking around," he repeated. "You led them right to me."

"I'm working with the police. I have a detective, a good man we can trust. He's here. Can you make Sadie believe I'm on the level? Then I'll call him up."

Bannerman shook his head, and I thought he was going to interrupt, but he held off and let me finish.

"I can't do this on my own. We need the authorities," I said. "You have a million dollars cash. That's not a crime, but how you got it is. Plus, Walton won't stop. He can't. If he lets you get away with this, it's open season on him. You need to return the money."

Bannerman scratched his chin, drifted off, and picked up the beer. He twisted the tab until it snapped off. "I underestimated Sadie's addiction."

"Meth?"

"And other things ... She needs professional help. Treatment at a facility or something. Otherwise, she's going to use again. I've been letting her drink, which helps, but it's a short-term solution, at best."

"I'll make sure she gets help," I said. "Let me talk to my man."

***

Sadie sat on the bed next to Bannerman, holding my phone. She looked tiny as he rubbed her back. It had taken Bannerman fifteen minutes to get her to hang up the phone, and another five to convince her to come out of the bathroom.

Duke had texted me three times from the lobby, asking what room number. Tony must have played dumb or refused to help Duke. Either way, it took balls and years of hardening to remain loyal to someone you didn't know under questioning from the police, and I respected that.

When I finally sent Duke the room number, he knocked, opened the door, and for a split second, I wondered if he might go the hard route. Thankfully, he introduced himself and shook hands with everyone. He sat beside me at the table, across from the thieves.

"I need time to sort this out," Duke said. "I'm going to speak with my deputy chief, and then we need to take what we have to a Crown attorney, that's the person responsible for charging Brad Walton." He looked around the room. "You can't stay here. Jake found you, and it's only a matter of time until Walton does. I'm going to place you in a safe house. No one will know you're there. Jake will stay with you until Walton is arrested."

"Then what?" Bannerman said.

"Then, hopefully, we'll get the RCMP involved and arrange protective custody. I can't guarantee they'll get on board, but that's the plan."

Sadie and Bannerman looked at each other, nodded, and an hour later, the three of us arrived at a small house on Garfield Street in a neighbourhood on the edge of downtown called Wolseley. Duke asked if I wanted a constable at the house. He said he had a young guy that he trusted, but I said no. The less people who knew our location, the better.

The house had been equipped with supplies–towels, new toothbrushes, phone cords, clothes in various sizes, canned and frozen food, coffee, bottled water, and a stack of used paperbacks. Sadie and Bannerman took one bedroom, and I took the other.

After we'd settled in, Duke said, "I'll be in touch," and turned to leave, but stopped. "I need to see it."

I knew what he meant and led him down the hallway to where Bannerman had brought the suitcase. I knocked.

"Come in," Bannerman answered.

Duke and I stood near the doorway.

"Let's see the dough," Duke said.

His words were smooth. It wasn't a demand, it was a simple request, one that the people on the other end of it were happy to oblige.

Bannerman got the suitcase out of the closet, Sadie stood, and Bannerman laid it on the bed. He opened it.

Duke's smile got even bigger, infringing on his eyeballs. "So that's a million bucks ... Thought there would be more cash."

"All hundreds," Sadie said, her voice surprising everyone. Duke and I looked up at her, and Duke nodded like he had seen her for the first time.

***

I ate a can of ravioli while reading texts Nia had sent me since the phone call with Sadie.

Is everything okay?

Where are you?

Text me. I'm worried.

I typed a response, erased it, and typed a new message. Then I re-read what I'd written, edited it, and hit send.

Sadie and Bannerman are safe. Duke is going to sort this out, but it takes time.

The bubbles calibrated.

Where are you? Nia texted.

I can't tell you that. We'll talk tomorrow. Good night.

I went to bed around midnight and tumbled into a restless sleep. The vivid dream was about the one and only time I'd seen my dad cry. I was ten, and he hadn't come home the night before. When he arrived the next morning, my mom greeted him with a barrage of shoes that flew toward his head like scud missiles. He dodged them until one connected with his forehead and he swore. I don't recall most of the argument that followed, but I remembered the tears.

In the dream, I came out of my bedroom and tried to hug them as they fought. I reached out, arms spread, and leaned in for an embrace, but they were holograms, and my body fell through theirs as it landed on the floor.

I awoke at 2 a.m., startled, and threw on a sweater. I put on shoes and stepped onto the back porch to smoke. The snow continued, sparkling like tiny lights in the night. The cold air and smoke burned my lungs, but I welcomed it. I checked the forecast, something I hadn't done in days. They were calling for a blizzard, more than twenty centimetres of snow and strong northerly winds, with the worst of it hitting the city tomorrow late afternoon. Unusual for late October, but not unheard of.

Why do I care so much about Sadie?

Well, Nia, for one, but it was more than that. What if it was my calling, my duty, to search for the lost souls?

The ones nobody looked for.

To show they mattered.

For as long as it took to get an answer.

I tossed the butt and went back in, praying the dream wouldn't return.

36

Thursday, October 24 (one day found)

I awoke just after six, and this time I was up. There would be no more sleep, not today.

I found Sadie on the couch, reading *Different Seasons* by Stephen King. A mug on the coffee table steamed.

"*Stand by Me* or *The Shawshank Redemption*? No, hold up," I said, contemplating her. "You strike me as an *Apt Pupil* person."

She dug her nails into her forearm, scratching like there was something alive under her skin. "I think you mean *The Body* and *Rita Hayworth and Shawshank Redemption*."

"Am I right about what you're reading?"

"*Apt Pupil*," she confirmed, and smiled. "There's coffee."

In the kitchen, I poured myself a cup, added sugar and powdered whitener, and returned to the living room. The tan-coloured carpet and a couch that had a checkered pattern were old but in good shape. There was no TV, generic paintings on the wall, and an oak coffee table. The room comforted me, like a grandparent's, full of familiarity. I sat in a chair that matched the couch, sipped coffee, and leaned back. I could ask her if she was willing to go to rehab, but as I watched her sip coffee and read, scratching like a dog who'd just emerged from the bush, it felt wrong, like it could cause anger to flare up, and that's the last thing I wanted to do.

"So?" I said.

Sadie dog-eared a corner of one page and placed the book on the table. "So ..." she echoed.

"What's on your mind?"

She paused and assessed me, perhaps weighing the pros and cons of letting me into her world.

"I'm trying to wrap my head around giving a million dollars to a man who pimped me out," she said. "That's fucked up."

I nodded, unsure of how to respond.

"Is that yours or was it here?" I said, meaning the NOFX T-shirt she wore.

"Mine."

"Have you seen them live?" I asked.

"You know them?" she said.

"I've seen them six times. Greatest punk band ever. And I do mean ever. Even the Sex Pistols and The Ramones are brief moments in the movement when compared to NOFX. I met the guitarist, El Hefe," I said, "in Calgary. He was in the beer gardens."

"That's awesome. I'm jealous."

"I grew up on bands like NOFX. Offspring. Green Day. Pennywise."

"Another Stephen King reference."

"That's right," I said, remembering the name of the band had been taken from the clown in It.

I wanted to tell her how sorry I was that she'd been abused, mentally and physically. I wanted to support her and get her some help. I wanted to say the right words in the right way.

But the words wouldn't come. Instead, I kept it in the moment.

"What could be more punk rock than returning a million bucks you stole? It's a big 'fuck you' to Walton, like you don't need his money, and you stole it just to fuck with him. There's something about that I like."

After a moment, Sadie said, "A shift in perspective."

"Yeah, but it's action, too."

"Good morning," Bannerman said, and strolled into the living room, hair wild. There was more colour in his cheeks, and the life had returned to his eyes. He kissed Sadie. "What are we talking about?"

"Returning a million dollars ..." Sadie said, and Bannerman shook his head.

"Kills me," he said. "Just guts me."

"I think I'm okay with it," Sadie countered, and turned to Bannerman. "Maybe we don't need it."

They kissed again, and Sadie looked at me.

"What if Walton tries to kill us at the exchange?" she asked.

"You won't be there," I said.

"What? He's going to expect me. That's how these people are. Everything is about something else. This is a personal slight. He's going to want you there, too, and Dustin. All of us."

There was no way Duke would let her go, and neither would I.

"The way I see it," I said, "Bannerman and I will go."

"Why would Walton put himself in jeopardy like that?" Bannerman said. "Won't he know we're working with the cops?"

"I don't know," I answered. "He might suspect it, but I think it's like Sadie said, it's personal, and he's willing to risk it. I also think he's going to set the meeting somewhere he feels safe. Where that is, who knows?"

"What if we choose the place?" Bannerman said.

"He'll never go for it. At the same time, it's good if he thinks we're working with the police. It provides us with a measure of safety."

The lightness evaporated, and a pensive air swept into the room. For perhaps fifteen seconds, we sat like that while the snow fell outside. The temperature had dropped ten degrees overnight, and it would remain cold. Our minds settled into a frenzied, heightened state, waiting for whatever came next.

***

Three cups of coffee and ninety minutes later, we'd each showered, dressed, and eaten. Sadie fidgeted, irritable when she couldn't get comfortable on the couch. She opened the book, put it down, and barked at Bannerman to leave her alone when he asked if she was okay. Bannerman retreated to the kitchen, and I read the paper on my phone, sitting in the recliner.

Old houses have creaking floors, shifting walls, and loud, angry furnaces. There's a constant series of aches and groans, so I ignored the popping noise from the basement.

Sadie didn't.

She flicked back the curtains, peered outside, and stormed into the kitchen. There, she examined the backyard, then returned to the couch and peeked out the window again. She stayed that way for a minute and showed no signs of leaving.

"Sadie's off," I said to Bannerman. "She's paranoid."

"Yeah, she gets like that when she hasn't used in a while." Bannerman didn't look up from his phone. "It comes and goes until she gets a longer stretch of sobriety."

"Sadie," I said.

She ignored me, finished her examination of the front yard, and sped back to the kitchen. I followed.

"Hey," I said to her. "Are you okay?"

"Yeah, but I heard something."

I dismissed her at first, then paused.

"Did you tell anyone we're here?" I said, feeling a slight surge of panic.

"Nia," she said.

"Are you kidding me?"

"She's my sister."

We heard footfalls on the basement stairs, and Bannerman looked up. He'd heard them, too.

"Someone's in the house," Sadie said.

At this, she turned, and Bannerman pulled a knife from a drawer. I foolishly considered going room to room, double-checking doors and windows, but it was too late.

A man walked into the living room holding a gun in a gloved hand. He wore black boots, pants, and a hooded sweater pulled up. His face was covered by a Deadpool mask. He pointed the gun at Bannerman.

"Put it down," he said, the words fuzzy through the mask.

Bannerman placed the knife on the kitchen table.

"The money," the man rasped.

I pointed down the hallway. "It's in the bedroom."

"You," Deadpool said to Sadie. "Get it. Slowly."

Deadpool moved past Bannerman and me, and backed down the hallway to follow Sadie, facing us, the gun pointed in our direction. He got to the bedroom, looked inside, then backed up and made way for Sadie. She walked out, pulling the suitcase.

"Leave it," Deadpool said. "Join them."

Sadie hesitated, but left the case and walked toward us, arms raised. Deadpool pulled the suitcase with his left hand, holding the gun in his right, trained on Sadie. She made eye contact with me, then shifted her gaze to Bannerman. Sadie still had her back to Deadpool when, at the end of the hallway, he turned toward the front door.

"Brad Walton says thank you," he said.

The comment struck a nerve, and I watched Sadie make brief eye contact with Bannerman–anger splashed across her face–and then look away.

She dove to her left and lunged at Deadpool, tore at his face and tried to remove the mask. Deadpool fired, and a loud bang reverberated through the room, deafening in the small space. Sadie held her stomach and stumbled backward until she fell. Spittle had drooled from her mouth to her chin, and she looked silly, like a little kid. I remember feeling bad for having those thoughts.

Deadpool latched on to the handle of the suitcase. "I didn't want to ..."

We didn't move.

The man left the house, and I watched the suitcase bounce down the front steps as my faculties returned and Sadie's screams registered. She pleaded for help, and Bannerman knelt by her side, covered in blood, on the phone with emergency services.

I hurried to the bathroom, returned with towels, and Bannerman plugged the hole in Sadie's abdomen, but there was too much blood, and the towels were soon drenched. Sadie's face had no colour, and she drifted in and out as Bannerman filled the room with words that I don't think Sadie even heard.

"Stay with me, baby."

"I need you to stay with me."

"I love you so much."

"Don't you dare die on me."

"Please ..."

37

I called Duke from the ambulance on the way to the hospital. He arrived with Gleeson twenty minutes after us, and I persuaded them to step outside onto a balcony that extended from the third floor, even though the snow hadn't let up and a pounding wind created drifts that soaked our shoes. I tried not to let my mind wander as a wet cold crawled into my bones. I kept repeating to myself: *Easy does it. Easy does it. Easy does it.*

You couldn't smoke on the balcony, but I lit up anyway and closed my eyes. I listened to traffic for a moment, people navigating icy roads while listening to the radio deejay read the local news or discuss sports and pop culture. Shit that mattered so little.

I opened my eyes.

Gleeson paced back and forth, a bird on a branch. "How'd this happen?"

"That's the question," Duke said. "The list of people who know about the Garfield house is small."

I turned to Gleeson. "Is there an internal list of safe houses? A list that Walton's cop–"

Gleeson cut me off. "He doesn't have a cop!"

"You don't know that," I said, then tried again. "Is there a list of safe houses accessible to police of a certain rank?"

Gleeson swiped at the air in frustration. "Aw, Christ ..."

"No," Duke answered. "That's not how it works."

"Could the shooter have followed you from the hotel?" Gleeson said.

"Maybe," I said. "But if he was at the hotel, wouldn't he have taken the money there? Why wait until the safe house?"

Duke furrowed his brow, deep in thought.

Gleeson finally stopped pacing, struck by a bright idea. He looked at me. "You said Sadie gave the address to Nia. What if he got it from Nia?"

"You think Nia gave the address to Walton?" Duke said.

Gleeson nodded.

"You think she'd do that?" Duke asked me.

"No ..." I opened my mouth, closed it, and opened it again. "But anything's possible."

"Maybe she gave it to him without knowing," Gleeson said. "Maybe her phone was hacked."

"Call her," Duke said, liking it. "Ask if we can see her phone." He looked at Gleeson. "We'll get Forensics to run it."

"And if Nia doesn't let us have the phone?" I asked.

"Then we know it's her," Duke said, "and she's working with Brad Walton."

***

Nia answered right away.

"What's going on?" she said, urgent. "Sadie's not answering her phone. I have a bad feeling ..."

Duke and Gleeson headed inside, giving me privacy.

"Sadie's been shot. She's in surgery. Doctors are optimistic, but she isn't out of the woods yet."

Nia moaned, a low, animal-like whine. It was an awful sound, truly awful, and guilt fanned over me like smoke.

"I'm so sorry," I said. "The shooter came in from the basement with a gun, wearing a mask. Sadie made a move, and–"

"You were supposed to protect them!" she cried. "You ..."

"I ..."

My first reaction was to make excuses, but what was the point? She was right.

"I'm sorry," I said again. I'd been apologizing a lot, and the words sounded empty, wimpy, and wilted. I felt like a pussy.

"We can't figure out how the guy knew where we were," I said, thinking about how to ask my next question. "Sadie told me she gave you the address of the safe house. Did you tell anyone?"

The crying became sniffles, and finally, an ominous silence on

Nia's end of the line. Then she said, "I didn't tell anyone."

Her voice wasn't angry, though.

"I knew you wouldn't have told anyone on purpose," I said, "but I had to ask. We need your phone so the police can look at it. It might have been hacked."

"Hacked?"

"Or something else, I don't know," I added.

"Okay," she said. "Where is Sadie?"

"Health Sciences Centre, floor three, but that's not where you'll bring the phone."

Duke had told me Nia could bring it to a station on Henderson Highway, and that she was to speak with an officer called Lou Birmingham. I relayed the information to Nia, who said she'd be at the station soon. She hung up, and Duke informed me twenty-five minutes later that Lou had Nia's phone.

When Nia arrived in the waiting room of Emergency, she ran to the desk, spoke to the receptionist, then lowered her head until it was resting on the counter. She picked herself up, turned to the rows of chairs–I was on the far side of the room, and she didn't see me at first–and took a seat close to triage. I stayed put, giving her time.

Police usually need to crack the passcode of a cell phone before they can get in to see what's on it, but Nia provided hers, so it made the process a whole lot easier. Lou Birmingham got the phone to Forensics, and they examined it, communicating their findings to Duke in less than an hour. Duke updated me, and I took the information directly to Nia.

"Hey," I said. "You mind if I sit?"

Nia motioned to the chair next to her, I sat, and then she melted into me. I held on to her for a long time, until my shoulder was wet. She eventually let go.

"Have you heard anything?" I asked, knowing there had been no updates.

"No ... They said it could be hours until she's out of surgery."

"Sadie's tough. The doctors here are good. They'll do everything in their power ..."

Nia wiped her eyes with a tissue. "So, my phone?"

"I recommend you get a new one," I said, smiling, trying to lighten the moment, but it didn't work. The creases of her face deepened and her eyes narrowed.

"What do you mean?"

"Your phone has a spyware app downloaded on it, tucked into the Extras folder."

She tried to speak but nothing came out. Eventually, she said, "How didn't I know?"

"Like most things," I said, "if you aren't looking for it, you'd never know it was there. But for this software to work, the person had to be in possession of your phone to install the app."

Nia leaned back, looked away, then sat forward and rested her elbows on her knees. Her head hung low, and for a moment I thought she might cry. There were no tears when she looked up, though, only rage.

"Bergel," she said.

"I don't understand."

"I was with Bergel, a little over a week ago. We killed a day watching *Suits*. Ordered food. Slept."

"What happened to 'just a casual relationship'?"

"What can I say? I lied." Her eyes glazed over, peering into mine. "I woke up and my phone had been moved. I always put it one inch from the edge on both sides of my night table. Call me OCD, but it's a thing. A ritual, I guess. When I woke up, the phone was like two or three inches away."

"That's hardly proof."

"I never would have left it like that. Never. I would have adjusted it until it was an inch away."

"Could you have bumped it while you slept? Maybe you turned and your arm pushed it over?"

"No. I charge my phone in the bedroom. I napped on the couch in the living room."

"Okay, let's say you're right. How'd Bergel open your phone? You use a passcode."

"Yeah, but he's watched me open it dozens of times. He probably memorized the numbers. It's not hard to do."

I paused, sorting it out for myself.

Bergel gathered the digits over time, waited for an opportunity to use the phone without Nia around, and downloaded the app. That gave him access to every text, social media alert, post, and all internet searches on Nia's phone. He had access to her notes, calendar, and even payment information. He had it all. Nevertheless, there was one major problem with this theory.

"When I spoke with Bergel at Soul Patch, he seemed to genuinely care about you," I said. "He showed up at my house to fight me after he learned we–"

"Is that what happened to your face?"

"Yeah," I said. "Why would he want to spy on you? That's not something you do when you're in a relationship, even if it is on-and-off. I sort of understand a parent placing the app on their child's phone, or an employer using spyware on their employees' company phones, because in both those scenarios, parents and the employer have lots at stake. There's a reason for it. I don't know, maybe I'm wrong, but reading your messages is a short-term plan, a stupid idea if he wants you to trust him. The truth always comes out." I paused. "It doesn't make sense unless he knew about the money. Does Sadie know Bergel?"

A new expression removed the crevices on Nia's cheeks, and they shifted to her forehead. Her face grew longer, her eyes and mouth opening aghast. "Holy shit."

"What?"

"Sadie went to Soul Patch. I saw the stamp on the back of her hand. I asked her about it, but she shrugged it off. It was ladies' night. Maybe she told Logan what she had planned with Bannerman."

"Was this before or after you killed that day watching Suits?"

Nia shook her head, lining the parts up. "Before."

Bergel's offer to me made sense now.

"Bergel said he'd give me money if I found Sadie and let him know first."

She paused. "How much?"

"Ten grand."

"He knows about the money. Sadie must have told him about it." Nia sat up, wiped her eyes, and a vacant stare swept across her face. "That was him in the safe house. He shot Sadie."

"Duke will arrest him," I said. "He won't get away with it."

"I need to get some air."

Nia stood up, and I watched her walk toward an exit as two paramedics wheeled in a man in his twenties on a stretcher. The man was covered in blood, oxygen mask on his face. When you really thought about it, it was a miracle that any species lived together and survived. It just seemed so improbable.

38

I let Duke know that Logan Bergel had been the shooter at the safe house, and that he most likely had the money. Duke asked where I thought Bergel might be, and I gave him Soul Patch and the address of his condo on Waterfront Drive, which I'd gotten from Nia. Duke sent officers to each location, and I wondered if Bergel had taken the money for Walton, or if it had been for himself. My bet was the latter. It wasn't in Bergel's nature to do someone else's dirty work. I told Duke I needed to ask Bannerman if he knew that Sadie had spoken to Bergel, and Duke said Bannerman was being held at an undisclosed location, and it might not be possible. They weren't taking any chances this time.

In the waiting room, I watched a doctor approach Duke and Gleeson. The conversation lasted less than a minute, but the doctor's shoulders, cast back and confident, and continuous eye contact revealed more than words ever could. Sadie made it. She'd live. When finished, Gleeson sped away on the phone, and Duke walked toward me.

"Sadie's got serious challenges ahead of her," he said. "Might shit into a bag for life, but she's alive."

"That's good," I said, but any relief I felt was overshadowed by what came next.

***

Nia wasn't answering, so I called Katz a minute after 11 a.m. to see if he wanted to go to a meeting. I hadn't spoken to him since yesterday, and when he asked how I was, I told him the truth, that I'd been keeping busy so I wouldn't think about drinking.

"I'll pick you up at the hospital and we'll do a nooner," Katz said.

On the way, I described Tony's call from The Fairlane, and what had transpired at the house on Garfield.

"Why'd they do it?" Katz said. "Why'd Sadie and Bannerman take the money?"

"Payback. For what Walton did to Sadie. And the money didn't hurt."

Katz always drove fast, with the assured confidence of a professional. Turn signals were optional, even in the snow. He wore Carhartt pants and jacket, a Jets toque, and thick work mitts. His Sorels squeaked as he placed his foot on the floor mat.

"What deal are Sadie and Bannerman getting?" he asked.

I exhaled a long breath I'd been holding on to. "Immunity in exchange for Sadie's testimony against Brad Walton. Gleeson secured protective custody with the RCMP, so they'll also get new identities. But this all hinges on Walton's arrest. No arrest, no deal."

Katz whistled, pulling into the lot of a commercial building on Pembina Highway with ground-floor shops. One of them was the Winnipeg Group.

I planned to keep my phone on and in my hand, but inside, Katz nudged my shoulder with a stern look that said "shut that fucking thing off." I did and settled into the meeting. Readings. Prayers. A basket went around. Sharing.

It was fine, but I spent most of it imagining all the ways I could get drunk. Whiskey, gin, vodka, sambuca, beer, and wine. Stumble drunk. Piss-your-pants drunk. Black-out drunk.

When I was able to shake those thoughts, I worried Duke had called and that I'd missed it. I placed a hand in my pocket, ready to turn my phone on, but stopped myself.

In the lot, post meeting, I turned it on, and the thing flickered and flashed, messages popping up in rapid succession. Duke, Duke, and Duke.

Where r u

Answer your phone

The screen blurred and my vision faltered as I read the last text.

"What's wrong?" Katz said.

Cars sped by, but I couldn't hear them.
"Bergel is dead."

***

Katz drove at breakneck speed as I spoke to Duke on the phone. Bergel had been stabbed in the back and neck with a butcher knife. The knife had been left in him, but the suitcase had been taken.

I hung up and watched the snow fall, my brain surprisingly clear. Well, not clear, but absent of the dark thoughts that had plagued me during the meeting. There, my mind ran, and I couldn't seem to put the brakes on. Now, I didn't feel calm, but I did feel emptied of the desire to drink.

Sadie's testimony and the notebooks from Remple, an admitted drug dealer, provided soft evidence, but a decent lawyer would rip it to shreds. And the testimony of Sadie would sound like lies created by a scorned former member of the church.

Sadie would live, and that was good, but there would be no exchange without the money. Without the exchange, the police couldn't arrest Walton. Without the arrest, Sadie and Bannerman wouldn't receive protective custody. They could leave on their own, but Walton would track them down and kill them.

What can I do?

Katz's truck pulled to the curb in front of my building. I got out and walked toward the exterior door, contemplating how I'd tell Nia about Bergel, when Katz's voice boomed across the threshold: "Get on the ground! Now! Get on your knees!"

I thought he'd spoken to me, so I dropped and laced my hands behind my head.

"Jake, get up!" Katz said. "It's Nia ..."

I stood and turned and saw the blood as Katz pointed a gun at her. Even the suitcase she pulled had blood splattered on it, and her hands and jacket bore the brunt. A diagonal spray across her face, in combination with a look of utter dismay, made Nia look insane. She knelt, and Katz pushed her to the ground, face-first, quickly patting her down. He pulled a pair of zip ties from a back pocket, cuffed her, and brought her to her feet. The snow mixed with blood to create a red paste that smeared the front of Nia's clothes. She looked like the work of an experimental body artist.

Katz tucked the gun into the waist of his pants, dragged Nia to his truck, and propped her up against it, facing us. I took the handle of the suitcase, head on a swivel, looking for anyone who might be with her.

"Nia," I said, "what happened?"

I'm not sure if she didn't recognize me or if she was in shock, but when she tried to run, I dropped the suitcase and bear-hugged her from behind. She kicked and screamed and pried my hands from her torso.

"Stay calm ... shhh ... I want to help you ... Stay calm ... I'm here to help."

I tried to make sense of it all, tightened my grip, and spun her toward the truck.

"You okay?" Katz said to me.

"Yeah. Nia's okay, too, isn't that right?" I said to her.

Her body relaxed a little, enough so that I could slowly loosen my hold and step away from her.

"I killed him ..." Nia said. "I ..."

"What?" I said, feeling stupid, like I knew the answer but couldn't remember it.

Katz stepped in when he saw me struggling.

"You killed Bergel?" he said to Nia.

"Yes."

"Why would do that?" Katz said, puzzled.

I wondered if it was an answerable question. Do people know why they do what they do? In my experience, they bounced from one thing to the next, stumbling around, blind and mostly without a plan. Even if they thought otherwise.

Nia told the story as if Sadie was an innocent victim, and maybe she was, but she'd also stolen a million dollars from a drug dealer. She'd pointed guns at men, threatened to use them, and then walked away, thinking all would be fine. Well, it wasn't. It had never been and never would be.

I listened, shifting from Nia to the snowflakes that blew down from the heavens, feeling like I'd been teleported to the moon, trapped on an unfamiliar planet.

When she finished, Katz looked at me. "What do you want to do?"

"I don't know what to say ..."

I wasn't sure if I'd spoken to Katz or Nia.

Both, I guess.

"If you want my opinion," Katz continued, "there are two options. You call Duke and he arrests her, or you let her go but keep the money so we can use it to lure Walton. Nia takes her chances on the run." He paused, considering what he'd said. "The latter definitely leaves you open to prosecution, but it might be worth it to you."

He implied it depended on how I felt about Nia. He knew I felt something, but truth be told, I didn't know what that was.

"Why'd you come here?" I asked Nia.

She shrugged, like she hadn't thought about that.

"Sadie's going to live," I said. "She survived the surgery."

"I-I didn't know," she said. "I–"

I was carried away on the crest of an appealing image of Nia and me on the run, the million dollars funding our adventures. There was a romantic quality to it that I liked, but it was ridiculous.

"For Sadie to be safe, the police need to arrest Walton," I said to Nia. "It's the only way she gets protection. A new life. I'm sorry." I dialed and Duke answered right away. "I got the money."

"What the fuck?" he said. "How?"

"Just get over here. It's Nia. She did it."

A pause.

"She killed Bergel?"

"Yes."

I gave him the address and hung up.

39

The woman on the radio forecasted "high wind conditions," and Portage Avenue looked like the setting of a dystopian movie. A small number of brave people battled the elements, holding hands up and leaning forward, sheltering themselves from the wind and snow. They moved robotically, like droids from the future there to hurt me. I shook my head, waiving off the thought. Katz's truck had four-wheel drive, but even so, a couple of the higher drifts forced him to go slowly.

The need to talk arrived.

"I don't care what happens to the suitcase," I said. "But I want Walton in prison."

The snow came down in blankets as we stopped at a red light.

"Do you think he knows that Sadie's been shot? That Nia killed Bergel?"

"I don't know," I said. "Probably. If he has a cop, then he knows. Maybe not about Nia and Bergel, but he knows about Sadie."

My head hung low, and I shuddered.

"Look at me," Katz said. "Hey–look at me, Jake."

I did.

"You got this. I'm in this thing with you till the end," he said, and held up a fist. I bumped it as the light turned green. "Tell me what you're thinking."

I explained my fears that Walton would take the money, kill Sadie and Bannerman, and maybe us, too. Katz said we could only control our actions, not Walton's.

"How far are you willing to go?" Katz asked me, pulling into the lot of the Silver Heights Restaurant.

"I've been asking myself that," I said.

"And?"

"I'm in all the way."

I gazed across the street, watching the snow, mesmerized. A text arrived from Duke.

Get your asses in here.

***

Duke nodded as we entered the bar, tapped his watch in mock anger, then smiled. He walked toward us, leaving Bannerman alone in the booth. Katz and Duke eyed each other. It was like seeing two jungle cats cross paths, and neither wanted to back down.

The men shook hands, and Duke pointed a finger at Katz.

"The infamous Bogdan Katzmarek," Duke said. "I love what you decided to wear for the occasion. There's a real hillbilly quality that I admire."

"Archie Jansen."

"You miss me?"

"Yeah, like a hole in the head," Katz responded, but there was no hostility in his voice.

"Your first name is Archie?" I asked Duke

He laughed. "Archibald. It's a family thing. You see why I go with Duke?"

I nodded.

"You mind pointing that thing elsewhere?" Katz said. "And I don't mean your pecker."

Duke kept the finger aimed in Katz's direction. "If my pecker was pointed at you, you'd know."

"You wish," Katz said, and smiled, patting Duke on the back with an enormous hand.

I admired their ability to laugh while under stress, but I wasn't built like that.

"As much as I'd like to stand here making dick jokes with you guys," I said, "we have work to do."

It took convincing, but Duke agreed that Bannerman's presence at the exchange made it more likely for Walton to attend.

I chin nodded toward Bannerman. "What does he know?"

"He knows Sadie's out of surgery, and that she's going to live.

He knows we've got the money back but doesn't know Nia killed Bergel."

We joined Bannerman in the booth and spent forty-five minutes discussing where we wanted the exchange to take place, and if I'd argue with Walton when he asked us to meet somewhere we didn't like.

Could I disagree with him? Could I debate? Was there wiggle room or did I just accept what he asked of us?

In the end, Duke felt being too agreeable would be unrealistic, so we decided on what he called "some pushback." I thought that sounded right.

We wrote out a script, and I moved to a table across the room, reading and re-reading what we'd come up with, memorizing the words.

Earlier, I'd called and left a message with a secretary at Watershed Moments, making sure to sound urgent. We had no way to know when Walton might return the call, or even if he would call, although I felt confident he would because I'd told the woman it was a "million-dollar situation."

There was no time for subtlety.

When Duke asked Bannerman if he could keep his anger in check and remain calm in front of Walton, Bannerman said he'd "grin and bear it."

What a guy.

***

Walton called from an unlisted number at 3 p.m.

"Mr. Joelsen," he said. "How can I help you?"

I steadied my nerves. "Can you talk freely on this line?"

"Yes."

"I found Sadie and Bannerman. They have your money. With some help from Sadie's sister, I've convinced them to return the money to you."

We had plotted the opening as succinctly as possible.

"Okay, what do you want?" Walton said.

"I want you to guarantee their safety. The money is for this guarantee, and a promise they won't talk to anyone, ever, about Watershed Moments."

"If you understand my business, and my role at Watershed Moments, you'll understand this is not about the money. It's about preserving what we've built here."

"I understand," I said, fighting the urge to rebut. "I just want this to be over, and for my client and her sister to be safe. Think about what you can do with that money. This guarantees Sadie and Bannerman keep quiet. It's a win-win for you. I know what happened to Tracy Remple and Delilah Moore, and I don't want any more losses."

Walton didn't take the bait and acknowledge my reference to the murders.

"How can you guarantee their silence?" he asked. "Sadie is not the most reliable person."

It had been one of the most difficult parts of our preparation. We knew he'd ask the question, and in the end, we played to his ego and self-interest.

"I can't guarantee it, but I don't need to. If you don't believe me, you can always go back on the deal. But I'm asking you not to do that. If Sadie and Bannerman hold up their end, you fulfill yours. It's way less risk for you if you let them live."

I glanced at the other men at the table. Katz smiled, Duke looked on, focused, and Bannerman was frozen in time. I don't think he inhaled or exhaled once. He didn't move.

After a long pause, Walton said, "I accept your offer."

I looked out the window of the bar at a car that lost control and slid onto the curb, luckily missing other vehicles, street signs, and light standards.

"When can I get the money to you?" I asked.

"Seven tonight. I'll text you with the location at six. And Jake, it doesn't need to be said, but this is a business transaction, and police don't belong at a business transaction."

"No cops," I agreed.

"I'll hold you to that," Walton said, and hung up.

***

Walton would text in two hours, but until then, we had no idea where the exchange would take place.

We were still in the restaurant, finishing late lunches. Duke did pastrami on rye, and Katz ordered a burger and fries. Bannerman got a salad and grilled chicken, for which he took a verbal beating from Katz and Duke. I ordered a clubhouse and fries. When each of us had taken our last bites, wiped our mouths, and plates had been collected by the server, we ran through specifics.

"How many officers can you get on this?" Katz asked Duke.

"None."

"What?" Katz said.

It was the first note of concern I'd heard in his voice.

"Just me," Duke said.

"We need a tactical unit. We have two hours, that's it. We don't know the exact location, but we can plan for type. Hotels, bars, restaurants, malls, grocery stores, box stores, arenas. They each have patterns of design. Similar points of entry and exit, offices, open spaces. All that. You're telling me it's just the four of us?"

"Gleeson won't budge," Duke said. "After the clusterfuck that was the raid, he says we don't have the money, and he's not going to risk a second embarrassment."

I breathed deeply as my heart rattled around in my chest.

"Why the fuck didn't you tell us this sooner?" Katz asked, louder than I'd expected. "Where is he? This Gleeson asshole."

"Call him if you want," Duke said, "but when the guy makes a decision, he sticks to it. It's just us."

"Just us ..." Katz shook his head but seemed to slowly accept it. "Okay, but we're going to need one hell of a plan."

Duke laughed. "That's the understatement of the century. Can we use any of your people?"

Katz blew out a breath, considering it. "What we're doing here, it's too dangerous. I can't ask my people to risk their lives."

The four of us exchanged looks, and I thought about Nia and the night we'd danced to Neil Young. I willed the images away.

40

Sadie asked for Bannerman from her hospital bed, and he asked me to go with him. At first, I tried to shirk. I didn't want to go back to the hospital, not for any reason. But then I thought about it, realizing Bannerman wanted me to convince Sadie it would be okay, that by the time she left the hospital, Walton would be in prison.

Duke okayed it and assigned a female constable called Rodriguez to escort us there and back. Rodriguez, who I'd put at twenty-six or seven, didn't say much in the car, and she remained in the hallway when we got to Sadie's room, watching us through the small window in the middle of the door.

Sadie lay in bed with her eyes closed as we entered the room, but woke up when Bannerman ran in. He bent at the waist and leaned forward, unable to hug her with any strength because of her injuries. He pulled away, kissed her forehead, and sat.

It was so touching and intimate a moment that I turned away, feeling self-conscious for being in the room, like I had violated their privacy. I stepped into the hallway and swore to myself that I'd get clean, a promise I'd made too many times to count.

When I returned, I noticed how Sadie looked tiny, even smaller than she had at The Fairlane. Rings beneath her eyes added to the sickly overture, but she smiled as tears ran down her face.

"Sadie, it's good to see you," I said.

She swallowed, then sleepily motioned to a cup on the table next to her bed. Bannerman picked it up and held it in front of her face. She closed her eyes and sipped from the straw.

"Nothing but a flesh wound," she managed, pronouncing each word slowly.

I smiled.

"The worst part," she said, opening her eyes and catching her breath, "is that my NOFX T-shirt was ruined."

I laughed. "Good band."

"Great band," she countered.

I stood at the doorway, as far from her as the space would allow, and ran through the plan in limited detail, making sure to focus on the part where Brad Walton ended up in cuffs.

"I need to tell you something," I said to them.

Neither one knew Bergel had shot Sadie, and they didn't know Nia had killed Bergel, either. I looked at Sadie.

"Logan Bergel is the one who shot you. Earlier today, when Nia thought that you were going to die, she–" I paused, then tried again. "She killed Bergel."

Sadie's mouth opened and she covered it with both hands.

"How?" she said.

They sat there like statues as I explained how it happened. I finished, and they continued staring at me, like someone had hit the pause button. They wore awful expressions, a mixture of shock and disgust. Maybe I shouldn't have told them yet, but they deserved to know.

"Sadie, Nia told me she saw a stamp on your hand from Bergel's club," I said. "Did you talk to him before you robbed Walton?"

Sadie met Bannerman's eyes, and his mouth opened slightly. He didn't know.

"Yes," she said, and it sounded like a death note.

"Why didn't you tell me?" Bannerman said.

"I didn't tell you because ... I thought he'd be able to help us."

"And what did he say?" Bannerman asked.

"He said no. That he didn't want to get involved."

"He was lying," I said. "He put spyware on Nia's phone. That's how he got to us at the safe house."

Sadie shook her head and Bannerman remained frozen. When I couldn't take it anymore, I stepped out of the room and stood with Rodriguez.

***

We were in Duke's office at police HQ when Walton's text arrived at 5:59 p.m.

442 Selkirk Avenue

Go in the front doors

I Google-mapped the address and learned Aerial Manufacturing inhabited 442 Selkirk Avenue. It looked like a warehouse. Duke got on the phone, and not long after, we had access to schematics and holdings for the building. Walton was not the owner, nor did he appear in the paperwork at all. I wondered if the name on the lease or the owner was a member of the church, but there was no time to worry about that.

Duke stood and retrieved copies of the schematic from the printer. He handed them to us.

"Take one and study it. Study it like your life depends on it. We think Walton will be there, but we can't be sure. Whoever it is will be there before us. Aerial Manufacturing does machining and power coating, whatever that is. It's a thirty-five-thousand-square-foot building with two massive rooms, probably rows of machinery, and the usual offices, washrooms, and other places for someone to hide. Jake, Bannerman," he said, looking at us, "you're going in the front doors, alone. Katz and I will park and wait in vehicles on separate side streets out of the range of cameras. Jake, text me when you get to the building. If you're not out fifteen minutes after that, we're coming in."

Duke paused and checked the time.

"It's six-oh-five. We'll be mobile in ten."

Duke and Katz both hit the can, and I looked at the paper.

Aerial Manufacturing had a good-sized lobby that opened from the main entrance. Washrooms and offices broke from the lobby to a large space on the north side of the building. There was a second warehouse that branched off that initial space, another huge rectangle.

"Hey," Bannerman said quietly. "Hey ... Jake."

It took a second for me to hear him.

"We won't have weapons, right?" he said.

I sat back and gauged where he was headed with this. "I can't see Duke letting us bring any. There's no point. We'll be patted down as we enter the building."

"I agree." Bannerman leaned forward, closer to me. "Walton isn't going to let us live. I don't care what he said on the phone. It just wouldn't make any sense. I'd kill us if I was him."

"You don't know that."

"Yes, I do."

We watched through the glass as another detective walked past Duke's office. Bannerman waited until the man's footsteps faded before continuing.

"But there's always opportunity," he said. "There's always an opening. Be ready. When one presents itself, I'm going to make a move."

I shook my head, and my first thought was to tell him "No, don't do that. Smarten up." But maybe he was right.

"I'll be ready," I said.

The storm raged outside, and through the window it looked like an alternate universe waited for us. Already dark, you couldn't really see the snow, only surges of wind whipping white streaks across the horizon.

In a stall in the bathroom, I got down on my knees and prayed for the first time in years. I prayed for my mom, that no matter what happened to me, she'd be okay. I prayed for the safety of Katz and Duke, and I prayed that no harm would come to Nia in prison. I prayed that Sadie would recover, healing wounds both physical and emotional. I even prayed for Bannerman.

Then I prayed for the strength to make quick decisions, and for the ability to act with precision and accuracy amid the chaos I knew was coming. I'd been through tough times before, but this felt different. I didn't know if I'd make it out of this one.

***

The snow stung as it hit, making it impossible to focus on anything for more than a second before having to blink. Cars stuck in the drifts had been abandoned along the street. They were parked diagonally, some half covered. A glimmer from the lamps of a streetlight looked as if an alien spaceship hovered in the sky, the glow like a forcefield. Icicles grew on my eyelashes, narrowing my vision. I wiped them away and kept going. No one else was out.

Bannerman led, shoveling a narrow path, and I dragged the suitcase as we trekked through a barren wasteland. Or so it seemed. Duke had dropped us off at Tim Hortons, which should have been a five-minute walk away, but was taking much longer. Bannerman and I wore snow pants, winter parkas, gloves, toques, heavy-duty winter boots, and bright-orange vests. We had to stop every few minutes to catch our breath.

I found myself thinking about Sadie and Bannerman in the hospital. Their affection reminded me of Nia. The professional way she spoke until she trusted you. Then her guard dropped, and she revealed a sarcastic sense of humour, along with a kindness I didn't think many people got to see. Where was she now? With the blizzard, I doubted she'd seen a judge. And what had she been charged with? First-degree murder, most likely.

I thought about my mom, and how she'd never been in a healthy relationship with a man in her life. Lying. Cheating. Abuse. That's all she knew. I was supposed to protect the people I cared about, yet my actions had led to the deaths of Tracy Remple and Delilah Moore, and Nia's situation was at least partly my fault. If Bannerman was willing to risk his life for Sadie against Walton and his men, then I'd do the same. How could I not?

41

The walk took twenty-five minutes, and we arrived ten minutes late. The building loomed over us, daunting and unafraid. My fingers froze as I texted Duke.

Here.

Cameras rested above the door and higher up on either end near the roof. The door opened and we gazed into white light. For a moment, I thought I was dead.

Then someone spoke. "Come in."

We entered the main doors, coated in snow, wet and shivering. A man I hadn't seen before held a gun on us. He was small and thin. Slight is the word that came to mind.

"Leave the suitcase," he said.

"No," I responded. "I'll give the money to Walton."

He didn't make an issue of it. "Fair enough. Arms out."

We followed his request, and he patted us down. He put our phones in his pocket, then directed us past the front desk through a door and into a hallway I'd studied on the schematic. The man walked behind us as we entered the warehouse.

The high ceilings and open layout made the space feel empty, even though it held intricate machines on one side, with shelves, cabinets, hoists, forklifts, and skids full of materials on the other. We walked fifty yards to an elevator.

"Hit the down button," the man said, and I did. A moment later, the elevator arrived, we got on, and the man clicked the button marked B. Five seconds later, with a flick of his gun, the man motioned us to get off.

Down the hall, a turn, and we got to a lunchroom. Walton stood at the far end, leaning against the wall, alone. Most of his swollen nose caused by Duke's punch days earlier was hidden behind a bandage kept in place by two strips of medical tape. The grooves under each of his eyes were the colour of a plum

"Thanks for coming," he said. His demeanour was what my dad used to call "all business."

I stepped forward, hefted the suitcase onto a table, and opened it. I turned the case toward him, expecting his eyes to expand as a pillar of light rose up from the suitcase. I pictured nylon gloves, money counters, and paper band straps for wrapping cash. I thought there'd be a scene. Instead, Walton didn't even look at the money.

"Where's Sadie?" he said.

"She couldn't make it," I said. "Not feeling well."

"That's too bad. I was hoping she'd be here."

I wasn't sure if Walton knew Sadie had been shot, but his reaction seemed genuine.

"I get it," I said, "but believe me, she's in."

Walton nodded, and I ventured a glance at Bannerman. His arms hung loose, his knees slightly bent.

The new man walked to the table, inspected the contents of the suitcase, closed it, and stood to the left of Walton.

We heard footsteps approaching in the distance, and a moment later, Duke strolled into the room and joined Walton and the new man. It didn't click until he placed a hand on Walton's shoulder. A tap of the shoulder, that's all it took to trigger a reel in my head.

Meeting Duke for the first time at The Original Pancake House.

Waiting for Delilah Moore in his shitty car.

The Ellice Motor Inn with Tracy Remple.

It was Duke.

Duke was Walton's guy on the force. The inside man. The dirty cop.

That's how Walton knew about the warrant, and why he'd had time to clean out his production room in the basement of the church.

They couldn't have known Bergel would show up at the safe house, and that threw a monkey wrench in their program, but I'd gotten the money back from Nia, gift-wrapped it even.

I listened, hoping to hear Katz's voice, knowing I would not. I wondered if he was alive.

"I'm sorry," Duke said, which blew my mind.

How could you fuck someone over so badly, then apologize? It didn't make sense to me, and I couldn't accept it.

"What's wrong with you?" I said.

"I tried to make this work," Duke said, like he had exhausted all avenues of possibility. "I really did. I just couldn't get it done."

"So you killed Remple and Moore?"

He shook his head. "No, not me."

"But you knew about it."

Duke shrugged.

"You fuckin' prick," I said.

I wanted to smack him, beat him senseless, wrap my hands around his throat and choke him into unconsciousness.

"Were you always dirty?"

"Dirty? Clean?" Duke said. "Man, it's practically the same thing."

"I'm going to rat you out."

Walton stepped in. "No, you're not. This is the end of the line for you."

The new man pointed the gun at me.

"What?" I said to Walton. "We had a deal."

"I changed the deal."

"This is a bad idea," I said, breathing to keep calm, trying to think of something, anything to say to stall. "It's a blizzard. How do you expect to dispose of ... the bodies?"

"Don't worry about that," the man with the gun said.

"I'm due in court in a matter of days. What happens when I don't show? A judge can't let that go."

Walton motioned for Duke to answer.

"A judge will think you ran," Duke said. "They'll issue a warrant, but that will be the end of it. As far as Bannerman goes, he's got no family here. The only person to kick up a fuss would be Sadie."

"And what about her?" I said. "You can't–"

"Can't what?" Duke added quickly.

Walton's eyes flicked to Duke, a brief look, but I caught it.

"You're going to kill her, too," I said.

Walton spoke casually in a humdrum tone that sent shivers up and down my arms. "Yes," he said, nodding to the new man, who came forward.

"You can't kill us all. It's too much of a coincidence."

"Let's go," New Man said, and we followed him out of the room, down the hallway. Our footsteps echoed as we arrived at a small room that had been cleaned out. It might have been a janitor's room or a storage space at one time. A tarp had been set up on the floor, and plastic lined the walls, taped at the seams. I stopped at the open door, causing Bannerman and the others to stop behind me.

"Woah, woah, woah, that's it?" I said to Walton. My whiny voice made me sick. "You're really going to kill us?"

"Did you actually think I'd let you walk?" Walton asked.

What had I felt? I didn't know. I felt unsure, but part of me believed Walton would let us live. I had convinced myself he would, but now it struck me as the stupidest thing I'd ever done.

"I wasn't sure ..." I said.

"That was a costly error." Walton pointed to the room. "In–"

I didn't move. "No."

"No?"

I looked at Duke. Maybe I could get him to change his mind, help us in some way. Otherwise, it was Bannerman's plan, and that felt impossible.

"I sent the notebooks to the *Free Press* and *Sun*," I said abruptly.

That got their attention, and Walton hesitated, but remembered something.

"No, you didn't," he said. "Duke gave them to me. I disposed of them."

I looked to Bannerman for help, but it was like he wasn't there, a spectre floating alongside me, quietly brooding.

"I made copies," I added.

"Nah, you didn't have access to them," Duke said. "Even if you did, who'd believe you? You're a drunk."

He made a good point. My credibility was low.

Walton took three steps until he stood beside the new man.

"I don't think you're a heathen," he said to me, "but things happen in this business. Mistakes are made. Bad luck. Bad faith. Duke's interests and mine are aligned. He's good at what he does. So am I, son."

Duke opened his mouth, but I cut in before he could speak.

"Don't call me son," I said. "I had a dad."

"I heard about that," Walton said. "John Joelsen."

I met his eyes. "Do you even know how sick you are?"

Anger flashed across Walton's face. "Your deaths are judgments come from above. The Lord chose me to remove anyone that is a threat to his holiness. He *chose* me, and he chose my people."

"Chose?" I said. "You interview people before they can join the church. That's not the Lord choosing, that's you. You're–"

And that's when Bannerman made his move.

I dropped low on instinct as Bannerman speared the new man. A gunshot rang out, deafening, and someone screamed. I spun and kicked Walton's left knee. He wailed in agony, and I pounced, punching him twice, then scrambling to my feet.

Bannerman swatted the new man's gun arm to the side and latched on to his forearm. The gun kicked again, *pop-pop-pop*, firing three times before Bannerman was able to force it inward, aimed at the new man's chest. Bannerman slid his finger inside the trigger guard, forcing the new man to fire a fatal shot into his own chest. The man slumped, bleeding profusely, and Bannerman let his dead weight and the gun drop to the floor.

I was vaguely aware of Duke as I moved to pick up the gun.

"Don't," Duke said, and I froze.

Bannerman lay motionless on the floor, bleeding from a hole in his shoulder. The new man was dead. I wanted to take Walton's life, like the bullet entering his body would cancel out the pain, but Duke would shoot me before I could get to the gun. Walton's moustache dripped blood from his re-broken nose. He pointed a shaking finger at me from the ground.

"Shoot this piece of shit," he said.

Duke shifted his arm toward Walton and fired. A crimson patch spread across Walton's chest, and the light in his eyes went out. He fell next to the new man.

I gasped.

"Listen," Duke said to me, lowering his gun, but ready. "We can make this work."

I steadied my nerves. "Where's Katz?"

"I tasered him, then tied him up in his truck."

"Jesus ..."

"He'll live."

The scene laid out before us was a mess. Walton and the new man were dead, and Bannerman lay there, bleeding out. Blood spatter covered the walls, pools of it next to each body. I looked at Duke, ready to listen to what he had to say.

"Here's the story: We set up the meet with Walton, money in exchange for safety. You and Bannerman brought the money to the warehouse, and I jimmied the door and followed you inside. When I heard gunshots, I came running. Bannerman and this guy killed each other, and I had to shoot Walton because he had a gun on you," he said. "I didn't want this. You won't believe me–why would you?–but I think you're a stand-up guy. I know you'll keep your mouth shut."

"What about Katz?"

"We go get him right now, before we call this in, and you convince him it's the right play."

There was an intelligence in Duke's voice that had always been there. He was thoughtful, and I believed him to be a good cop. Now, though, I wondered how long he'd been dirty, how many of his cases he'd sullied, and if I could get past it.

How much do I want to live?

"And I just let you keep your job? Keep fixing cases?" I said. "What else have you done?"

"Nothing. This is it. Walton and Watershed are my only sidepiece. I'm a loyal man. I'll continue with them after this, and to be clear, you'll owe me when you get out. When I need a favour, I expect you to be there."

I contemplated his offer.

"How can I trust you?"

"I don't know. The other option is I shoot you now." He squinted, weighing it out for himself. "It complicates things without a second person to back me up and tell the same story, but I'll take my chances if I have to. Think about your mom. She needs you, man."

He was wrong to mention my mom. She'd had a hard life, and in the eyes of most people, she was a loser. But my mom wasn't dishonest, and both my parents had taught me the value of that, even as they drank, as they neglected me. I couldn't agree to what he was asking.

"I won't do it," I said. "I can't." I braced for impact. "Do what you will."

I closed my eyes and accepted my fate.

A gun roared, and I heard a wheeze, then a sudden gulp of air, but it wasn't me. I opened my eyes and saw Katz standing over Duke's body. Katz was cuffed at the wrists and barefoot. He noticed me looking at his feet.

"My boots squeak like a motherfucker," he said.

I nodded, tried to smile but couldn't produce one.

Katz placed two fingers on Duke's neck, feeling for a pulse. He did the same with Walton.

"Both are dead," he said, moving to Bannerman's body. "You okay?"

"Yeah," I said, feeling like my brain had been cut out, tossed in a bag, shaken, and then reinstalled in my cranium. I felt dizzy.

Katz checked Bannerman next. "He's alive."

I reached for my phone, remembering the new man had taken it. "You got a phone?"

"No, Duke took it."

I knelt beside the new man's body, took a deep breath, and began patting him down, searching for our phones. I found them just as the suitcase caught my eye. Katz noticed me.

"Don't do it ..." he said.

"What?"

"You know what. Don't take the money."

"That's all my problems right there. Poof, gone."

"Yeah, and a new batch just waiting for you. If you take that money, you're profiting from Walton's fucked-up church. The drugs he made and sold, the people he hurt."

"But my mom ..."

Katz shook his head. "It's your decision, and I won't stand in your way. You have thirty seconds to decide. Then I'm calling this in or Bannerman dies."

Katz walked out of the room.

I looked away from the money, leaving it where it was.

***

At the station, I answered Don Gleeson's questions.

Who was in the warehouse?

What happened when you got there?

Who shot the new man and Bannerman?

"Tell me about the moments before Katz shot Duke. Details," he said. "I want details."

I gave him what I could, answering with short, precise sentences.

"And you are, without a doubt, saying Detective Jansen killed Walton? That Duke was corrupt? Is that what I'm hearing?"

I said yes, describing what I knew and how I knew it.

Gleeson paced back and forth, stopping often to scoff at what I'd said. "How did Katz free himself from the steering wheel?"

I said I didn't know.

The conversation took more than two hours, and Gleeson made it clear it was well within his power to charge me with something. He said he wasn't sure yet, but let me leave. I got to my apartment a little after 1 a.m., but I couldn't sleep. I was dead inside, hollowed out. I contemplated the aftermath.

The new man, Walton, and Duke died at the scene.

Bannerman was in surgery.

According to Gleeson, Nia had been charged with second-degree murder, not first, which was the only minor positive in a never-ending list of shit.

I stared at the ceiling until dawn, when I made coffee, drinking a pot at the table, looking out the window blankly, smoking cigarettes like they were keeping me alive.

42

Saturday, October 26 (two days after the warehouse)

The meeting began at 9 a.m. Hardly any empty seats. Loud conversations competed with laughter. Everyone knew each other. We stood, progressed through the routine, and the meeting opened with a reading. Outside, snow drifts three feet high blocked the faces of most buildings, and a miserable wind spun loose powder in circles.

The shootout at the warehouse had hit the papers, local and national. The religious angle, the polygamy, and Brad Walton were featured prominently on the front pages, and had been the lead story on the six o'clock news last night. But there were surprisingly few details of what had happened in the warehouse. None of the specifics. Gleeson painted Duke as a cop gone rogue, a bad apple, and not indicative of the quality of officers in the Winnipeg Police Service. There were whispers of an internal investigation, but I didn't think it would amount to much. These things rarely do. Katz and I declined every interview request.

It was too much for me, and I had developed an ache behind my eyes I knew wouldn't subside until I spoke to Nia. I got in touch with her through her lawyer, told him that I needed to see his client, and he set it up. That morning, I'd gotten an anonymous text.

11:00 today.

Instructions followed.

I figured I'd need to be as calm and strong as possible, hence the meeting. As people shared, I listened closely, but my head felt unsure, and I couldn't focus on anything. The words didn't register. My hands tingled off and on throughout. When it was my turn to share, I breathed deeply and found the words.

"My name's Jake ..." I said.

"*Hi, Jake.*"

"And I'm an alcoholic."

***

The remand centre is downtown on Kennedy Street, across from the Law Courts building, a pre-trial detention centre with inmate offences ranging from assault and theft to murder, and everything in between.

At the desk, a woman in her late forties told me the rules, then ushered me through to the security checkpoints. A friendly guard showed me to the interview area. Each cubicle had a Plexiglas divider that acted as a window. Nia sat on a metal chair, waiting. The grey prison fatigues hung loosely from her body.

I sat down and picked up the phone. She did the same.

Nia's usually bright eyes had faded. She looked weary, and without much fight.

"Hey," I said.

"I got your message." Her voice was strained, like she was holding back. "You wanted to talk?"

"Yes."

I wasn't sure what to say; the plan I'd made earlier felt empty now.

"I wanted to see how you're doing," I said. "I got the payment you sent before–"

I stopped, realizing my error.

"Before I killed Bergel?" she added.

I nodded.

"I also wanted to tell you that Brad Walton is dead," I said.

"I know. I read the paper." Nia held the phone to her forehead, closed her eyes. "Tell me what happened ... and not the version in the paper. The real story."

I told it from my point of view, a streamlined version of events.

"Sadie and Bannerman are safe," I said.

"He'll make it?"

"Yeah, he's going to be fine, the tall prick," I said, and smiled.

The lights in the room were dull and repetitive. Lifeless. They didn't care, want, or feel, and seemed completely unnatural.

"I thought about something you said the night we went dancing," Nia began. "You said people exist on a spectrum, and that they can only change in small ways. You were wrong." Her mouth puckered rapidly, fighting back the tears.

"I didn't say people couldn't change," I said. "I said that without a major event in one's life, change is not possible. This"–I looked around the room from floor to ceiling and back–"is a major event."

Nia made intense eye contact, a permanent grimace on her face.

"How have you changed?" I asked her.

"I'm angrier." Her cheeks trembled. "I'm–I regret what I did. I no longer have hope."

Tears crept from her eyes as she spoke. Angry tears. Hurt tears. They ran down her face and dripped onto the counter. She let them fall.

"I'm sorry you're hurting," I said. "I'll speak on your behalf if there's a trial, or if you plead out, I'll write a letter of support. You're young, and you'll have a life when you get out. It won't be the life you had, but it will be a life. There is hope in that."

She nodded, and the phone felt awkward in my hand as a sense of peace washed over me. The discomfort in my brain wrangled its way to the base of my skull and exited in vapours of grief.

At least it felt that way.

I let go.

"Take care, Nia. I'll miss you."

I placed the phone in the holder, stood, and walked out.

43

Monday, October 28 (four days after the warehouse)

I stepped off the bus, dodged a patch of ice, and crossed the parking lot to the main building. A man whose hair hadn't had colour in it since the late nineties directed me to the far side of the property. The sprawling landscape roamed for miles, and it took seven minutes to walk to where the white-haired man said they'd be. The service had begun.

Katz's wife, Naomi, had died two days ago–as I'd been sitting with Nia–and it threw me off-kilter again.

Why?

Why had this woman died the way she had? And why had I lived?

Why had I been given another chance?

A clergyman spoke of the afterlife. People stood close to one another, held hands, and wrapped arms around themselves, anything for a little warmth. The family wept in the front row, but an open chair sat next to them. I turned and saw Katz. The snow crunched under my shoes, and I could see my breath as I walked toward him.

"Jake ..." he said.

I smelled the whiskey from a distance, and Katz's suit looked like he'd folded it up and launched it from a cannon. It had deep creases, smears on the forearms of the jacket, and a stain on one pant leg. A bottle swung loosely from the fingertips of his left hand. He smoked with the right. We stood a hundred feet from his wife's funeral.

"Jake, Jake, Jake ..." he said, and took a swig. "I'm drunk six ways from Sunday." His eyes swept over himself, assessing. He shrugged. "I look awful. She'd always say 'look good, feel good.' I must be such a disappointment to her."

I'd never seen him like this, drunk and disheveled. It was strange. He sat down on the hard ground and I joined him.

"Give me the bottle," I said.

"Isn't this a role reversal? It's usually me taking bottles from drunks."

"You're going through a tough time. An impossible time. You lost your wife."

"That's right, I did," he said, brief anger taking over until he shook it off. "Now, I'm a drunk and a widower."

I didn't know what to say, so I put a hand on his shoulder.

"Are you ready for this?" Katz said. "You strong enough?"

"I don't know. Today is my sixth day sober, whatever that's worth."

"I had twenty years." He took another sip. "Pissed away."

"It's not pissed away. You didn't lose those years. They still count. Think of all the people you've helped, including me. This is just a slip."

"A slip is when you fall on ice. A drunk deciding to drink is inevitable. It's the opposite of a slip. It's almost planned. Destiny!" he sang.

I remembered Bannerman's words from what seemed like months ago, what he'd said about people coping.

"Maybe, but we deal with life on our own terms," I said, extending my hand. "Give me the bottle."

Katz put his head down, then he laughed. "Six days ... such a newbie."

Six days wasn't much compared to twenty years, but it's what I had.

"Did I ever tell you the one about the drunk in bed?" Katz asked.

I shook my head no.

"So, there's this hopeless drunk, and he refuses to get out of bed. He's been fired from his job, been through rehab and A.A., and his wife has had enough. She calls his old sponsor, one last-ditch effort before she packs up and walks out." Katz took a sip. "The sponsor shows up with a newbie not unlike you, and the two of them go into the bedroom where the drunk is sleeping. It smells like sweat, stale booze, and puke in the room, just nastiness. The sponsor shakes the drunk awake and sits on the edge of the bed. The newbie stands.

"The sponsor introduces himself and the newbie, and tells the drunk how long they've been sober, and how A.A. has changed their lives. The newbie's got a week sober, the sponsor's got thirty years. The drunk looks at the newbie, then the thirty-year man, and with a look of disbelief, says to the newbie, 'One week. How'd you do it?'"

I laughed, and a smile spread across Katz's face.

"You get it?" he said.

"I do. Now give me the bottle."

On cold, crisp days on the prairies, the amber liquid burns. It alters personalities, drowns sorrows, and changes the course of history. It sucks the soul right out the afternoon, bakes worry into your mind, and stains your thoughts with selfishness.

Katz passed me the bottle and I read the label. Jim Beam. Kentucky Straight Bourbon Whiskey.

I'm not religious, and I go back and forth on many of life's big questions. For a while, I believed in God, then I didn't. I'm not sure what I believe now, but in that moment, I was struck by something, a detail that didn't make sense. Call it a higher power or a random thought, a coincidence. I poured the booze into the snow.

"After the warehouse, you went to the hospital, right?" I asked.

Katz looked at me, a note of sober suspicion on his face. "Yeah, as a precaution. Because I'd been tasered."

My thoughts raced. "Did you tell the paramedics you'd been handcuffed to the steering wheel?"

He shook his head, thinking, waiting a moment until he had confirmed it in his memory. "No, I told paramedics that I'd been tasered, but I didn't say anything about the steering wheel, not to them. I spoke to Gleeson at the station, told him, but that was ... well, almost two in the morning. Why?"

"Gleeson interviewed me around ten thirty. He asked how you freed yourself from the steering wheel. *Steering wheel*. How would he know you'd been cuffed to the steering wheel if you didn't tell anyone until almost two?"

Katz considered the question. "Could he have guessed?"

"Maybe, but it's unlikely. Tasered, sure, a paramedic could have delivered that information to him, but cuffed to the steering wheel? The paramedics didn't know. That's specific, too specific. Why'd Gleeson say steering wheel?"

"I don't know ..."

"I think Duke told him, before the exchange, what he was going to do."

"You're saying Gleeson was in on it with Duke? As in they were working together?"

"That's what I'm saying."

The whiskey on the snow looked like syrup.

"What a world," Katz said, and I wasn't sure if the comment was about Gleeson and what I'd speculated, the emptying of the bottle, or if he'd said it in response to another private thought.

"I'm going to prison tomorrow," I said.

Katz looked up at me.

"Jake, you'll get through it. You're a good man. A very good man. Whether it's a year, two years, or in between. You'll get through it." Katz tilted his head and smirked. "My ol' man was a beauty. An absolute beauty. Huge man, and funny. A hard man, though. He used to say 'Sometimes you have to do wrong to do right.' Maybe this is one of those times. You broke that man's jaw, and maybe it was wrong, but then again, maybe it was right. I think it was both."

And then he hugged me.

"Let's go sit down," I said. "Your kids need you."

Reluctantly, Katz stood. We walked to the gathering, and Katz took his place in the front row. I stood in the back and listened to the remainder of the service.

Afterward, Katz rode in a cab with me, where he promptly fell asleep. The cab arrived, and I draped him on my shoulder and dragged him into his house, down the hall, and plunked him into bed, pulling the covers tight.

***

My mom smiled when she saw me in the monkey suit and silently ushered me into her apartment to a familiar display. Sink full of plates and cutlery. Half-drunk drink on the go. The place smelled like cigarettes and body odour. I sat at the kitchen table.

"Mom," I said. "This is my last day ..."

"I know."

Mom stubbed out the butt and lit a fresh one. Sipped from her drink.

"I love you," I said.

She played with a ring on the pinky finger of her right hand. Her legs were crossed, the upper leg bobbing up and down.

"I love you, too," she replied, but I wasn't sure if her heart was in it.

Then I shared, and this time, I included every detail.

Logan Bergel. How we'd met in group, and what had happened with Pete Argyreos. The trial, and that I'd lied on the stand to keep him out of prison.

Katz.

Sadie and Bannerman.

Tracy Remple and Delilah Moore.

Brad Walton.

Duke.

And Nia. Of course, Nia.

I included the drugs, booze, sex, murder, arrests, and the events at the warehouse on that cold, fucked-up evening.

Then I explained that Katz would pay her bills, provide her with spending money while I was inside. He'd agreed to take care of it, and I trusted him despite his drunkenness at the funeral. Nia's tab was more than ten thousand dollars, and with the money from the sale of my truck, couches, and TV, I had thirty-one grand for my mom, seventeen short of what I'd calculated she'd need. I asked Katz to kick in a little extra here and there if he could, to keep a record of it and I'd pay him back when I got out.

She listened as she smoked and drank. When I finished,

she nodded but didn't say anything. I wanted emotion, a hug, and maybe a "thank you." Sometimes, though, it's best to toss expectations and accept things as they are.

We said our goodbyes and I left.

44

Tuesday, October 29 (five days after the warehouse)

I called police HQ and asked for Don Gleeson at quarter after nine that morning. I wasn't sure if he was in, but someone had delivered the message, because ten minutes later he returned my call. Leonard Cohen's "Who by Fire" played in the background of my apartment, as if planned. I stood as the call came in, surrounded by the wares of packing, my clothes and belongings fitting into three bankers boxes.

"Good work the other night," Gleeson said, sounding like he'd eaten gravel. "That said, I'm still processing what happened, you know, with Duke."

"That's what I want to talk to you about."

"What's up?"

"At the station, after the warehouse, you said Katz had been handcuffed to the steering wheel. Who gave you that information?"

"He was still wearing the cuffs," Gleeson blustered. "Paramedics told me he'd been tasered."

"That makes sense, but did the paramedics also tell you Duke handcuffed Katz to the wheel?"

Heavy silence, then breathing, and Gleeson took his time. He was composed, you'd have to be to rise all the way to deputy chief.

"You know, I thought about calling you myself," he said.

"Oh yeah?" I moved to the window and watched people treading carefully on the sidewalk that skirted my building. The sidewalks had been cleared, but most people wore boots. A few wore dress shoes or sneakers, like they refused to acknowledge the storm. Often, an early snowfall causes a hassle, drains part of the city's winter budget, and then melts, gone like it was never there. Not this year. This year, it seemed committed.

"Yeah," Gleeson said. "I almost called you. Almost. See, life is a tug of war. I forget who said it, a smart man, no doubt, that life is the constant tension of opposites. Pros and cons. Balance, and all that. Guy wants to be the best looking, funniest, and most athletic. Wants to know music and art and explore the inner workings of his soul. Wants the corner office and, of course, as he ages, he wants a relationship and maybe a family."

He laughed and it wasn't a nice sound. It felt mean.

"It's impossible to be all those things," he added, "so most people do them all a little bit and do them poorly. They go to the gym until they get into a serious relationship, then fade. Get district manager and make a good salary, then lose motivation. They change jobs, buy a new house or car, get divorced or have another kid. It's all pointless unless you know who you are. Me? I make decisions, and I never waver. I don't back down, and I don't let people fuck with me." He paused. "Are you fucking with me, Jake?"

"I'm asking questions," I said. "Katz went to the hospital with the paramedics, and yeah, he told them he got tasered, but he never mentioned the steering wheel. Not until he spoke to you at the station, hours after you spoke to me. You couldn't have known Duke cuffed him to the wheel when we talked, unless–"

"Unless Duke told me."

"That's right."

"Listen, I don't give a shit about religion," Gleeson said. "A church like Watershed Moments makes me sick, but I'd be a fool not to recognize their influence. Their power in the political community. Their potential to do harm. A church that size? They need to be under constant supervision. Constant. That's all Duke was. Eyes and ears."

"People died."

"People will always die. That's part of the tension of opposites. Change is inevitable, but the more things change, the more they stay the same."

"I don't know what that means, but I need to know: Are Sadie and Bannerman safe?"

"It depends."

"On what?"

"If you accept a gift from me. Then I'll make sure Sadie and Bannerman end up in protective custody. It's already arranged with the RCMP, and we are just waiting for them to get well before they can travel, but now that you've brought this to my attention, I need more leverage."

"What kind of gift?"

"Oh, it's about a million little gifts."

"The money? What–Why?"

Then it struck me, so obvious I felt dumb for asking. If I took the money, I couldn't blow the whistle on him. The money implicated me as part of whatever Duke had going on with Brad Walton.

"And if I say no?" I said.

"Then I'll squash protective custody like a bug."

"And I'll go public with this."

"If you do, Sadie and Bannerman are dead by sundown that same day."

He let that hang in the air like a grenade.

"Am I safe?" I said.

"The situation is fluid. But if you take the money and keep your mouth shut, you're safe. Plus, I understand you're short on cash, what with the extended vacation you're about to take. Just think about how much this money can help your mom."

I'd said I'd never take money for nothing, but what choice did I have?

"Understood," I said, feeling ill. "I accept the deal."

"Good. It will be delivered to you promptly. I'm sure we'll see each other again."

***

The rest of the morning passed quickly, and I didn't think about Sadie, Nia, or Don Gleeson's offer. I cleaned out my office, then shaved my head at home with clippers and smoked a satisfying cigarette on the back stoop of my apartment building with a guy who told me his name was Dice. He was one of the people who refused to recognize the storm, wearing gym shorts and a Metallica zip-up hoodie, no T-shirt underneath. I asked if Dice was a reference to Andrew Dice Clay, and he looked at me like I had a booger. He said no, the name just sounded cool, and I had to agree, it did, if you were a rapper or a street artist. Maybe he was.

Then again, what did I know?

I finished my smoke and Dice walked away, leaving a gym bag at my feet. In my apartment, I unzipped it slowly, like a dress, to reveal stacks of cash. I closed the bag and placed it in my closet.

***

The needle burned my skin, a slow, steady vibration. The motion of the artist's hand was minimal as she let the electromagnetic coils move up and down, branding my shoulder forever. I relaxed in the chair, settling in.

Two hours later, the artist stopped. "I'm going for a cigarette. Be back in five."

I scratched my head, the hairs fine to the touch. I didn't say anything and checked the work in the mirror. I'd found the image online, a black bear, snout closed, looking straight ahead. The eyes weren't fierce, but gentle, and that's what I had wanted.

The artist returned, fired up the gun, and the needle played its song. Another hour and it would be finished.

At five that night, I brought the cash to Katz. He was doing okay, sober, and although he didn't like that I'd taken the money, he promised to use it to take care of my mom when what I'd earned ran short. We hugged and both shed a few tears.

Inside Stony Mountain Institution, I took one last look at social media and checked my Gmail.

"You Jake?"

I looked up into the face of a man in his forties.

"Yeah, I'm Jake."

"I'm Matt Rooney, your PO. Would you please come with me?"

I stood and followed him to a room where he took my phone,

keys, and wallet. He described what the rest of my day would look like, but I didn't hear a word.

I was too busy thinking about what I'd do when I got out.

Maybe I could dedicate my life to helping people find their loved ones. The lost. The broken. The missing.

Rooney patted my shoulder, and the pain from the tattoo flared, letting me know I was still alive.

ACKNOWLEDGEMENTS

Writing a novel and seeing it in print has been a dream of mine for a very long time. But it's a long road, one paved with rejection and a steep learning curve. This book wouldn't be here without the following people who I'd like to thank:

The online crime fiction community for sharing their work with the world, supporting my writing, and for their friendship based on our mutual passion for stories.

Authors kind enough to read *The Broken Detective* early and provide blurbs: J. Todd Scott, David Swinson, A.J. Devlin, Amber Cowie, J.T. Siemens, Matt Phillips, M.M. DeLuca, and Thomas Trang.

Warren Layberry for his expert developmental edit that led to the CWC shortlist nomination.

Vern, Gary, and Krysta from Run Amok Crime for their professionalism, talent, and guidance along the way.

My parents: thank you for everything you've done for me. Words can't express my gratitude.

To Grady and Emmy: thank you for bringing joy and honesty to the world, and for teaching me about love.

Most of all, Meagen: thank you for your love and support, for letting me 'run ideas by you,' and for accepting that I'll always be someone who walks around the house talking to himself, lost in a story. We've built an amazing life together.

I'm indebted to you all.

About the Author

Joel Nedecky is a high school teacher and writer based in Winnipeg, Manitoba. He has always loved stories, yet most of his childhood was spent playing hockey. It was not until university that he discovered a passion for all types of fiction. *The Broken Detective* is his first novel.

For more, check out jnedecky.com.

www.ingramcontent.com/pod-product-compliance
Lightning Source LLC
Chambersburg PA
CBHW032237310726
48973CB00008B/2176
* 9 7 9 8 9 9 0 4 8 5 1 3 6 *